PEN

ENTWINED

ENTWINED

A.J. ROSEN

PENGUIN BOOKS

PENGUIN BOOKS

UK | USA | Canada | Ireland | Australia
India | New Zealand | South Africa

Penguin Books is part of the Penguin Random House group of companies
whose addresses can be found at global.penguinrandomhouse.com.

www.penguin.co.uk www.puffin.co.uk www.ladybird.co.uk

Published in Great Britain by Penguin Books in association
with Wattpad Books, a division of Wattpad Corp., 2020

001

www.wattpad.com

Printed and bound in Great Britain by Clays Ltd, Elcograf S.p.A.

A CIP catalogue record for this book is available from the British Library

ISBN: 978–0–241–45579–1

All correspondence to:
Penguin Books, Penguin Random House Children's
One Embassy Gardens, 8 Viaduct Gardens
London SW11 7BW

For my dad, Joe, and my mom, Myke. I love you both infinity times infinity. My angels and those who have this book in their hands now, thank you for giving *Entwined* a chance and may your dreams come true.

PROLOGUE

The words *soul mate* send chills down my spine. The average person might find comfort in the idea of having someone who shares every aspect of their life, but I know better.

I belong to an ancient race of humans descended from the Greek gods and goddesses—the Hellenicus. My ancestors are also closely tied to the origin of the soul mate. I have seen the torment caused by the existence of soul mates, and so, I dread the day when I'll be reunited with mine.

Of course, not all of my people feel the same way. We have been taught to take pride in our history, to be gracious about our ability to reconnect with our soul mates. As Hellenicus, we learn from a young age where we come from and where we sit in the hierarchy of our community. Reciting our history in my sleep was nothing; that was how much it had been drilled into me over the years.

Centuries ago, before the Golden Age, there were the three parents—the Sun, the Earth, and the Moon, and each of them had offspring. The Sun produced the men, the Earth produced the women, and the Moon produced the androgynes. The original human form was a hideous sight to behold, having one head with two faces, four arms, four legs, and two sets of genitalia. These humans rolled, hand over hand and foot over foot, by manner of cartwheels at double speed. These original humans had been created to be strong and fast and free and powerful, and they roamed the earth with a great deal more freedom and power than humans have now.

The power eventually went to their heads. They thought that they could stop giving offerings to the gods and goddesses and be gods in their own right. They decided they deserved a place on Mount Olympus alongside the gods; a rebellion broke out and humans scaled the mountain to attack. Obviously, it wasn't a good idea and it led to an inevitable defeat. The Hellenicus commemorate this battle as the Day of Prideful Folly.

Because of the humans' audacity, the gods, with their limitless power, pondered how to punish them. Zeus could burn them to dust with his lightning bolts, just as he'd done to the giants. Poseidon could drown the fools with an enormous wave. Or Hades could lock the creatures in the depths of Tartarus for eternity.

But the gods loved a little drama for their own amusement, and they also loved to be worshipped. Zeus realized that humans weren't the real threat—it was their oversized egos that needed adjustment. He stripped them of their arrogance by splitting them into two with his lightning bolts, making them half as fast and half as strong. Not only would it put them in their place, but it would also double the number of those giving tribute to the gods. Problem solved, right?

Well, no. The halved creatures ran around frantically, looking for their other halves, seeking them out, embracing them, and trying to be one again. The creatures who had been double women naturally sought out women. Those who had been double men sought out men. And the androgynes sought out members of the opposite gender. But, unable to rejoin, they lived in utter misery and began to starve to death in their sorrow.

Mindful of his need for worshippers, Zeus instructed Apollo to create a means for the creatures to reunite, if only briefly. Apollo did so by turning the genitals toward the belly side of the body. According to the legend, when the two halves finally found each other, they would have an unspoken understanding. They would lay with each other in unity and know no greater joy, and when each of them was reincarnated after they died, they would be reunited in their next lives.

To complicate things further, the gods and goddesses mingled with the newly divided humans, fornicating with them and producing demigods. These demigods would then have children of their own, and so on, until clans were built. These clans became known as the Hellenicus—my ancestors.

Over the generations, the Hellenicus spread out around the globe. We were taught to take pride in our history, and so, despite the diaspora, we have always held on to our traditions. But one thing has kept us divided: the three castes. Pure Royals, Royals, and Regulars.

Pure Royals retained the top shelf of our hierarchy because they were the descendants of the Big Three: the Lord of the Sky, Zeus; the Lord of the Sea, Poseidon; and the Lord of the Underworld, Hades. It was easy to tell who belonged to the Pure Royals by looking at their eyes. Pure Royals who had blue eyes were from the Christoulakis family, Zeus's descendants. Green eyes belonged to the Ambrosia family, Poseidon's descendants. And finally, those with dark brown, nearly black eyes, were from the now-extinct Stavros family, Hades's descendants.

Slightly below the Pure Royals were the Royals, the descendants of the remaining Olympian gods and goddesses. Unlike the Pure Royals, who maintained their original ancient Greek family name, the Royals' family names were influenced by the culture and language of their geographical locations. For example, Hera's descendants were originally known as the Themistoklis family, but in Australia, it was Tavoularis, and in Bulgaria, it became something entirely different: Petrova. I didn't even bother trying to remember all their names, though. Most Royals would jump at the chance to let you know their royal lineage, anyway. Besides, it was also obvious who was a Royal from the size of their wallet.

Then there was the lowest caste, slightly above your standard-issue humans. That was where I fit in: the Regulars. Look it up in the dictionary and it was precisely what I was supposed to be: average, common, uniform, consistent, and fixed. No overflowing bank accounts, no exotic vacations, no sports cars, or big houses. There was a god for everything under the sun, but of course, us Regulars didn't share a lineage with the fancy, powerful ones. We came from the many gods and goddesses who didn't have a seat on Mount Olympus. They were the gods and goddesses of regular things, like the god of sleep, Hypnos, and the god of the west wind, Zephyros. It was next to impossible to keep track of a Regular's lineage—there were too many minor gods and too many of us.

Other than being the descendants of the gods and goddesses, the Hellenicus had one other thing in common: to honor our demigod lineage, Apollo wanted to set us apart from normal humans—or, as we called them, the Nescient—and awarded us an extraordinary ability to help us find our soul mates. Our gift allowed us to read our other half's mind, something the Nescient couldn't do. That way, even though we were continuously reincarnated, we would always be able to find each other.

Every year, the Court—a heavily guarded compound located in Denali, Alaska—held a revered event known as the Gathering. It was a chance for all the Hellenicus from around the world to come together in the hopes of being reunited with their soul mates. In our eighteenth year, during our first Gathering, our clairaudient gift was awakened through a sacred ritual known as the Awakening Ceremony.

Then we would wait for the moment when we met our other half. A single touch could ignite what we called a click—a phenomenon that allowed us to hear our soul mate's thoughts. It was how we knew we had found the one.

I would be eighteen soon. Tomorrow I would officially go to the Court for the first time. And find out if my life would change forever.

CHAPTER ONE

"Remember to set your alarm, Avery," my mother shouted from downstairs. Despite Katherine Montgomery's small stature, she had a loud, stern voice. I was in the middle of brushing my teeth, so I couldn't respond to her right away. "Avery! Did you hear what I just said?"

"Yes, Mom!" I opened the bathroom door so she could hear me clearly. "I got it. I'm brushing my teeth."

"Tomorrow is a big day. You need to be prepared in case you meet your soul mate."

Soul mate.

I shuddered. That word alone ignited the same reaction I got from watching a horror movie alone in my bedroom at midnight. I could always turn off the movie, but there was no escaping my fate.

I was seventeen now, but I would turn eighteen on December 22. I would be attending my first Gathering to awaken my clairaudient ability. Thinking about the long procession, the formality, and the fact that I had to dress up for the occasion was exhausting. After all, there was no guarantee that your soul mate would be at the Gathering in your first year—or even your fifth or sixth. Or even at all. Sometimes a Hellenicus died still waiting to meet their soul mate. My mom came upstairs and we met in the hallway.

"Hurry up and get to sleep. Eye bags aren't attractive."

"Mom, relax. Maybe I won't meet mine this year," I said.

"But maybe you will," she said. "I met your dad during my first Gathering. Not everyone's so lucky to meet their soul mate at their first Gathering, but we're the descendants of—"

"Tyche, the goddess of luck," I said, having been reminded at least a dozen times a day. Everyone knew that it was impossible for Regulars to trace their lineage, so it drove me crazy that she insisted we were the descendants of Tyche. I had just about the worst luck in the world, which convinced me that my mom had no idea what she was talking about.

"Exactly. We're descendants of the goddess of luck! You should know better that—"

What if she was right? What if I did meet my soul mate this year? My body instinctively shivered at the thought.

The other Hellenicus would be surprised if they knew how repulsed I was at the prospect of reuniting with my soul mate. Most claimed that having a soul mate was romantic and that we should be grateful for Apollo's gift of the click. But for me, having a soul mate was more like being subject to an arranged marriage that I could never run away from, even if I wanted to. Once I was Awakened, it would be possible for me to have a click that would cause my soul mate's mind to be instantly linked to mine. I would always be able to hear my soul mate's thoughts, and they would always be able to hear mine. If that wasn't a total breach of privacy, I didn't know what was. And the idea of being tied to someone I possibly didn't even know existed until the day we were revealed to be soul mates was the icing on the cake.

Honestly, I'd prefer to be a Nescient. At least they could ignore the whole soul-mate situation if they wanted to. Of course, this was all merely wishful thinking. As a Hellenicus I was destined to be reunited with my soul mate in the most invasive way possible.

"—girls pray to Aphrodite, wishing to be reunited with their soul mate as soon as possible. You should be praying too. Let me see if I can get—"

"Mom." I stopped her before she signed me up for some obscure Greek ritual that I didn't even know about. "It's late. Didn't you say you wanted me to get to sleep early?"

"Yes," she said. "Go back to your room and have a good rest."

I quickly headed to my bedroom before my mom had a change of heart. It was rare for us not to bicker, and I knew that I should cherish this moment. As I lay down on my bed and stared at the ceiling, I thought about how impossible it was to escape my destiny. It was so disheartening.

The Fates shaped each of our lives. They were the three weaving goddesses—Clotho, Lachesis, and Atropos—who were in charge of assigning mortals to their destinies. From birth to death to how and when we would meet our other half, and even whether we would meet them in this lifetime—everything was in the hands of these three goddesses. If even the Great Zeus, king of the gods, could not overrule their decree, how did I stand a chance?

I reached for the shoe box hidden underneath my bed. This was my liberation. Since the day I had decided that I wanted none of this soul-mate business, I had been saving up every penny I had. There was a faded photo buried underneath the crumpled money stuffed inside the box. It was of a pale girl with insufferable auburn frizz for hair and dark-brown eyes that were too big for her small oval face. Next to her was an olive-skinned guy with dark hair. They were both smiling, wind blowing the hair from their faces, sunlight shining on their foreheads. Me and Bryan. Tears prickled the corners of my eyes, and I took a deep breath.

He was supposed to be here with me. We were supposed to escape together.

I wiped my tears away with my sleeves. I wished I could go a day, or even an hour, without thinking about him or being reminded of him, but it was impossible when everything and everywhere evoked something about him—even this room. He used to sit on the floor with me, and we'd spend hours talking about our dreams and what we wanted to do in life.

The Davises had moved next door ten years ago; they were Regulars too. While my house was always quiet, practically a ghost house, Bryan's had been the other way around. Every morning his mom turned on the radio and tuned into a country music channel while doing housework (I disliked country music because I'd heard more than my share of it). Despite going to the same school, Bryan and I never shared anything but awkward hellos for the first five years we lived next to each other.

But then his father kicked him out of the house. Six months ago, Bryan's mother had a terrible accident while hiking. She lost her footing and slid down the edge of the hill, hitting her head against a rock on the way down. She ended up in a coma. Instead of being there for his wife, Bryan's dad cozied up to a co-worker. Bryan found out about his dad's secret affair one day after coming home early from visiting his mom at the hospital.

With country music–free mornings, I had been getting used to sleeping in, but that morning, slapping, clacking, and crashing sounds jolted me awake. Bryan had confronted his dad bright and early, causing havoc before the birds had even started chirping. Everyone on our street heard the details of their argument, crystal clear. Disturbed by the noise, I ran to my window and caught sight of Bryan dashing out the front door, carrying nothing but his backpack. His usual slick, jet-black hair was disheveled, and his face was red with anger. Catching his breath, he brushed away a bead of sweat trickling down his forehead and looked back at his house before walking away. I watched him until I could no longer see any glimpse of his grey backpack and white sneakers.

My day went on much like it had begun, with my parents arguing. Most of their fight took place inside their heads, but every now and then my dad would shout, "Holy Zeus," and my mom would slam cupboards and doors. It wasn't enough to clue me in on the cause of their disagreement, but it was enough to make me want to lock myself in my room with my head hidden underneath my pillow. After I'd listened to them for the majority of the day, Mom called me downstairs to demand I go buy the sour cream that she'd forgotten at the grocery store. Something told me that they weren't arguing about the forgotten sour cream, but I was happy to have an excuse to get out of the house for some fresh air.

To avoid having to spend more time at home, I took the long route home after shopping and passed the playground. Bryan was sitting on the swing, his backpack flopped on the ground by his feet. He was staring at the ground, deep in thought, a frown wrinkled across his forehead and a yellowish bruise on his tear-stained cheek. It must have been tough to find out about your parent's infidelity and then, to top it all off, be kicked out for confronting them about it.

I must have said something out loud because suddenly Bryan lifted his face and our gazes met. The way he looked at me, with eyes the deepest shade of the richest earth, made me feel exposed. Neither of us knew what to say after what had happened earlier that day. *So, hey, I also happen to think your dad is an asshole. Kudos on standing up to him for your mom,* was definitely not a good conversation starter. Instead I squeaked out a lame, "Hi."

"Hey." He greeted me. "I'm sorry you had to hear all that. It probably ruined your morning and anyone else's who heard my fight with"—he paused as he appeared to have a battle in his head over what he should call his father, finally settling on—"Daniel."

"It's fine. I hope things get better, though," I said.

"I doubt it will. I mean, I'm here ready to sleep on the swing."

"I'd take the slide if I were you. At least you could lay on your back."

"Good idea." He smiled. His bottom teeth were slightly crooked but very white. "Maybe I'll do that."

I lifted my left wrist to check the time on my rectangle-shaped watch. If I stayed for another minute, my parents, particularly my dad, would call the SWAT team to look for me. He was *that* protective and paranoid. "Look, I have to get back. My parents will worry, so I'll see you around?"

"See you around, neighbor."

I felt guilty leaving him there, and I couldn't stop thinking about him for the rest of the evening.

For several nights in a row, once the sun had set, I would find something I needed to buy at the mini-mart—excuses to go out and meet Bryan. I'd bring him food and we'd talk about being Hellenicus and rant about all the Royal pain in the asses at school. One week went by and his dad had still not allowed him back home, so I offered to let him stay at my house. In secret, he'd climb in and out of my room using the tree outside my window. He'd sneak in late at night and leave early in the morning before my parents, or any of our prying neighbors, woke up.

We quickly became inseparable, partners in crime, each as silly as the other, and we did everything together. It was hard to describe the connection we had because I didn't fully understand it myself. It was as if we had always been friends even though it had only been a few weeks. He made me feel comfortable. I was myself around him, and he never judged me. Bryan was the only person I knew who understood what it was like to have a turbulent family life. I trusted him with everything.

Our friendship continued even after his mom finally awoke from her coma, returned home, and brought him home. Bryan would still sneak into my room when the rest of the neighborhood was asleep, and we'd talk for hours. He vented about what was going on at home, his parents' divorce, and how his mother cried herself to sleep every night, haunted by the fact that she was able to hear his father's thoughts about the other woman. Bryan cried as he poured his heart out. Together, we agreed that neither of us would ever experience the click—the invasion of privacy was too much. We had seen how it could all go wrong. If only his parents' minds were not linked, perhaps his mother could have moved on.

Then one night, while sitting on our favorite swing in the nearby park during one of our usual conversations, he told me he had feelings for me. I was stunned. I'd come to think of him as a brother. I couldn't say the one thing he wished to hear: that I felt the same way about him. The heart-wrenching look on his face, as if his whole world had crashed and burned, was one I would never forget—no matter how hard I tried.

The next day he texted me from our Hellenic school's library, saying he needed to tell me something urgently. I told him to come over, dreading the awkward conversation that would ensue. As I waited for him to arrive, an uneasy feeling grew in my stomach. Something, maybe intuition, informed me that something terrible was about to happen. Still, I waited and waited.

He never showed up. Bryan died in a car accident. That was over a year ago now, but I still missed him every second of every day. I also couldn't help feeling like it was my fault; if he hadn't been on his way to see me, he would still be alive today. We would be working on our escape plan together—counting our combined savings and deciding whether New York was too expensive for our budget. We had already agreed that a big city was our only option if we wanted to avoid being found by our parents. We could live peacefully among the Nescient, blissfully click-free.

I couldn't bear to look at the photo any longer so I put it back inside the shoe box, closed the lid, and pushed the box to the dark corner underneath the bed. I hated the idea of someone reading every passing thought I had inside my mind. I couldn't go through what Bryan's mom had. As cliché as it sounded, I wanted a normal life—free from all the sacred rituals and important celebrations. The fact that I'd also be free from all the Royals who always looked at me as if I was below them—as if I was *less* than them—was a generous bonus.

Without Bryan, though, I couldn't escape on my own. The thought of being on the road alone terrified me, and I hadn't saved up enough, anyway. It seemed like I was stuck going to Court after all.

My parents were busy preparing for my first Gathering. My mom insisted it'd help to take my mind off of Bryan's death if I immersed myself in the rituals. While everyone with royal blood in their veins received an invitation, Regulars had to travel all the way to Court a year early to sign up and get their photographs taken in order to participate. My dad had made me go to Court with him so I could sign up. Getting my photo taken as I stood against the wall next to a water dispenser had been embarrassing enough—the photo looked like a mug shot—but the worst part of the whole ordeal was that I had to wait for hours outside the gate at the security office while my dad was inside finishing the necessary paperwork. Those who were not of royal blood and had not been to their first Gathering couldn't enter the Court, which was why we had to have our parents come with us.

I'd spent the first hour alone. Then *he* was there with his hazel eyes and raven hair, exchanging some heated words with the guard at the security gate. He was undoubtedly the most handsome person I'd ever seen. His whole demeanor changed from frustrated to intrigued when he noticed me gawking, and he strolled confidently over.

"What was that about?" I asked.

"Some bullshit about me not being able to get back into the Court grounds after leaving. I was only outside for a minute! I needed a little walk to get some air. But apparently I need to wait for verification to get back in." He glared at the guard before softening his expression again. "But it looks like I'm in good company now. I'm Carlo."

"Avery," I said, my face flushing.

We had only used only our first names. I didn't know his family name, and he didn't know mine. We didn't know each other's Hellenicus status, and for the first time, it felt normal and refreshing to be Avery—*not* Avery Montgomery, the mere Regular.

I lost track of time as we sat outside the gate of the security office, chatting for hours. Carlo reminded me of Bryan in so many ways. He had a way of speaking to me, just as Bryan had, that made me feel safe, and the conversation flowed naturally between us. In the short time we spent together that day, we learned so much about each other.

"When you finally become a pilot, where will you fly your plane first?" Carlo asked.

"I don't think I can choose where to go. I'll have to go wherever they tell me to," I said.

"Maybe. But it's your dream, right?" Carlo grinned. "Maybe you could work for the Court? I heard they recently bought another jet. They will let you go for your first trip."

There was no way I could handle having snobby Royals as my passengers. Since Carlo could be a Royal and might be offended by this sentiment, I didn't say this out loud.

Perhaps my true feelings showed on my face, because after a short while, Carlo said, "Probably not a good idea." It was almost as if he had read my mind. He leaned forward and whispered in a conspiratorial tone, "There are a lot of vexing people around here—some might even call them assholes." I couldn't help laughing, and his eyes lit up, knowing he was the source of my amusement. "Anyway, it's your dream, Avery—you can be and do whatever you want. You just have to have enough courage and willpower to pursue it."

"What about you? What do you want to be?"

"I want to be a teacher."

"What kind of teacher? Math? Biology? High school or college?"

"High school teacher, and yes, you guessed right, I want to teach math. I love math, and I want to break the perception that it's a boring or tough subject."

"Good luck with that. With the math mark on my report card, I won't be changing my mind about that subject any time soon."

"I'll take that as a challenge," he said. "Are you nervous about this whole thing? You're preparing for your first Gathering, right?"

"Yeah." It took a while for me to find my voice again, suddenly feeling uncomfortable. If Bryan were still here, I wouldn't be going through any of this. My heart ached as the memories of Bryan came flooding back to me. I looked up, trying to keep my tears from spilling. A soft, warm hand cupped mine.

"You lost someone you love."

It was more of a statement than a question, but I answered it nonetheless as I shook my head. "I lost someone who loved me. I didn't have time to figure out my own feelings. But I think I lost my chance at happiness."

"Do you think this person was the *one*?"

"I don't know." I shrugged helplessly. "We aren't supposed to know until we have a click, are we not?"

"Yes. We have to have a click to know for sure." A look of disappointment flashed across his face. "This year will be my fourth Gathering, but I still haven't met my other half. We just have to trust the Fates, I guess."

The Fates. The mention of them got me frustrated in an instant.

"Don't you get tired of waiting? You've wasted four years waiting for your soul mate." He looked like he was about to interject in protest, but decided to simply clamp his mouth shut and listen. "What if you don't meet your soul mate again this year? What if next year you don't either? And the year after that?"

It was only when he squeezed his hand that I realized he was still holding mine. "Avery, I understand what you mean, and these four years haven't exactly been filled with patience either," Carlo said, shaking his head lightly. "Maybe for you it's a waste of time, but for some people, for me anyway, it's not. After all, we're not waiting for a pizza delivery; we're waiting for our literal other half, the other half of our soul. Whoever it might be, they will make it worth all the years I've spent waiting."

"You can just as easily meet a nice person and have a shot at happiness."

"Maybe," Carlo said. "But they wouldn't be my other half. Besides, what if one day I have a click? I would end up hurting two people, not just one."

"You're just going to wait?"

"Of course."

"What if your soul mate never comes? What if you waste your whole life waiting for someone who never shows up?"

"Then I shall meet my soul mate in my next life."

He noticed the disbelieving look on my face, "Look, I'm not trying to change your opinion—I believe each of us can have our own—but don't feel sorry for me by thinking that I'm wasting my time because I don't think of it that way."

We were quiet for a moment before he cleared his throat. "Can I ask you something?"

"Sure."

"I'm just curious. You know if you don't go through with your first Gathering you could live as a Nescient, and your gift will never be awakened, right?" I nodded. "Then why are you signing up for your first Gathering if you think that this is a waste of time?"

"Because I have no choice," I answered matter of factly.

"That's where you're wrong, Avery." Carlo's kindness danced in those hazel eyes. "You always have a choice."

Ω

My dad showed up moments later, but not before Carlo and I had exchanged phone numbers. After a few days, he texted, telling me he hadn't met his other half. Even though I *still* wasn't entirely sold on this soul-mates business, I couldn't help feeling relieved that he hadn't met his. With Carlo, I felt a spark of hope. I met him exactly when I needed to, and he offered me a new solution to my fears. There was this small, yet unwavering thought growing inside my head that maybe, if my soul mate turned out to be someone I knew—and actually liked—then maybe clicking with them wouldn't be as horrible as I had thought.

Maybe the reason why I was still here instead of on a bus heading to New York or Seattle, anywhere but Denali, was because I had feelings for Carlo. Unlike me, he was one of the Hellenicus who thought that having a soul mate was a gift. And his trust in the process planted doubts in my mind that I couldn't shake off. As if knowing that I was thinking about him, my phone buzzed. Carlo. I quickly unlocked my phone and pulled up his text. It started with his usual greeting,

Buonasera, cara mia.

That night, I decided that I wanted, more than anything, to know if Carlo was my soul mate or not. If by my birthday we did not have a click, at least I wouldn't have to live the rest of my life haunted by what-ifs.

It was risky to have hope because hope led to expectation, which could also lead to disappointment. I'd heard about it often, how a Hellenicus went to their first Gathering certain that their significant other was their other half only to be heartbroken when they discovered their beloved was meant for someone else. And there was no guarantee that things would work out—look at Bryan's parents; look at mine fighting all the time. I was also aware that if I went to the Gathering and my soul mate turned out to be somebody other than Carlo, my whole plan was ruined. But if I didn't click with anyone, then I still had my savings. I could escape before next year's Gathering, and my original plan to live in hiding among the Nescient would remain intact.

After spending most of the night mulling the pros and cons over in my mind, I woke up to the sun peeking through the slits in my blinds, my alarm ringing, and my mom's voice shouting through my bedroom door telling me to get up. I had chosen to stay. I would go to my first Gathering. When it came to Carlo, I simply had to know.

CHAPTER TWO

It was barely eight o'clock in the morning and I'd already lost my temper.

"Mom, I've told you, I'm done packing!" I hissed through gritted teeth. My mom slid the zipper around the suitcase, then dumped the contents onto my bed—every piece of clothing that I had spent hours ironing and putting neatly inside. "Why. Did. You. Do. That?"

Ignoring me, my mom tossed aside all of the old T-shirts I loved so much. She pulled out dresses and some faux-fur coats from the plastic bag she'd had with her when she had barged into my room and packed them in place of my choices.

"I'm not going to wear *those*."

"You will," she said as she turned on her heels and rummaged through my wardrobe. "You won't have a choice when these are the only clothes you have with you."

"If *I* am the one who has to wear them, don't you think that *I* should be the one deciding what *I* wear?"

"Nope."

This was too much. We had already fought during breakfast an hour ago, and I really did not want to have another argument now.

I left, paying no mind to her yelling as I raced downstairs, took my coat off its hanger, and dashed out the front door.

My mom and I had never had a stable relationship, and without anything in common, it was even harder to build one. We were doomed to clash. Our personalities were too different: I was fire and she was water. If I was lucky, I could use my fire to evaporate her water. But if she held her ground, she would put out my fire with her water. It entirely depended on who was more stubborn at that moment. We could never reach an agreement because neither one of us was willing to compromise—maybe that was the *one* thing we had in common. We didn't even agree on small things, like what we should have for dinner or who would take a bath first. Most of the time my dad had to come between us with a solution that we'd both accept.

Taking a left turn at the junction, I headed to Bryan's swing and sat there for a few minutes before pulling out my phone to call my best friend, Kristen Ambrosia. Although Bryan had been my partner in crime, Kris was the one person I shared all my bottled-up feelings with. We had been best friends since her first day at my Hellenic school. She had walked toward me—the fat girl with ginger hair and freckles all over her nose—stopped by my desk, and asked to sit with me. She ignored everyone else who had tried to befriend her simply because she was a Pure Royal, and chose me, a Regular.

Other than glorifying soul mates, the Hellenicus were obsessed with status and how to promote themselves. I never understood it; it wasn't like you could elevate your caste based on who you hung around with. Still, Royals tended to be even more status hungry than us Regulars, who had accepted our place. Besides our love for mystery novels and detective TV series, Kris and I had bonded over our shared dislike of the Hellenicus caste system and how it made some people so shallow.

After trying to phone her several times and having all my calls go straight to voice mail, I slid my phone into the front pocket of my jeans and decided to go to her house, which was only a few blocks away, in a fancy gated community.

The house looked like a cutout from an architecture magazine, looming proudly behind creaky iron gates and flanked by rows of skeletal trees swaying gently in the December wind. At its threshold stood a delicate marble fountain. On summer days the soft gurgling of the clear water resonated melodically in the surrounding silence, but now that it was winter the water had frozen, and all that could be heard were my footsteps crunching on the snow of the front walkway.

Cloaked in blankets of white snow and days of little sunshine, winter was a long season in Alaska. Although it only took fifteen minutes to get to the Ambrosias', my feet were numb thanks to my stupid choice of footwear. I should have worn extra socks.

I was about to ring the bell at the grand entrance to the Ambrosia house when someone turned the lock. I hoped it was Leopold, the gardener's handsome son, who might answer the door again. Last time I hadn't been prepared and had parsley from my salad stuck between my teeth. Leopold had awkwardly pointed it out. Zeus, it was embarrassing. But I had learned my lesson and ran my tongue along the front of my teeth to make sure nothing was stuck in there. When the door swung open, I had my most dazzling smile on . . . only to have it dissolve immediately.

The gods loved to torture me—always throwing obstacles in my way. This time it was in the form of a six-foot-tall guy with tousled brown hair and mesmerizing green eyes who was looking down at me from his lofty height. Vladimir Ambrosia, Kris's older brother. I tried to stand up a little taller, stretching my five-foot-two frame and refusing to show deference to a Pure Royal, despite having spent my whole life being trained to.

The last time we had been in the same place was two years ago during Hermaea—a festival with an athletic contest held in honor of Hermes. Vladimir had come to support Kris, who played tennis. I had been cheering on my best friend, minding my own business, and doing my best to ignore him. But before the match was over, we had managed to bicker. As usual, he had started it.

I still don't understand why people who know nothing about tennis feel the need to shout out during the game as if they know what they are talking about. It just makes them look stupid.

Excuse me?! His passive-aggressive comment was directed at me. *I'm only here to support my best friend, who also happens to be your sister. Got a problem with that?*

Yes, if you're going to shout "That's cheating" like you did a minute ago when you know nothing about the rules.

My finger shot toward Kris's opponent. *But what she did was cheating!*

It actually wasn't. And I'm simply pointing out how embarrassing it is for Kristen to have to listen to you shouting ridiculous accusations without any legitimate basis.

After the game, I asked Kris and she agreed with me that her opponent hadn't been playing fair. Vlad was unnecessarily being an ass.

That wasn't the first time he had acted like a smart-ass either. He always provoked me like that. He started with something condescending that triggered my anger and then would somehow manage to make me look like a brat for arguing without knowing when to stop.

I hated him so much.

Holding my stance, I looked up. Way up to his thin lips, straight nose, and green eyes that reminded me so much of damp moss after the autumn rain. Had he always been this handsome? He was better looking than I'd remembered. It irked me to realize that I didn't find his face repulsive.

"Just my luck," Vlad said flatly.

What. A. Jerk.

"Can you please be less of an asshole and get Kris for me?" I said.

"There's a gadget called a phone, you know. We're not living in the Golden Age, Avy. We've evolved, technology has evolved. You don't have four legs and four arms anymore either."

It seemed that since we had last seen each other he had perfected his irritating tone and saved it just for me. And to make it worse, he had used the nickname that I *severely* hated. It sounded so much like gravy—which was perhaps where he had derived it from. What was so difficult about saying *Avery* or *Ave*?

"I've called her a hundred times, but she isn't picking up. Is she home?"

"Have you ever considered that maybe there is a reason why she didn't answer any of your *bajillion* phone calls?" he said. "Maybe she needs some time away from you."

Completely fed up, I pushed past him to go see for myself whether Kris was home or not. Stomping through the door, I not-so-accidentally tromped on his left foot as I made my way into the warmth of the house. He groaned, but I couldn't have cared less.

A sparkling chandelier hung in the grandiose hallway and I could see the spacious living room where social gatherings were usually held. Kris's mom had an eye for interior design, and everything in their home was meticulously placed. I headed up the spiral staircase on my left, making my way to Kris's bedroom on the second floor, where she was stuffing clothes into her suitcase. I immediately crouched down to help.

"Geez, Zeus, how come your charming family has such an asshat of a son? I mean, come on, apart from him, all of you are practically saints!" I didn't bother lowering my voice. If he heard me, perhaps he would fix his manners.

"I know, right?" There was affection in her beautiful green eyes, indicating she didn't mean anything she said except her next sentence. "But you know we all love him."

"Hold on there. I'm not included in that 'we.' You and your parents may be bound to love him by blood. Me? I can hardly tolerate the guy."

Perhaps if I had a brother I would know the feeling of unconditional love for a sibling. Or maybe not, considering Kris and I were nothing alike. She behaved as graciously as a princess with a heart of gold to boot, while I had a hot temper and a level of stubbornness that could tempt Mother Teresa herself. Our looks were distinctive too. She was the pretty, platinum blond with jade-green eyes, and I was her brown-eyed, redheaded sidekick.

"Why do you guys fight like cats and dogs now? I don't remember you being like this when we were kids."

"Oh please. Don't you remember third grade and all those horrible nicknames he created for me?" Kris pointed at the orange dress on my left, and I handed it over. "Or that time he ruined our first time hosting a party here by kicking everyone out?"

Kris neatly put the dress inside her suitcase then reached for a white tunic. "We would have been in deep trouble if he hadn't done that, Ave. That party got out of control."

"That's not the point. The point is he ruined it for us." I reached for Kris's pajamas. "He even dragged Raymond out by his ear. Like, who does that?"

This time, my best friend laughed. "My brother, apparently." She leaned back against the wall. "Do you remember what happened to Nikki, though?"

"Yes! How could I not? That's the only time your brother did something that I actually approved of."

Nikki had been a bully at our Hellenic school, and somehow, she had managed to sneak into our party. When she tried to make a move on Vlad, he flat out rejected her. It was a small piece of revenge after all the nasty stuff she had done to Kris and me over the years. As we talked about all the funny things that happened at that party, my tension dispersed until the anger ebbed away. Talking to Kris always had that effect on me.

Kris sat on top of the suitcase while I slid the zipper shut. "Hey, I just realized—I can't text you since my phone died and I can't find the charger." She tapped her forehead. "Here's the thing, Mom and Dad can't come with me today—they have something to take care off. Do you want to come with me or would you rather go with your parents?"

"*Yes!*"

My best friend giggled. "Which one?"

"Joining you, of course."

"Cool. I'll let my parents know." Kris looked down at her clasped hands.

"Let's hear it," I said. "I know you have something on your mind."

"You can always tell, huh," she said. "You're my best friend, more like a sister, and I want you with me, of course I do, but are you all right going to the Court?"

I opened my mouth to answer, but nothing came out. "Ave," Kris continued, "I know it takes so much for you to change your mind once you've set it on something. I understand your feelings about the soul-mate thing. You know, after what happened to Bryan's parents, not to mention Adrian."

Adrian Ambrosia was her cousin, who had also suffered heartbreak because of this stupid "gift."

"Kris—"

"And I've never asked you to change your view, and I'm not going to do that now. But how are you feeling, Ave? If you don't want to go, we can call this trip off. We can postpone our first Gathering until you're ready."

I knew how much the Gathering meant to Kris. She had been looking forward to her first Gathering since the day I'd first met her. There was no way I'd let her sit this out just for me. "No, Kris, I can't do that. I'd never do that to you. You've wanted this for so long."

"I don't mind delaying it a year or two for you."

I shook my head, about to tell her that I had already made up my mind, when we heard a knock on the door. "Are you girls done?" Vlad's voice echoed in the hallway in front of Kris's bedroom. "The driver is ready and waiting for you downstairs." He pushed the door open and stuck his head in. "Kris, do you need help with your bags?"

I mouthed *I'm fine*, and that seemed to erase at least some of her worries. "Sure," she replied.

Vlad's gaze lingered on me for a few seconds before he broke it off and reached for Kris's suitcase. "Only one?"

"Nope." My best friend grinned mischievously. "Two more." Kris and I broke into peals of laughter.

Ω

An hour later, I found myself relaxed alongside Kris in the back seat of one of the Ambrosias' fleets of cars. My dad was riding shotgun. People attending their first Gathering had to have an adult present to help with the check-in process, so there was no getting away from him for the time being. My mom was still mad about our last fight, so she refused to come. I wasn't sure if she'd even bother to show up for the Awakening Ceremony. But at least I didn't have to worry about her for now.

One of the downsides of having my dad with us was having to listen to him kissing my best friend's Royal butt. He was obsessed with anything Royal, and always went overboard to try to please Kris and her family. It was *excruciating* to watch. But it was still way better than riding in awkward silence with him in his Toyota Yaris all the way there.

Kris reached over and placed her hand on top of mine. I looked up to see her smooth profile—the shiny white skin of her forehead, straight nose, and full lips. Her long platinum-blond hair framed her face perfectly, and the sun shining through the side of the window gave her a luminous backdrop. She was the definition of stunning, and being born an Ambrosia meant she would always stand out in a crowd.

One lock of her blond hair slid across her cheek, and she raised her free hand to push it behind one ear.

"I'm so excited, Ave." Her smile widened. I turned my palm up and squeezed her hand, grinning back at her before turning my gaze out the window as our neighborhood rolled by. We were leaving behind our normal American-teenager façade and preparing ourselves for the centuries-old compound we were heading toward.

"So, Ave, tell me . . ."

I could sense by the way her eyes glinted that she was about to bring up something I didn't want to talk about. "Hmm?"

"What did he say?" she said, blatant curiosity etched across her face.

"Who?

"Carlo. We were in so much of a hurry that I didn't get a chance to ask you about him." I glanced at the front seat where my dad had his eyes glued to the road as if he was the one driving. She lowered her voice, "Don't worry, he can't hear us."

"What do you want to know?" I whispered.

"Everything. How's the long-distance relationship been working out?" Kris teased.

"He said he's coming and he . . ."—I pulled up his last text on my phone—"Don't freak out, okay. He said he hopes that I'm his other half."

Kris read the text. I didn't need to look at it again—I remembered every word by heart. After all, it had helped me make my decision to go to Court.

Buonasera, cara mia. Even without you saying it aloud, I know how you feel about soul mates. You always swiftly changed the subject whenever I brought it up during our calls. That's why I'm sending this text. Bottom line, all I want is for you to be happy. I don't know whether you're coming or not, but my gut tells me that I'll meet my soul mate this time. With these feelings I have for you, I can't help thinking that maybe my other half is you. Whichever decision you make, to come to Court or not, I'll respect it. That's what we do when we love someone.

Kris let out a gasp. "Avery Montgomery, how can I *not* freak out? Dear Poseidon, he's in love with you!"

Shaking her head in wonder, she passed my phone back. "I need to meet this Carlo guy. I can't believe someone finally got through your stubbornness. He must be special," she said. "How on earth don't you have any photos of him?"

"His family is part of the whole no-social-media-for-Hellenicus movement." I shifted in my seat. "It's not like I'm head over heels for him. Well, hardly. It's probably because no guy has ever paid any attention to me."

Kris laughed. "Please, Ave, guys practically throw themselves at you. You're just really picky."

I snorted. Unlike my best friend, I had not been blessed with delicate, proportionate features. And we both knew there had only been one guy with a crush on me: Bryan.

With the memory of *him* fresh in my mind, the cruel gods seized the opportunity to remind me of his demise as a truck cut right in front of us. The driver braked abruptly, and I slammed up against my seat belt and my dad cursed. As if I was hypnotized, I breathed out in a whisper, "Bryan."

It was always like that. Nearly every single thing, every place, brought back a memory of him. My chest tightened. It had also been winter the day he'd taught me how to drive—the day we'd taken his dad's Mustang. I had been sulking in my bed with a ton of homework piled up when I heard the soft thud of a pebble hitting my window. Thinking it was the naughty kid from across the street, I was about to tell them to knock it off but found Bryan, looking up, car keys dangling in his hand.

I ran downstairs, grabbed my coat, and jumped into the car. His dad flew out the door in a rage when he heard the roar of the engine in the street. We laughed as we drove to an abandoned parking lot where I could practice without disrupting anyone. That time, I had also hit the brake too soon, throwing us forward against our seat belts. It was as if it had been a premonition of what would happen to Bryan only a few weeks later. My parents lectured me for two hours when we got home, but it had been worth it to spend the afternoon with him. I didn't know then how little time I had left with him.

"Avery!" My dad frantically called my name. "Avery! Are you all right?" His dark-brown eyes were filled with concern, and his voice sounded like he genuinely cared about my well-being.

Only then did I noticed that the car had stopped at the side of the road and there were three pairs of eyes staring at me. I swallowed back my tears. "I'm fine."

"Good." His parental concern was gone in a flash, his face instantly returning to normal. We moved again.

Hearing him clicking his tongue, I knew I would hear about this later when Kris wasn't around. He would somehow find a way to make this my fault. I could feel my dad's stare as he watched me like a hawk in the rearview mirror, but I pretended not to notice. Outside the window, I could see the mountain range coming into view, the landscape becoming more and more forested as we traveled closer to Denali. Now, just like Kris, but for very different reasons, I couldn't wait for this journey to be over.

CHAPTER THREE

This was it. I would finally see inside the Court, home of Queen Christoulakis and all the Hellenicus relics we'd learned about at school. Kris, who had been coming here forever—her family's ancestral residence was here, and she had lived at Court until she was ten—tried to answer my millions of questions. But seeing it first-hand was the only thing that would truly satisfy my curiosity.

I was on the edge of my seat, leaning forward, as the driver handed our IDs over to the guards at the massive black metal gate that barred the Court compound from the surrounding dense forest. The secrecy and security were just as intense as when I'd come to sign up for the Gathering. The guard returned our documents and ordered us inside. The car was barely through the gate when it began to close. It was evident that no one could come in—or leave—without the Court Guards allowing it. Carlo had had to wait outside the gate for verification, and a smile crossed my face. Now that I was inside the Court walls, the fact that I would be seeing him again soon felt more real.

As we made the long drive through the woods, I recognized some of the buildings from photos Kris had shown me of the Court. Her family owned both a suite and a mansion inside the

Royal High Court—a secluded, heavily guarded area where many of the Royals lived.

The Royals' building—the Royal Quarters—looked gigantic even from a distance, like a European castle. When I had signed up for the Gathering, I had been given a handbook that explained how I could enter the quarters as an invited guest of a Royal, but that there were rooms and archives that only Pure Royals could enter by proving their lineage—a drop of blood, maybe? They didn't let Regulars in on the details.

Next to the Royals' castle was the beyond-boring building for the Regulars who worked at Court—it screamed all business, no glamour. The stark contrast between the two buildings served as a reminder of how Regulars were treated so differently from those of royal blood.

As the car made a final turn, the Hyped came into view. The Hyped was where Regulars who lived outside of Court could stay during the Gathering. Most of the events would take place there as well. From the outside, it looked like a five-star hotel, galloping impossibly high up to the low-lying clouds, at least thirty floors tall. To be honest, I'd been expecting something old, something that looked like it had been there for centuries, but boy, was I wrong. It was completely modern. And it would be my home for the entire month of December.

We finally made it through the lush, forested drive and the driver parked the car in front of the Hyped before getting out to help us unload our luggage.

"Lady Ambrosia." A polite smile accompanied my dad's overly formal greeting to Kris as he offered his hand to help her out of the limo. Watching her back, I knew she was fighting back a cringe. "Do you wish for me to accompany you to your family unit? I'd be happy to oblige."

Kris shook her head, her platinum-blond hair brushing her shoulders lightly. "No, it's okay, Mr. Montgomery." She nodded toward the bellhop who was walking toward us, ready to escort her to the Royal Quarters.

"Of course. As you wish."

I scrambled out of the back seat with no offer of help—not that I needed it, but c'mon—and took in a deep inhale of crisp air, happy to be out of the stuffy car and in the chill of the mountains.

Kris pulled me into a big hug and whispered in my ear, "Text me as soon as you can escape!"

"Wish me luck!" I gave her a squeeze before watching her walk away, the bellhop trotting after her and probably hoping for a Pure Royal–sized tip. I grabbed my suitcase and faced my dad, dreading being alone in his company for even five minutes. He had his phone out and the usual furrowed-brow look on his face. I cleared my throat to make it obvious that I wasn't going to stand there all day, ignored.

"Right. Avery. Stay here. Don't move," he said to me like I was a poorly behaved puppy. "I have to take care of some things and get access to our suite. I'll be back in ten minutes."

I nodded my assent. Satisfied I wasn't going to give him attitude, he marched off toward the Hyped. Letting out a long sigh of relief, my rebel alter ego took over—time for a self-guided tour of the Court.

I had never seen *this* many Hellenicus in one place—people were bustling around everywhere I looked. Wandering past the Hyped and the crowds toward the center of the Court, I found a beautiful garden. The big oak tree standing in the center of the garden must be the Whispering Oak of Dodona—the oldest Oracle and Zeus's sacred oak, from which, through the whisper of its leaves, priests had interpreted messages from the gods to mortals. People used to travel from all over Greece to Dodona, where the tree first grew, to worship Zeus and the goddess Dione, whom the city was named after.

But centuries later the sacred oak was in danger of being cut down. So Zeus moved the soul of the tree here, far away from the religious struggles of the time to a land where the natural world was respected. It has remained here ever since, protected by the Court walls and our people.

Every December the tree bloomed. It was rare for any tree to bloom in the middle of winter, but this was no ordinary oak. Every time a pair of soul mates met a bud would grow. When their souls were finally reunited, a flower would blossom—catkins for a male pair, small flowers for a female pair, and a pale pink and white flower inside a catkin for mixed-gender soul mates. Kris, who had always spent a week of December visiting her grandparents here, told me that by the end of the month the tree would have dozens of flowers.

Even though I should have gotten back to where my dad had ordered me to wait, I had to see the tree. There were a few small buds already there, and I wondered if one of them was for Kris. Since I wasn't yet eighteen, my bud wouldn't appear for at least a few weeks. That was, if my soul mate even existed, and if they were at Court as well.

A muffled voice, like a whisper in the wind, echoed, and I turned to see if someone had approached without me noticing. I was all alone. As I moved closer to the tree, the whispering grew louder. The breeze whooshed in my hair and as I strained to hear it again I ignored the strange lingering feeling I had. Swallowing the lump in my throat, I held my breath and reached out my hand to touch the rough surface of the trunk. My fingers were mere inches away when a hand grabbed my shoulder and pulled me back.

"What the—" I turned around, a murderous glare prepared for whoever was rude enough to grab me like that. "Mom?"

Maybe I was going crazy, but only a few hours earlier she had dramatically yelled at us to leave her behind, stating that she would rather come with her friends and would meet us here tomorrow—which meant she would miss my induction as an Awakened. Yet here she was, standing in front of me.

"Mom, what are you doing here? Weren't you supposed to be arriving tomorrow with Kiara?"

"Her name is Tiana," my mom grumbled. "But the question is, what are *you* doing here? This is not a tourist spot. You're not here for a vacation." Here it was, another lecture about to go down. "You can't be here. This is the *Court*—you can't just go wandering around like you own the place. Behave as you were raised. Do *not* embarrass your father and me," she hissed as she dragged me away.

"I'm not trying to embarrass you. I just wanted to hear what the tree was saying."

She came to an abrupt halt, and the look in her eyes was deadly. There was something there I'd never seen before, something that I recognized as fear, and it confused me. "Never say that again, Avery Zosime Montgomery."

She just *had* to use my full name. "Mom, let go of me." I planted my feet firmly on the ground. "I was just joking."

Noticing how many people's investigative stares were now glued to us, she folded her arms over her striped white-and-blue sweater.

"There you are, Avery." My dad handed me a piece of paper and a folded map. "That's the password for the suite's keypad and the emergency code. Save it on your phone just in case. And that's a map. You're going to need it if you don't want to get lost."

He exchanged a quick look with my mom, and for the briefest moment, it felt more loaded than their usual mind communication. Something was off and I couldn't figure out what it was. All I knew was that they were way too stressed out about me being at Court.

Like if they let me out of their sight I might burn the place down or find the secret stairway to the Underworld or something.

With Mom and Dad leading the way, I entered the Hyped and suddenly understood how it had earned its nickname. I had expected the lobby to be ornate, but it was pretty sparse, more geometrical than classical. The floor was tiled in fine marble, making every step echo and reminding me that it was a privilege for a Regular like me to be allowed to stay here for the Gathering. The light hitting the chandelier made rainbows dance across the floor, while Hellenicus lounged on luxuriant silk couches scattered around the room. There were stunning floral arrangements in the queen's signature shade of pink complementing the rest of the interior design.

But it was the massive mural on the far wall that made my jaw drop. It must've been two stories high and just as wide, and it depicted the origin of the Hellenicus, when our ancestors had stormed Mount Olympus on the Day of Prideful Folly, with Zeus revealing his plan to his fellow Olympians, then the grisly bit—the hideous creatures being split in half—and finally, the soul mates being reunited. I blushed at the rather detailed depiction of this steamy piece of our history. Our schoolbooks had not been so . . . visual.

As I moved toward the elevators, a prickling feeling of someone staring at me caught me off guard. Three stern-looking women sitting behind the Hyped's mahogany desk had their eyes transfixed on the papers on their desk. Were they the ones who had been staring at me? After another minute of observing them and deciding that they weren't anything out of the ordinary, I quickly fled to the set of elevators where my mom was waiting, no doubt ready to give me a piece of her mind.

Surprisingly, by the time we arrived at our unit—two bedrooms with en-suite bathrooms, a simply furnished living room, and a kitchen—there was no lecture. My mom told me to go to my room and get ready, saying that she and Dad needed to discuss something in the living room. I, being all too happy not to get another scolding, dashed to my bedroom with my suitcase in hand.

CHAPTER FOUR

The Gathering was officially starting in an hour and I had to appear somewhat presentable, but my hair was nothing but a bird's nest. Standing in front of the bathroom mirror, I cursed under my breath. A halo of auburn frizz framed my face, and after spending the last twenty minutes trying to tame it, I had failed miserably. I was neither a stylist nor a miracle worker, and I was racing against the clock.

In a decisive moment, I pulled my hair back into a loose, high bun, figuring this was as good as it would get, and moved on to brushing my teeth. At least here at the Hyped I didn't have to share a bathroom with my parents.

Back in my bedroom, I threw on the floor-length cerulean dress my mom had insisted I wear tonight. The queen would be present, so I had to do *formal*. I moved to the dark-purple velvet couch, leaning against the arm and stretching my legs out in front of me. I had a few moments to myself before the insanity began and I was going to cherish them.

I had never even been to a hotel before, and I couldn't believe how quiet it was in my room, especially when I knew there were Hellenicus all around me, hustling to get ready for the queen's speech, which marked the official start of the Gathering. I was used to the quiet and to be being alone. At home, my parents were always working, and they were strict about letting me go out. It was quite lonely. Before Bryan, I used to wish for an annoying little brother or a bossy big sister because it sucked to be in the house all by myself, and now that he was gone, some of that loneliness had returned. I was thankful that I still had Kris, though. She had been my very first friend, my sister. After losing Bryan, I wouldn't have been able to pull myself back up on my feet again without her.

What am I doing here?

The closer I got to potentially being linked to a soul mate, the more nervous I felt. Doubts crawled out from their hiding place and clouded my mind.

What if it wasn't Carlo? What if I couldn't escape next year because I met my soul mate this year? What if it was someone who didn't have any of the same interests as me? Or, even worse, what if they were one of those Royals who looked down on Regulars? Then what? How would I live my life being tied down to a person like that—to have that sort of person reading my every thought and having to suffer reading theirs? Was I making the wrong decision being here?

My phone buzzed. Kris. I swiped to answer.

"Ave! I'm so nervous about this whole thing!" Her hair sparkled in the sunset coming through the window behind her, but she looked so worried. She pulled her phone away to show me her outfit—an elegant but kind of boring dress in green, her family's signature color. "Do you think I should wear this or the orange one? You know, the dress with the spaghetti straps?"

"Orange! It's your favorite dress and you look amazing in it."

"You're right. If my other half is at the party tonight, I want to make a good first impression—and look like myself, not like every other Ambrosia in the room."

Sometimes I forgot how insecure Kris was. Sure, her platinum-blond hair and hourglass figure always drew stares, and she'd been scouted by modeling agencies, which she always turned down, not wanting to risk exposing our race to the Nescient. But, just like everyone else on the planet, she had her self-doubts. And with something as important as the Gathering, I could see those fears had multiplied.

"Kris, you're beautiful. Inside and out. No matter what you wear, they will love you. Your soul mate will be the luckiest person on earth."

"Thanks, Ave. You have no idea how glad I am that you're here. I know this isn't your thing, but it really means a lot to me."

"You don't have to thank me. I'm glad I'm here." I hadn't realized how true it was until I'd said it.

Kris told me she was going to change and would meet me in the lobby in five minutes. As I hung up the phone, my mom yelled for me to hurry up from the other side of the door, and I took a deep breath, mentally preparing myself.

Ω

Kris and I met in the lobby, ready to join the ceremony. She had changed into her orange dress and had fastened the family crest that all Royals and Pure Royals had to wear on the left side of her chest.

We took the short trip to the Hyped's Royal Hall. Kris's nervous energy buzzed as she walked alongside me, and I linked my arm through hers as a gesture of my support.

"Wow, there are so many people," Kris whispered as we entered the Royal Hall. She was not wrong. The immense space was crowded with Hellenicus from all over the world. The ceiling soared high above us, and its artwork was even more impressive than the mural in the Hyped lobby. Hand-painted mountains and skies encircled the room, with the Big Three (Zeus, Poseidon, and Hades) watching over us all, while the rest of the Olympians were dotted around the room—Hera, Demeter, Athena, Apollo, Artemis, Ares, Aphrodite, Hephaestus, Hermes, Hestia, and Dionysus. Vases of blooming flowers gave off a cloying scent as we made our way past them, and my nose twitched as I held back a sneeze.

Those of us who were to be inducted as Awakened tonight were corralled to one side of the hall, and I was happy to ditch my mother and her fussing over every detail of my appearance. She needed to chill. No one would be looking at a Regular like me. No one except for Carlo, who'd join later for the after-party since he had already gone through all of this four years ago. Those who had already experienced their first Gathering could come anytime during the month of December, unlike us first timers, who had to spend the full month participating in all the Court-organized activities. The only escape was a click—then we'd be exempt from everything.

We gathered at the foot of the golden staircase that twisted upward in a perfect spiral. Royal Guards made a not-so-subtle semicircle around it, discouraging anyone from getting too close. A stressed-looking official noticed that Kris and I were standing together, and without saying a word, sternly pointed at me and motioned for me to stand at the back. Of course—it was Pure Royals, then Royals, then Regulars. Kris gave me an apologetic half smile in sympathy, and I shrugged. Typical Hellenicus baloney.

At the back of the group I couldn't see a thing over the heads of everyone else—short people problems—so I hiked up the skirt of my dress and climbed onto the base of the massive statue beside me. On my perch tucked behind the sculpture, there was no way my judgmental parents would be able to spot me. It was perfect.

The sound of a harp filled the hall. The excited murmuring quieted as all eyes were drawn to the top of the golden staircase. The awestruck crowd gasped as the most beautiful woman I had ever seen in my entire life appeared at the top of the stairs. Queen Rhea Christoulakis. With perfectly symmetrical features and piercing blue eyes, her looks transcended time. I could hardly believe she was even a real person and not a goddess standing before us. But more than her classically beautiful looks, it was the grace of her presence that made me forget to breathe. She carried herself with such poise.

I watched, mesmerized, as she descended the staircase. The way the bottom of her sparkly silver dress moved as she took each step made it appear as if she was floating. Once she reached the last step, to my surprise, she looked right at me with her icy-blue Christoulakis eyes—or so it seemed, at least. As she came to stand at the podium, she said, "You may rise." Only then did I realize that everyone else had bowed before her, and on her command, were now respectfully standing. I blushed and mouthed, *Sorry*, and I swear I saw a hint of a smile on Queen Rhea's face before she turned her attention to the huddle.

"Welcome, everyone—those who have been in the Court before and those of you for whom today is your first time.

"We, the Hellenicus, are graced by the gods, as we have been since time immemorial. And we welcome the newest among us to find their true wholeness, their one body with their soul mate, in this most sacred of Hellenicus traditions."

The queen explained how important it was for us to keep our tradition and to always remind ourselves that we were still bound by the rules of the gods—subject to their favor and their wrath. She called upon her steward to bring forth a chalice and explained how the ceremony would proceed.

The Golden Chalice was one of our most cherished relics. It was created by Hebe, the goddess of youth, prime of life, and forgiveness, and then blessed by Eros, the god of love, eroticism, and sensual desires. Engraved with the Fountain of Youth for Hebe and wings for

Eros, the chalice was used in the ritual awakening of the Hellenicus. Only after a Hellenicus drank wine from the chalice would their clairaudient ability be activated.

The ceremony unfolded as the Pure Royals were invited to be the first to drink the nectar of the gods and be awakened. The Royals followed after them. And then lastly, the Regulars.

I hopped down from my perch to find my place in the line that had formed. One of the organizers hurriedly asked me my name before ushering me to stand behind a girl I'd never met before. We slowly moved closer to the front of the line as each of the Awakened accepted the chalice from the cupbearer, took a sip, and bowed to the queen, who looked on attentively. I realized it was simply another way to segregate Regulars from Royals, as rank determined the order in which we went up for the nectar of the gods. Each caste received a different type of nectar, and apparently, Regulars couldn't drink the Royals' nectar (or vice versa) without getting sick. *Please.* It was probably everyone's backwash that made people sick! As if a Royal's backwash was any less disgusting than a Regular's.

Finally, the girl ahead of me went up. This was it. I was next—no turning back. If my soul mate was eighteen or older, and they were also on the sacred grounds of the Court, I would be able to read their mind, and they would be able to read mine. Once I drank from that cup, I would be fully Awakened. My hands trembled and my heart pounded, telling me to run, but my stubborn head told me that I was not a coward—that I had made my decision and I should stick to it.

The girl in front of me drank from the cup and stepped aside. It was finally my turn. I looked over one shoulder to see Kris beaming at me. The cupbearer, a guy only a few years older than me, refilled the chalice and brought it forward, ready to hand it to me so I could take a sip. Bracing myself, I reached for the cup and brought it to my lips. I shut my eyes as I drank, letting the rich, sweet, fermented grapes mix with a slight bitterness as the liquid rolled over my tongue and down my throat. Almost as soon as I swallowed it, I started coughing.

The cupbearer looked at me with an odd expression on his face, as if it was the first time he'd witnessed someone choke. I wanted to tell him how sorry I was, but my throat felt weird. In the end, I could only give him a regretful nod, and walked to the line of those who had had their share, standing behind the girl who'd drunk right before me.

After everyone had finished drinking and the Golden Chalice was safely stashed away, the queen bid her farewell, wishing all the best for us, and ascended the stairs just as gracefully as she descended them earlier. The organizers informed us about the after-party. I wanted to go back to my room to change and continue reading my Agatha Christie book. I was dying to find out the resolution of *And Then There Were None*, and I didn't want to be worried about tripping and breaking my neck while walking in this dress anymore.

Over the crowded space, my eyes found Kris. I knew how excited she was and that she wanted me to stay. Seeing the glint in her jade-green eyes and the smile forming on her beautiful heart-shaped face, I realized my wishes would have to wait.

CHAPTER FIVE

I had thought Carlo would be here, but he'd texted during the ceremony to say he couldn't get here until tomorrow. I was disappointed; the thought of him being here was part of the reason why I'd agreed to stay for the after-party. But, at the very least, the party was the best way to avoid my parents until tomorrow, and so I turned my ringer back on and looked around at the party. As I suspected, it was obnoxious as hell.

Despite seeing a lot of Regulars at the Awakening Ceremony, I didn't see that many of them here. Instead, the ballroom was crowded with a bunch of drunk Royals. Even though Alaska's legal drinking age was twenty-one, Hellenicus law allowed us to drink at eighteen, the legal age in Greece, while on Court Grounds. The smell of expensive perfumes and booze in the air, coupled with the ridiculously loud music, should have been red flags that this party wasn't going to be my cup of tea. Still, I reminded myself that I had promised Kris I'd try my best to enjoy myself.

A girl I didn't know came up to me with two of her friends in tow as I looked for Kris. They wore high heels that made them so tall that I needed to crane my neck to meet their eyes. "Hey, aren't you the one who choked on the wine?"

Great. Apparently that small incident had not gone unnoticed.

"Yep, that's me. It went down the wrong pipe." My nervous laugh met dead silence.

One of the girls squinted her eyes as she stared me down. "You do realize choking on the sacred nectar is considered blasphemy?"

"What?"

"You're being disrespectful," said the one with curly brown hair. "You'll have seventy years of bad luck."

I found this to be hilarious, considering I already had so much bad luck in my life. "Let's hope I really am Tyche's descendant then."

The three of them gasped loudly enough that several people around us looked over in curiosity. "You're a Regular!"

Their eyes dropped to where my family crest would be if I were a Royal or Pure Royal. The absence of a crest confirmed their suspicions, but I answered them anyway. "Matter of fact, I am. I was in the lineup for the Regulars, remember?"

"Dear Aphrodite, I can't believe I wasted my breath talking to a Regular," said the first girl before turning around and saying, "Come on, ladies."

I spotted Kris standing by the refreshment table with a tall, blond, wannabe-surfer dude who wore an unusual gold-band necklace. Kris introduced him as Damian Tavoularis. He was from Sydney, Australia, and he was Hera's descendant. At first, he struck me as an okay guy, but I soon changed my mind as he ignored me whenever I spoke and would jump in when Kris tried to turn the conversation my way. I imagined he had decided that a measly Regular wasn't worth his time, just like those other girls had.

"I mean, the Gathering is great, and our queen is so thoughtful to have this in the Hyped so Regulars can join in, but I still think it would be better if Royals and Regulars had separate Gatherings. We could have ours in the Royal Quarters; Regulars could stick to the

Hyped. The Hyped is so boring in comparison. Besides, it would be less crowded, and you wouldn't have to force yourself to mingle with them. That's why the Olympians reside on Olympus while the minor gods and goddesses live elsewhere, right?"

Damian was *obnoxious.*

I couldn't put up with him anymore. I'd already made a scene once tonight with my already-famous chalice moment, and I knew if I stayed any longer I might cause another scene by arguing with this douchebag. The fact that some Royals believed they were above everyone else pissed me off. Did it really matter which god's lineage you were a part of?

He opened his mouth and started talking about how a line must be drawn between Royals and Regulars so we'd know our place. Ignoring him, I asked Kris if she wanted to go to the bathroom and she quickly accepted. Kris, polite to a fault, informed Damian how sorry she was that she had to cut it short, but she needed to find her brother.

"Okay, I don't actually need to go to the bathroom," I said once we had enough distance between the sulking Damian and us. "I do need some fresh air, though. Do you want to go outside?"

Kris shook her head. "I wasn't lying. I really need to find Vlad. He should've arrived thirty minutes ago."

"Okay. You go find your brother. I'll be outside." I pushed through the crowd, which was halfheartedly moving in time to the blaring music, and found my way to the courtyard.

In the wintery mountain air it felt like a different world altogether. I hadn't realized how nauseated I had felt closed in with all the others. Out here I could see the tree in the middle of the courtyard. I was interested to see if any more flowers had grown since the Awakening Ceremony. I wondered how many newly Awakened were inside having clicks as they chatted up their soul mates.

Not wearing a coat, I shivered in the chilly night air, but I didn't care. At least out here it was clean air and—a cloud of smoke blew straight into my face.

"*Chocolate brownies!* So much for fresh air," I exclaimed through a cough. I used to have the vocabulary of a drunken sailor, but after being scolded numerous times by my parents, I now censored myself.

Smoke hanging around him like a toxic grey cloud, there was Adrian Ambrosia, Kris's cousin. He was the first guy I'd ever had a crush on. He looked at me for a moment, puzzled, as if he was trying to recall who I was.

"Seriously?!" It may have been a few years since I'd last seen him, but I liked to think that he would remember me. At least my first name, anyway.

He did better.

"Avery Montgomery?" He winked.

"Yes. The one and only." Being on the receiving end of his smoke waste had piqued my annoyance to the point where I almost forgot that seeing him here at Court during the Gathering was actually really weird. "What are you doing here?"

Two years ago, Adrian's love had taken a tragic turn, and Kris told me that he had sworn never to set foot back here as a result. He thought he'd found his soul mate—his girlfriend, Marsela Costas—and came to the ceremony believing that soon they would have the click, validating their relationship. To his utter shock, she'd clicked with a Russian guy she'd never even met before. Adrian wanted to ignore the gods and begged to continue their relationship. Still, despite all the promises they had made to each other beforehand, Marsela broke up with him and moved to Russia, carrying the proof of her betrayal inside her belly. From what I'd heard from Kris, he hadn't had a serious relationship since. Adrian's heartbreak was a harsh reminder that nothing was certain until the day the Fates decided it was.

Adrian ignored my question, put out his nearly finished smoke, then reached into the pocket of his designer pants and pulled out a pack of cigarettes. He lit the end of a new cigarette with his lighter. As he squinted against the flame, I took the opportunity to check him out. His emerald-green sweater matched his eyes perfectly, and a pair of black jeans hung on his hips. Adrian was still as good looking as he had been four years ago. No wonder my fourteen-year-old self crushed on him. Of course, he had never noticed me because he was completely head over heels for Marsela.

"Do I pass inspection?" Adrian asked. The lighter closed with a snap of his wrist, and he stuffed it back into his pocket along with the rest of the pack of smokes.

Being caught blatantly eyeing him up, I wanted to climb up the oak and hide there for a while until my cheeks were no longer the same shade as my hair. Instead, I had to make do with playing it cool. "It's been a while," I said. "I didn't expect to see you at the Gathering, that's all."

"I'm not here for the Gathering. But I'm *very* curious which unlucky Hellenicus will have to tame you."

I stuck my tongue out. So much for playing it cool.

As if he remembered something from the past, pain flashed in his eyes for a brief second before he gave a lazy smile. "Don't worry, Montgomery, if you don't like the guy, I could help kick his ass for you."

"I don't need your help kicking anyone's ass, Adrian. I can take care of it myself, you know that."

"Actually, I don't. It's been a while since I last saw you, Montgomery."

And if he wasn't going to put out his cigarette, he wouldn't be seeing me for much longer. I'd had just about enough second-hand smoke. As if he'd read my thoughts, he took one long, last drag then dropped the butt to the ground and stomped it out.

"Hey, no littering!"

"No escaping your Awakened after-party either. Why are you out here? You're supposed to mingle, meet people. Maybe one of them is your other half. Aren't you excited to find your Romeo?" he said sarcastically.

"Not really," I said. "The whole thing freaks me out."

"I get that." He, surprisingly, agreed. "I don't think this soul-mate bullshit suits you, anyway."

"What do you mean?"

"You are Avery Freaking Montgomery. You're fiery. You're the type of person who makes decisions on your own accord. There is no way in hell you would willingly wait around for your soul mate to show up."

Damn. He was right. Even though I'd said to myself that I wanted to find out if Carlo was truly my soul mate and tried convincing myself to go through with this Gathering, deep down I knew that this was *really* not my thing. It was crazy that Adrian of all people understood that about me when I'd always thought he had never even given me a second glance. What else did he know about me?

"But seriously, why are *you* here?"

"For the brat."

"Caitlin?" Adrian's eighteen-year-old sister, whom he *always* referred to as brat, Caitlin was every bit the spitting image of Adrian—maybe that was the reason why she annoyed him so much, they were too alike. But here he was, swallowing his pride and coming to the Gathering to support her.

"You're a really good brother," I blurted.

"Look," he scoffed, "someone's met their destiny."

There before us, like magic, a bud blossomed into pink and white around a catkin. We stood in silence in the cold night air, taking in the tree. I didn't want to admit it, and maybe it wasn't cool, but there was something dreamlike about being here. It was almost as if I was not on earth but in some mythical place where magical things could happen. The air grew lighter, and just like when we first arrived this afternoon, I had to fight the urge to reach out and touch the tree. The ring of my cell phone broke the silence. It was Kris.

"Ave, where are you?" I could barely hear her over the noise of the party. "A click just happened and everyone is congratulating the new pair."

"I'm outside with Adrian." I looked over at him only to find him lighting up a new cigarette. Geez, Zeus.

"Wait, Adrian's here?"

"Yeah. He's busy inhaling toxins to shorten his life span, polluting the air, and making me feel like I'm going to puke."

Adrian elbowed me and I gave him a murderous look before taking a few steps away from him and the influx of carbon monoxide.

"Tell him to put it out and come inside!" Kris yelled, then ended the call.

"We've been commanded by Lady Ambrosia to come inside to party," I said. The only time Kris was ever bossy was when she'd had a couple of drinks. It was quite hilarious to see her personality completely change.

Adrian grabbed my wrist to stop me from walking away and pulled me closer to him. I could feel his warmth, and inhaled the scent of cigarettes mixing with his cologne. I was ready to tell him to buzz off, but his eyes silenced me.

"Ave, you know what happened to me and Mars. It's better not to have any expectations or hope."

"I know." A small voice, laced with worry and fear, answered, and I could hardly believe that it was mine. "I'm sorry it happened, but you don't need to worry about me, okay? I'll be fine."

I wrenched myself away and he let me go.

"Adrian?" I asked. "Will you do me a favor and come inside? I know you've had a rough start to this whole soul-mate thing, but if you keep letting that stand in your way, you might miss out on your chance of finding someone."

"Never knew you were so wise, Montgomery. I thought you were a brawler."

"I'm not *that* bad," I said.

"You're right. You're worse."

We bumped into each other lightheartedly. And there was less pressure walking back into the party with Adrian by my side. Maybe he was right—I shouldn't expect anything.

Kris was nowhere in sight. I was about to suggest to Adrian that we check the dance floor when I heard a familiar voice.

"Avery Montgomery."

"Nikki," I said coolly, nodding my acknowledgment. "It's been a while."

As soon as I'd seen Nikki take her turn with the chalice, tottering in a pair of five-inch stilettos, and surprisingly without her twin sister, Renata, I'd known this run-in would come sooner or later. She'd never forgiven me for breaking her nose the first week of high school when she had purposely shoved Kris to the ground during gym class. Since then, she'd been hell-bent on trying to make mine and Kris's lives a living hell. Nikki had even slept with Kris's first boyfriend just to hurt her.

Personality aside, Nikki was beautiful, even with her new nose, and tonight she was in a silver cocktail dress that accentuated her body in all the right places. Adrian took her in, inching a little closer to her, clearly wanting to be introduced. Guys really did judge the cover before knowing the contents.

Nikki noticed him and gave him a once-over before opening her thin lips. "Aren't you going to introduce us, Avery?"

"Adrian Ambrosia, this is Nikki Vidales. We—" I wasn't sure how to introduce her without outing her as the nasty piece of work she was. "We used to go to Hellenic school together."

How else could you describe your high school bully?

Nikki's eyes danced with excitement, and I realized it had been a bad idea to introduce them. Being part of that group of status-hungry Royals, the Vidales were suckers for Pure Royals, and Nikki was not an exception. Not really wanting to be involved in the conversation, I tried to scope out Kris until I felt a nudge on my arm a few moments later. "What?"

"I was asking if you wanted to go find Kris," Adrian said.

"You're ditching me? Seriously?"

"Let me rephrase." His voice sounded like he was trying his best to explain something to a toddler. "Do you want to go find Kris *with me*?"

"Yes," I said.

Adrian politely told Nikki that it was nice to meet her, but we had to go.

"Aww, so soon?" Nikki's voice sounded soft and silky, but I could see the annoyance in her eyes.

Once we were out of earshot, I turned to Adrian. "That's honestly not how I thought that would go."

"Why not?"

"Guys fawn all over her, and I saw you checking her out."

"Is this really happening?" he teased.

"Is *what* happening?"

"You're jealous of some random girl." He chuckled. "Damn, Montgomery. You're possessive as hell."

"No, I'm not!" I tried my best not to look like a brat, though I was kind of acting like one. "The thing is she's not *just* some random girl. She's my worst nightmare—and Kris's too."

I filled Adrian in on how Nikki had spent all of high school mean-girling us every chance she got. One time she even dumped Kris's Harry Potter collection into the toilet and tried to flush them down.

"Sounds like I dodged a bullet!" he said.

It was very crowded in the room, but it didn't take us long to find Kris on the dance floor. I knew she'd be there. In addition to tennis, Kris loved dancing. She spotted us and came over, enveloping Adrian in a hug before pulling us both onto the floor.

"What have you guys been up to?" she yelled over the music.

"Nikki. She was trying to sink her claws into Adrian. Until I saved him, of course," I shouted.

"My hero." He fluttered his eyelashes in a damsel-in-distress-like way.

Kris stopped dancing and grabbed Adrian's hand. "Please tell me you're not developing a crush on Nikki. She's—" Kris paused as she struggled to find the right word. "Not a very kind person."

Typical Kris. She always had trouble saying anything bad about people, even when it was the truth. I, however, never had that trouble. "And by that, she means Nikki is the worst."

"Ave!" Kris's eyes couldn't get any wider.

"Can't sugarcoat the truth."

"God, I miss high school drama," countered Adrian. "Golden days. When all the girls fell for me. Not a surprise, really."

"Ah yes. Those glory days. Until it all went downhill and now no one remembers you."

Kris laughed at this and I raised my hand for a high five. Adrian leaned forward and there was that smell again, musky aftershave plus smoke. Somehow the scent made me feel less queasy, more alive, even if it was only for a moment. His eyes looked wicked under the light, and his smile challenged me.

"Careful there, Little Miss Rebel, before you become one of those girls," he said.

"Dream on. Maybe you do belong with someone like Nikki."

"Montgomery, relax." He laughed. "You own my heart. There's no other girl, present or future." He patted my head before walking away, toward the bar.

Kris watched the exchange with an amused look on her heart-shaped face.

"What is it now?" I asked.

"Adrian likes you," she said knowingly.

"Yeah, and the rest of the female population." I shook my head in disbelief. "Weren't you the one telling me two years ago that he had lots of one-night stands to get over Marsela?"

Kris shrugged. "You're different."

Ω

It was around midnight when I woke up suddenly feeling nauseated. The room had shrunk, it was hard to breathe, and I had to get out of there—needed fresh air. I made my way downstairs, out of the lobby, and ducked outside. Immediately, I felt a little better as I took in deep breaths of mountain air. Maybe I shouldn't have skipped dinner? Maybe it was because I was completely worn out from the party? Maybe it was the fact that since I'd gotten here I'd been constantly surrounded by hordes of people when I was used to being alone. At any rate, I was in no mood for any more social interactions, so I walked toward the fish pond. Fish were about as much as I could handle at this moment.

I found a large rock on the side of the pond and sat down. There was a thin layer of ice on the surface and the koi were swimming in slow, languid motions. I leaned over to say hello to them, watching them minding their own business and not caring about the too-dramatic world of the Hellenicus. Perhaps I was too preoccupied with my own thoughts—and the fish—because when I felt a tap on my shoulder I nearly fell into the pond.

"What the—?"

Now on my feet and with one arm restrained, I used my free arm to jab my elbow into my attacker's stomach, hitting a solid wall of muscle.

"Zeus's lightning! Avy, why did you do that?"

Avy?! Holy smokes!

"Vladimir!" I said over my shoulder.

He let go of me and took a few steps away as I turned to face him. "If you're looking for Kris, she went back to the Royal Quarters over an hour ago. I'm just leaving now."

"To go where?" he asked softly.

His question startled me for two reasons. Usually, he would be happy for me to leave. Sometimes he even told me to run along, which never came as a surprise considering he was such a jerk. Also, he had asked me softly—not in the harsh, mocking tone he always used with me. That had never happened before.

"Are you feeling all right?" I asked.

He seemed to find my question humorous. Had I ever heard him laugh before? I began to wonder if he was drunk or if I was dreaming. Unlike Adrian's boisterous laugh, Vlad's was rich and deep. And apparently just as infectious, as I joined him, though I wasn't sure why.

"How terrible was the party?" he asked.

"It's not my scene." I leaned against the tree behind me, its cold bark sending a chill down my spine. "I didn't see you at the Awakening Ceremony."

He didn't reply but took off his jacket and wordlessly offered it to me, having noticed me shiver. Argh, I *was* flipping cold, but it felt so wrong to accept a kindness from *Vladimir* of all people.

"Don't be stubborn, Avy. Just take it."

Ah, there it was—the usual Vlad tone. I snatched the jacket from him and muttered a reluctant thanks as he moved to stand beside me by the tree.

"Are *you* all right?" His voice was gentle and laced with concern, and I didn't know which surprised me more: him asking me, or him being concerned about me.

"Yeah, I'm okay. Today has been . . . a lot. Awakened and all." Desperately trying to change the subject, I jerked my head toward the Royal Quarters, where some people were seemingly throwing an after-party for the after-party. "Don't tell me you're going to join those morons partying all night long?"

"No, I'm taking a walk around Court before I have to leave. There are things to be taken care of."

"You're leaving! What about Kris?"

"I got a call from the office; they need me to prep for a trial."

"Can't someone else do it? This is her first Gathering." Kris would never tell him, but I knew that she'd be crushed.

"She has Mom and Dad here. She doesn't need me."

"Of course she does!"

Second to me, Vlad was the closest person to Kris. She relied on him for advice and guidance. And he *knew* how important a Hellenicus's first Gathering was—it was literally a sacred ritual. A once-in-a-lifetime thing. Family members were always there to provide guidance through what was often the weirdest month of an Awakened's life as they adjusted to becoming a full-blown Hellenicus and learned to manage the heightened emotions of being imbued with the power of clairaudience. Even my unloving parents were here for me. I couldn't understand why he was being difficult.

"Kris needs your support; you're her brother. There's some stuff that she would *never* talk to your parents about—you know that! You've been through this!"

"Avy, stop."

He stepped away from the tree. I had to say something that would stop him from leaving. "Adrian's here. That's right, you heard me, the brokenhearted Adrian Ambrosia is here—even after he swore never again. He actually cares about his sister, so he's putting his own shit aside to be here for her. Why can't you do the same for Kris?"

"I'm a law intern, Avy. I don't have the luxury of taking off work for a whole month. I could lose my placement. Work is *important* to me. And, as I said, Kris already has you *and* our parents."

"*Vlad.*" My voice caressed his name in a way that it never had before. "I know you're a good, caring person. I know how much you value your work, but I know you love Kris more than anything. That she is the most important person in your world." My sincerity surprised even myself. Despite what a jerk he could be to me, he would die for Kris. "This is the most important event in her life. Please find a way to stay. I'm sure you can sort something out with your work. This is once in a lifetime. She needs you."

He stood quietly, considering my words. After what felt like an eternity, he shook his head adamantly. "I have to go. Tell her I'm sorry, Avy."

"Tell her yourself. You're the worst! How can there be anything more important than your own sister! I thought you at least had a heart when it came to her. I hope you enjoy your internship knowing that you've sacrificed Kris's happiness."

Walking away, I only managed seven steps before my legs buckled underneath me. Cold stone hit my cheek. Through the chill of the windy December night, Vlad's voice called out, using that nickname I despised. I tried to get up, but there was no power left in me. All I could do was roll onto my back. My insides were on fire, my stomach roiling. I looked up at the night sky; the clouds above were in chaos, mimicking how I felt. Something was very wrong.

I managed to pull myself to my hands and knees. Nausea crept up from my abdomen, clawing at my throat as I tried to force down the bile. It was too late. My stomach contracted violently and forced everything up and out. My face felt clammy and pale, and dripped sweat and tears. What was worse was that Vlad knelt beside me, and I must've looked disgusting—just after I had lectured him too.

Right when I felt like some kind of black hole was consuming my innards, dizziness came over me and I collapsed again, the world fading to black. I could only hope that I wasn't dead.

Ω

Adrian stood there in a pair of black trousers, a dark cashmere scarf, and a long coat. His white shirt peeked out from his coat. His eyes were trustworthy when he asked me to follow him. We passed many rooms as we made our way downstairs. I tried to analyze where we were to figure out where we might be headed.

We were in the lobby of the Hyped, passing the mural of the Hellenicus, and only then did I notice the silence and vacancy of our surroundings. He led me outside, and I came to a halt before the fully bloomed Whispering Oak of Dodona.

Hadn't it been buds just a few hours ago? Its beauty was captivating. I strained to hear its whispers; I knew it was trying to tell me something. My feet were rooted to the ground where I stood, until Adrian tugged on my arm.

"Montgomery, there's no time for that now. You have to get there before it's too late—before someone ruins everything."

I followed him to the door of the Royal Quarters. Fear gripped me. "I can't be here. I'm not Royal. It's prohibited."

Without a word, he took my hand in his. Warmth spread all over my body, like a burning fire. I knew I should pull my hand away; instead, I held his hand tighter.

When we passed through the entrance, a deep feeling in my gut me told me this was wrong, but with his hand in mine, I indulged my defiant side—my curiosity. We were the only souls here, our footsteps sounding across the marble floors as we approached two doors: an indigo-blue door on the left, a wine-red one on the right. Without hesitation, he led me to the one on the right.

"Why not the blue one?"

"It's not for you," he said simply.

At a security panel beside the door, he entered a long series of digits to unlock it. How did he know that code? I wanted to ask him, but the view ahead stunned me into silence. Three more doors awaited us inside. As we walked through, I could see that each door was engraved with a crest. They were the Pure Royals' crests representing the Big Three: Zeus, Poseidon, and Hades.

I let go of his hand and walked closer to admire them. The crest representing the Christoulakis family included a sky filled with clouds and Zeus's lightning bolt in the middle.

The door in the middle displayed the Ambrosia crest. Kris, Adrian, and Vlad's family. This one for Poseidon had a beautiful engraving of ocean waves with his trident in the middle.

Finally, I reached the last door: Hades. The god who reigned over the world of the dead. In the middle of what looked like havoc was the Helm of Darkness, a weapon so powerful that it made even Zeus and Poseidon pale with fear. It reminded me of a skull, which was enough to terrify anyone, even me. I might cry if I looked at it any longer.

Feeling that all this was too much to bear, I moved back toward the red door, but Adrian's hand stopped me. "Don't be afraid." He held a cloth in his hand and offered it to me. "You have to clean it."

"I can't," I whispered.

Adrian dragged me back to the last door. "Clean it. You have to."

The crest was covered in dust and spiderwebs. While the other crests were gleaming and well-cared for, the door of the Stavros family had been forgotten. A wave of sympathy washed over me as I raised the cloth and gently wiped the crest clean.

Underneath the thick layer of dust, it was coated with gold. It still looked like it belonged in the Underworld, but overall, I was satisfied. I turned to face him.

"Open it."

I didn't want to, but I knew I had to. I reached for the door handle, which was shaped like a dog with three heads. Why did they have to put all the creepy stuff in one place? Careful not to touch any of the heads, I grabbed the handle. A sudden jolt shot straight to my hand and pulsed through my body. The door clicked and opened wide. "Did Zeus lend you his lightning bolt?" I hissed under my breath, trying to regain my balance.

Pitch blackness laid inside. Filled with dread of what might lay in that darkness, I reached to steady myself against the door frame.

"I don't think I should be here."

Adrian's expression was blank, as if he were a puppet and someone was pulling the strings. Adrian pushed me inside and slammed the door before I had the chance to get back on my feet.

The last thing I heard was, "It has to be done," before the darkness engulfed me in its waiting arms.

Ω

I was in my own bed when I regained consciousness. Using both of my hands to push myself up, sweat running in rivulets down my forehead and dripping off my nose, I pushed the covers off. It had been a dream. But it felt so real. The last thing I remembered was staring into Vlad's worried eyes.

Staggering to the bathroom, I retched violently. Holding on to the sink for support, I breathed in and out several times to calm my angry stomach. After washing my hands, I grabbed the smudgy bathroom mirror and angled it toward my face. Staring back at me was a pair of swollen, bloodshot eyes, pores so enlarged my face could have been mistaken for a colander, and a complexion paler than death.

Splashing some water on my face to cool off, I reached for a drinking glass and filled it with water. I had not realized how thirsty I was until the water touched my lips. Through my foggy mind, images from the dream flashed across my mind.

That look on Adrian's face right before he'd pushed me through the door was off. His expression had been blank, but there was relief in his eyes—as if he had done the right thing, like it was meant to be. My mind spun and I felt dizzy. Everything was fuzzy, and I staggered back to bed. I hadn't even been drinking last night, so why did I feel like I had the world's worst hangover?

CHAPTER SIX

"Avery Zosime Montgomery, you have to wake up now!"

My head screamed in pain at the sound of my mother's voice. As sleep left me, my body felt sore everywhere.

"I assumed you were responsible enough to get yourself out of bed in time for the *Court-mandated* activities." She ripped the blankets off me and stalked away grumpily.

I forced myself to stand and walk to the bathroom. I quickly got into the shower and allowed myself a moment to relax as the hot water and the scents of lavender and rose washed over me.

"You have ten minutes to clean yourself up and be in the dining hall, or you'll miss breakfast entirely." My mom yelled from the other side of the door.

I shut the shower off and reached for the towel. As I got dressed, my mind replayed my argument with Vlad. How could he choose work over Kris? When Kris had first told me that her brother wanted to become a lawyer, I assumed he would work here in the Court. But he wanted to serve in mainstream society's courts, not under Hellenicus law. I wanted him to chose the latter—he'd still be around for Kris's first Gathering, but I'd see even less of him. A win-win situation, in my opinion.

The door of the suite clicked closed, which meant my parents had left for breakfast. At least I wouldn't have to eat with them. Maybe Kris was still in the dining hall? As I thought to text her, I realized I had no clue where my phone was. I'd had it at the stupid after-party, and when I went outside with Adrian. I rushed around the room, searching for it—no luck. I was out of time, and there was no way I was missing breakfast. My love for food always took precedence. I grabbed the map Dad had given me and headed outside.

The elevator doors slid open and I was about to step inside when a hand caught mine, making my skin tingle in surprised delight, almost as if it had been longing for this contact.

"Montgomery," Adrian drawled.

Last night's dream surfaced, along with the connection and the sense of inevitability that I'd felt. I had to find out if those doors really existed somewhere inside the Royal High Court and were not just a concoction of my wild imagination. I must have had a strange look on my face, and Adrian being Adrian thought I was enchanted by his good looks.

"Like what you see?"

The elevator doors were closing. I pulled my hand away from his and reached out to hold them open. "Please," I said as I stepped inside and stood next to him. "Don't flatter yourself. You're not as charming as you think you are."

It was a blatant lie and we both knew it.

"What are you doing here? Are you going down?" I asked. "Don't tell me you got lost on your way to the Royal Quarters?"

"I'm going for breakfast. I had a late night. Looks like you did, too, Montgomery."

"Sort of . . . more like really strange dreams. That's why I'm running late. But I'm heading there now, before the . . . *ephedrimos*?"

Adrian laughed at my feeble attempt to remember whatever Awakened event was happening today. "Nice guess, but it's *astragaloi* this morning."

"Astragaloi? As in knucklebones? For real?" He had been staring intently at me the entire time. The elevator felt *very* small. And very private.

"Yes, for *real.* Astragaloi, or knucklebones as you Regulars insist on calling it, is a beloved tradition—it's not only for little children. You'd be surprised how many Hellenicus have clicked with their soul mates while throwing jacks in the air and seeing how many they can catch on the back of their hands."

"And this is meant to be fun?"

"Some people believe that winning a game of knucklebones foretells a destiny filled with true love."

"Yeah. Right." Hellenicus could be so superstitious. Maybe it made sense centuries ago, but not today.

"So." Adrian raised one hand and scratched the spot above his ear, seemingly nervous all of a sudden. "If you're not interested in knucklebones, do you want to have breakfast with me?"

Before I could reply, my stomach growled, giving us the answer we needed.

Ω

December sun poured through the tall windows of the dining hall, bathing the room with light. There were chandeliers above our heads and well-polished marble beneath our feet. A huge buffet was set up in the middle of the room and the last of the Hellenicus were finishing up their breakfasts. Kris wasn't anywhere. It was so annoying that I didn't have my phone! Court workers in immaculate but plain, dull-brown uniforms decorated only with the Royal emblem, stood with their backs glued to the wall, waiting to be of any assistance.

Adrian grabbed us a table while I headed straight to the buffet to fill a bowl with cereal. As I settled into my seat, a waiter came up immediately to offer me a drink. "A glass of mango juice and a cup of steamed milk, please. Thanks."

"Odd choice," commented Adrian.

Scenes of the dream came flooding back, and I wondered if I should ask him about those doors. He would never let me hear the end of it if I told him I'd been dreaming about him, so I broke the connection. "It's not that odd."

"Nothing but cereal for you?"

"Nope. I plan to have cheesecake, brownies, and cupcakes too."

"Ah, a sweet tooth."

The waiter came with my drink order and I thanked him. "Why, what's your choice of breakfast food?"

"Steak."

"Steak is hardly an ordinary breakfast food, Adrian."

"When will you learn that I'm not *just* ordinary?"

"I don't know. Maybe when you run naked down the hall screaming." I ate a spoonful of Corn Flakes.

"Whoa. Do you want to see me naked that badly, Montgomery?" He pretended to look surprised. "You sure aren't wasting your time." Adrian leaned forward and the intense way he watched me sent a shiver up my spine.

"Not as badly as I want to punch your face," I replied, causing him to laugh.

Get a grip, Avery. Adrian flirts with every female breathing. He doesn't mean it, and it doesn't mean anything to you either. Yet somehow, that no longer felt true.

"I need to borrow your phone," I said, desperate to end this weird tension. To my surprise, he reached into his pocket and handed it over without saying anything.

"Hey, it's locked."

Adrian told me the passcode, and I repeated it out loud as I typed. The phone was unlocked, and a black wallpaper filled the screen. Why were those numbers so familiar? I gaped at him in disbelief. "Hey, that's my birth date! Why is it your passcode?"

"Because you own me—body, heart, and soul," he answered dramatically, putting one hand on the left side of his chest.

"Dude, I think you missed your calling. You should be in a soap opera. Such cheese!" I quickly texted Kris, letting her know what was up, and passed him back his phone.

A waiter approached our table and offered to clear our used plates and utensils. Once he was done, he looked at me and Adrian. "Anything for dessert?"

♎

I took my last spoonful of the chocolate mousse, savoring every last taste. We'd spent the last twenty minutes talking about food—to be more accurate, I'd been talking about my top ten favorite desserts while Adrian had been telling me about all kinds of aphrodisiacs.

Adrian's phone buzzed with a text. He scanned the message, sipped his coffee, and then fixed his gaze on me. "Kristen's at the knucklebones game. Shall we go save her?"

"She doesn't need saving." I finished my mango juice. "She loves this kind of stuff."

"Don't you know how thirsty Awakeneds can be during the Gathering?"

"What?"

"This could be their last chance of hooking up with anyone without their other half knowing about it. Makes for thirstiness. And desperation." Adrian shrugged. "Then there are those social climbers who figure they might as well take the opportunity to chase Royals while they have the chance. Knock them up so they can still have a connection with them. Dirty tricks like that, you know. And we both know Kristen is a target thanks to her royal blood and her looks."

"Geez, Zeus! Some people are just gross. I had no idea. Let's go. You should be the guide since I have no clue how to get there, and either this map is useless, or I suck at reading maps."

"Damn, ending our date so soon? Maybe I shouldn't have brought it up," Adrian said as we stood and walked out of the dining hall.

"This was a date? I didn't realize I was your type," I joked.

Surprisingly he didn't laugh but grabbed my hand instead. "You're a beautiful girl, Montgomery."

"Adrian . . ."

"Don't worry, Montgomery. I won't start something that I can't finish. Let's go find Kristen."

I found myself momentarily stunned and stared down at my hand, still warm from his touch. What was happening to me? I'd heard that being Awakened meant heightened emotions and desires, but this was getting a little too intense.

As I crossed the lobby of the Hyped, trying to catch up to Adrian, I saw the three stern-looking ladies watching me like hawks. I shivered, and distractedly walked right into Adrian's back. "Cheesy fusilli! Why did you stop?" I rubbed my forehead and groaned.

Adrian's face had hardened. His eyes glistened with pain as he stared at the entranceway to the Hyped.

"Adrian? Are you okay?" I grabbed his upper arm and gave him a hard squeeze. He didn't react to my voice or my touch.

"Avery?" said a silky female voice.

Standing in front of us was the stunning Marsela Costas, her thick dark-brown hair falling over her shoulders in loose waves, framing her heart-shaped face.

"Mars! It's so good to see you!" I embraced her in a warm hug.

"Geez, you're all grown up!" She pulled away to look at me and shook her head in awe. "And what a beauty!"

Besides possessing an allure that could match Aphrodite's, Marsela also had the kindest heart. Just like Kris, she never saw ill in anyone. I said, "You should see Kris. She looks like a legit model."

Adrian still hadn't said anything. Even with a few inches between them, I could feel the coldness inside him. It felt like the temperature had dropped a few degrees, and it had nothing to do with the December weather.

Marsela's eyes locked with Adrian's. So much was unspoken between them. "Adrian." She gave a curt, acknowledging nod. "It's been a long time."

Adrian responded in kind. The tension building up between the two of them was making me uncomfortable.

I cleared my throat, hoping to shake the awkwardness. "What're you doing here?"

The Costas, being one of the Royal families, had their own family mansion inside the Royal High Court. Both of Marsela's parents and her grandmother lived here. "We're here for Valeriya, Dimka's cousin. It's her first Gathering, too, but unfortunately, her parents couldn't come, so we'll be at Court all December."

Marsela had moved to Russia with her soul mate once she found out that she was pregnant, and her son was born soon after. The news of their child had sent Adrian spiraling, as if he had lost his mind. He quit college and used his trust fund to travel the world. His parents had let him, thinking it was better than if he were to remain at home, sad and lonely. Instead, Kris told me he'd spent his time jumping from club to club, attending numerous parties—trying to avoid thinking about Marsela, even if that meant being drunk most of the time.

"I'm glad she has you guys to accompany her," I replied, smiling.

Adrian grunted.

"It's really nice to see you, Marsela. I wish we could talk more, but I'm running late for the knucklebones thing and my mom will kill me if I don't get there soon."

"Try to have fun, okay?" She briefly glanced at Adrian before adding, "To be reunited with your soul mate is the most wonderful experience a Hellenicus will ever have."

I tried not to wince, knowing the last sentence must have felt like a dagger in Adrian's heart. Who would've thought that two people who had been madly in love with each other could become so cold and distant? Marsela headed out through the entranceway of the Hyped and in the direction of the Royal Quarters.

"Why did you have to start a conversation with her?" Adrian's voice broke. "You know how I feel about the bitc—" I elbowed his ribs so hard that it probably left bruises. "Ow! What the hell was that for?"

"I know she broke your heart, but refrain from calling her names. It's pathetic to be disrespectful to an ex. At one point, she was your everything."

"You want to know the truth? I wish I never loved her. It has ripped me apart and messed with my mind. I'm sorry, Montgomery." The elevator dinged. "I'm going to head back to my suite. Say hi to Kristen for me."

Before I could say anything, Adrian turned and strode across the lobby of the Hyped toward the entrance and disappeared into the cluster of people, out of sight.

"There goes my guide," I murmured to myself with a sigh.

CHAPTER SEVEN

Part of me wanted to go after Adrian, but I knew I had to get to the stupid knucklebones game before anyone—especially my mom—noticed I wasn't already there. Luckily, one of the elevator buttons was labeled Social Room, so I managed to find my way to the correct floor even without my guide—or my map.

As I stepped off the elevator, the feeling of being watched rushed over me. I caught the Royal surfer boy, Damian, as his eyes ran critically up and down my body. His behavior was nothing like yesterday when he had acted like I didn't exist. My gut told me he was one of the guys Adrian had been talking about, thirsty to sleep with as many girls as he could before he found his soul mate. Imagine clicking with him? I shuddered at the thought. Would his behavior even stop once he had a click? I shot him my best don't-even-think-about-it look and strode toward the social room.

Vlad was standing outside the door, looking more serious than the Court Guards, in a black suit, white shirt, and dark-green striped tie that was almost the same color as his eyes—moss in the depths of a forest. Despite the suit, he looked a little scruffy, not his usual clean-shaven self. Like he'd had a rough night too. What was he still doing here?

My stomach knotted, butterflies twisting inside. "Vlad. You're here," I said softly, as if afraid he might disappear if I spoke too loudly.

"I am." His voice sounded as hesitant as mine. He paused before he reached into the pocket of his coat and pulled out a black cell phone, which I instantly recognized. "Here."

"My phone! Thank you! Where did you find it?"

"In my coat pocket." Noticing my confused look, he elaborated, "I lent you my coat last night? You must've put it in there before you—well, before you passed out."

"Did you"—I paused and cleared my throat to hide my nervousness—"Did you carry me back to my unit?"

"I even cleaned you up and tucked you into bed."

"You what?"

"Don't tell me you forgot what happened last night?" When I didn't respond, he said, "That's okay. As long as you don't forget to pay for the cleaners."

"What?"

"You puked on my favorite shoes."

"I wasn't even drunk," I whispered to myself. "I'm mortified. How much do I owe you?"

One corner of his lips turned upward, forming a breathtaking smile. One that he had never given me. "Nothing. I'm just kidding. You don't need to pay for anything. I'm just happy that we're not yelling at each other."

"Are you going to stay?" I asked, hopeful.

"Yes."

"Why?" Surely my words last night were not the reason for his sudden change of heart.

"I was able to sort out a deal with my job after all. I'll be working from Court most of the time. But I still need to go in for the trial."

He paused before admitting, "You were right. I should be here for Kristen." He caught my eyes. "And for you."

Vlad had just said that I was right. That had never happened before, even when it was true. And second, he wanted to stay here for me. My phone presented an avenue for escape, and luckily there were tons of texts from Kris, but also three missed calls and a voice mail from Carlo. "I suppose we should probably head in there, then, and get this over with."

Vlad held the door for me. My eyes habitually scanned the crowded room for Kris. People on one side of the room were sitting on the floor, tossing all five knucklebones pieces into the air and trying to catch them on the backs of their hands. In the middle of the room, others were trying to throw the pieces into the opening of a small vessel. I had played both of these versions of astragaloi as a kid, but this was something else entirely. Vlad noticed my confusion. "They have to throw the dice onto the table thirty-five times. Each side of the die has a different value, but unlike the modern game of dice, it's not the side of the astragaloi faced up that counts, but the side that lands on the surface."

"Geez, Zeus, how do you know so much about this game? Do you remember all this from your first Gathering?"

He pointed at the table. "This one is my favorite version of astragaloi. I love counting those numbers."

This was surprising. I had thought that for him games were a waste of time. I was about to make a joke about how his first Gathering must have gone if he was so keen on counting numbers instead of courting women, when I heard a laugh I would recognize anywhere. I swiftly turned and saw Kris standing near the corner of the room, her face full of joy and her arms wrapped around someone I'd been dying to see: Carlo.

Emotion crashed over me. Pain, confusion, anger. I curled my hands into fists at the sides of my body, clenching so tightly that my palms started to burn. My nails dug in deep as I fought back tears.

"Hey, are you okay?" Vlad put his hand on my arm, but there was nothing that could ease the internal pain I was feeling. Without replying, I stalked across the room to Carlo. Adrian had been right: Kris did need protection . . . from this two-timing liar.

"Avery!" Kris beamed at me. Carlo put his hand out as if we were meeting for the first time. I didn't know how to react—damn, was he good. For the last year he'd been texting me, telling me all sorts of bullshit, and then suddenly here he was, wrapped around Kris. What a player.

"Ave, this is Domenico." Her green eyes sparkled.

Domenico? Did he think he could get away with not telling her his real name? Or maybe he had given me a fake name. Whichever it was, he had lied and that was far from okay.

Swallowing hard, I filled my lungs with a gulp of air, then exhaled as I plastered a sarcastically gracious smile on my face. "Hi, again," I said as casually as I could. "Sorry I haven't returned your calls. But I see you've found my *best friend*."

"Pardon?"

"Oh *come on*."

Carlo—or Domenico—looked at Kris, who shared the same look of confusion. My anger bubbled like hot lava as he continued his ruse. "You're really going to pretend that you don't remember me?"

"What's there to remember?"

That was it. I couldn't contain my fire any longer. I swung my arm back and hit him right across his stupid, pretty face. The sound cracked and he stumbled backward to land on his behind. The buzz of excitement around me died down—nothing but dead silence now. Kris looked at me then down at Carlo. Her expression morphed from confusion to shock. She apparently decided that Carlo needed more help, and crouched down on the floor next to him, staunching the blood pouring from his nose.

A hand came down on my shoulder and I turned, expecting it to be Vlad. Instead, I came face to face with a Court Guard.

"By order of the Court Guards, you are hereby in custody for an act of violence on Court Grounds." His voice was deep, and he didn't wait for me to respond before he pinned my arm behind my back.

I was about to yelp in protest when Vlad cut in. "Commander Hudson, I believe? I am Lord Ambrosia."

The guard bowed and nodded. No introduction needed. Everyone knew who Vlad was.

"I am Ms. Montgomery's legal representation. There's no need for handcuffs. I will escort her with you to holding."

Hudson gave him a nod and then let go of my arm.

"Are you okay, Avy?" Vlad whispered to me, putting one hand on my shoulder.

"Of course." I unclenched my fist then curled my fingers again. It didn't ache as much as I would've thought.

As I was ushered out of the social room, I heard Kris calling my name and I turned to catch a glimpse of her. She had to tell me something—I could see the urgency in her eyes. But I was yanked away before she could say another word.

CHAPTER EIGHT

Commander Pete Hudson had left us to wait for the verdict in a small waiting area in the Court Guard Headquarters. Vlad had immediately started furiously texting someone. The mystery of who he was texting was solved the moment Adrian strode into the waiting area like he owned the place, and sat down on the other side of me, sandwiching me between the two guys.

"Damn. What a rebel, Montgomery," Adrian said.

"Yeah, yeah. Go on, continue winding me up and I'll have to add your name to the bottom of my long list of rebellion." Two Court Guards were on the phone with the Court Hospital to find out how much damage I had caused. "You know,"—I turned to Vlad and gave him a look—"you just earned a new nickname. I'm calling you General from now on for putting Commander Hudson in his place." I rubbed my wrist, still feeling how hard Commander Hudson had gripped me.

"Can you not?" he said.

"You'll just have to deal with it, General. Sort of like how I've told you not to call me Avy and you never listened. Two can play that game."

We fell into silence and the whole thing felt more real. The Court Guards hovered over the administrative desk as I waited for one of them to come over and drop the bomb. Vlad must have noticed me staring at them anxiously because the next thing I knew, he fished his phone out of his pocket and said, "I'm calling your father."

"Whoa, whoa, hold on a sec there, *General.*" I held up both hands in surrender as I stared at his phone, hoping there was no signal here. "No one is saying anything to my dad."

"Listen, Avy, this is serious. And since you're under eighteen, a parent needs to be notified."

I wasn't happy about it, but I had no other choice. It was only a matter of time before my parents were informed, anyway. I suppose it would be better coming from Vlad than Commander Hudson. Vlad walked off to make the call.

"Man, this sure feels nostalgic. It's been a while," said Adrian as he took in the surroundings.

I couldn't help but smile—I needed a dose of levity, and I was glad he was feeling less crusty than he had been after running into Marsela. "What? You've been to jail before? Shocker."

Adrian laughed. "Not just me. Vlad was here too." I looked at Vlad, who had just gotten off the phone. Adrian *must* be joking.

"*Vlad* was in jail? What for?" I asked.

"We were in Royal Bar. He decided to play the knight and save a damsel in distress. Except this knight was drunk, and the damsel wasn't actually in distress. He took down every guy in the room who tried to stop him anyway." Adrian chuckled and Vlad looked mortified.

"Geez. I didn't know you were like that." I shook my head in disbelief. Vladimir, the dedicated law intern, involved in a bar brawl.

"They only locked him up for one night, but he got his own VIP cell since there was no sign of him calming down. The Court Guards felt it was best to put him in solitary where he couldn't beat anyone else up," Adrian continued. "He was a beast."

Unbelievable. I could barely picture Vlad in a bar, let alone in a fight. He struck me as the type of guy who spent most of his time studying in the corner of a library somewhere.

"Adrian, *enough*."

Commander Pete Hudson came back, along with two men in suits, all three wearing the same deadpan expression.

We stood up and I met Hudson's gaze. "Look, I know what I did was wrong. I'm sorry. I'll pay the fine. Though I'll need to ask my parents if it's more than two hundred bucks."

"It's not that simple, Ms. Montgomery."

"You want me to do community service too? That's all right; I love the elderly." The last comment earned a choking noise from Adrian, who tried hard not to laugh.

Vlad cut off my childish behavior and politely asked, "What was suggested for the penalties, sir?"

"There are stricter laws during the Gathering, as I'm sure you well know, Lord Ambrosia. There is no room for negotiation. We simply cannot tolerate anyone ruining the sacred month of December with any kind of violence. Therefore, by royal decree, we have no choice but to place Ms. Avery Zosime Montgomery under arrest and in a holding cell."

Surely my ears caught it wrong.

"Wait, for how long?" Adrian stood and fished out his cell phone, seemingly ready to send for more help.

Vlad looked very calm as he asked, "When is the trial, sir?"

"I'm afraid there won't be one, Lord Ambrosia." Commander Pete Hudson shook his head and continued, "It is a minor offense." When he saw me about to protest, he quickly added, "But an offense nonetheless. Minor offenses do not go to trial." To Adrian, he answered, "She'll be here for the week."

Two Court Guards went to my sides and I barely had time to say good-bye before they took me to my temporary home.

Ω

When the door closed behind me, the sound of the automatic lock turning reminded me there was no escape. These four concrete walls would be my residence for the next seven days. The cell itself was nothing like I had been expecting from all the crime dramas I'd watched. My imagination conjured creaking metal bunks, dark and dirty floors, one tiny barred window, a surly cellmate, and rats lurking in the corners. This was nothing of the sort. The cell was clean and bright to the point of blinding—making me want to file a complaint about their energy overuse. On my right, a metal bed was attached to the wall: no mattress, no pillow, just one thin blanket to keep me warm. There was a sink in one corner with something that looked like a chamber pot placed below. I was extra grateful that I didn't have a cellmate. No way could I use that thing with someone else in the room.

I wrapped my arms around myself and sat on the stone-hard bed, plonking down too hard and bumping my tailbone on the metal. I had given over my personal items—my phone! I hadn't even read Kris's texts yet—and changed into an all-black prison uniform, the color that represented the Underworld. The color of mourning, sadness, darkness.

Each new minute felt like an hour. After two hours—or twenty minutes, who really knew—of nothingness, I was bored of staring at the walls. Just as I was about to bang on the door, screaming came from another cell. The noise paralyzed me. I backed away from the door and knocked my right hand against the bed. *Ouch.* My palm was already red and swollen from giving Carlo a good head smack. But that hurt was nothing compared to the ache in my heart. All

I wanted now was to talk to Kris and let her know why I had hit "Domenico." I had to tell her that he was Carlo and he had tricked us both.

I should have known better than to allow myself to be vulnerable and give someone the chance to break me. It was like giving a murderer a gun and expecting not to be killed. Love was a myth. In the end, all that was left was agony, misery, and emptiness. I only had myself. And that thought was the loneliest one I'd ever had.

The lights in the corridor dimmed one by one, the only indication that it was nighttime. I lay down on the bed carefully, the cold metal pressing against my back, and covered myself with the blanket. It was a mistake to come to Court in the first place. Yes, I had wanted to satisfy my curiosity—but at what cost? I closed my eyes briefly, feeling overwhelmed by everything. I had let myself develop feelings for Carlo. I had believed his empty words and I had decided to come here. Now I had to face the consequences.

I tried to gather my thoughts, figure out my next move. But soon, I drifted to sleep.

CHAPTER NINE

I could only tell that it was daylight by the slim shaft of light penetrating the air vent. My whole body ached after sleeping on the metal bed, but I forced myself to sit up, ignoring my muscles as they throbbed in protest. For a brief moment, confusion spread through me as I processed my surroundings, until the realization hit me hard. Cheesy macaroni, I *really* was in jail. A feeling of hopelessness sank in, and I tried to shake it off as I stretched my arms above my head and then reluctantly got up.

The drowsiness still had not left me, so I stumbled my way to the sink. As I was splashing my face with water, I heard the door open followed by an upbeat voice.

"Are you enjoying your new digs?" It was the young Court Guard who had been with Hudson when they'd arrested me. "Remember me? I'm Officer Brad Warwick." He winked as one corner of his mouth stretched up into an asymmetrical smile that showed off his flawless white teeth.

Even though I remembered him, his cocky behavior made me refuse to admit it. "No."

"That's too bad. Because I certainly can't forget a pretty redhead like you."

"Is this what they pay you to do—harass prisoners?"

"Feisty." Raising one hand, he tapped on the panel and pressed several buttons all at once, so I had no chance of catching the passcode. One side of the door opened, and he leaned against it. "You have visitors."

Kris?

After the loneliness I suffered last night, I walked toward the door with newfound excitement. The feeling quickly plummeted back down when Officer Warwick added, "It's your parents."

I had to face them sooner or later. It was best to rip the bandage off and get it over with. And at least I would be out of my cell for the next little while. Officer Warwick brought me into a room with one metal chair facing a partition of glass that separated an inmate from their visitors. My parents waited on the other side of the glass. They looked as pissed off as I expected. I sat opposite them.

Dad was the first to make any movement, his eyes narrowing as he leaned forward. Without a *hello* or *how are you*, he said in a cold, detached voice, "I am glad they put you in a cell. I hope that will teach you something."

Dad sat back in the chair and Mom took over.

"Avery Zosime Montgomery," she said. "What. Were. You. Thinking?!" She balled her fist and slammed it on the metal surface a few inches from the glass partition. "Why on earth did you assault him? You know it is an offense to use violence of any kind on Court Grounds. So why the hell did you hit Lord Ferraro? He is of royal blood, the descendant of Hephaestus, god of blacksmiths, metalworking, metallurgy, fire, forges, the art of sculpture, and stonemasonry!"

"Geez, Zeus. Did you memorize all that before you came in here?"

She was in such a boiling fury that if someone were to draw an animation of her right now, fumes would be coming out of her ears.

If I had been five, seeing my mom this angry would've made me want to hide. But I was used to this by now.

"Tell me," she finally said after one minute of silence and murderous stares, "why did you do it?"

"He lied. He deceived me."

"How?" My dad laughed.

"He told me that—" I swallowed my embarrassment before continuing. "He liked me, but then I saw him with Kris and—"

"Can you blame him?" Mom said. "It's a choice between a pebble and a diamond."

I ignored her snide comment. "Maybe I shouldn't have used violence—that was wrong of me, but Carlo lied. He used a fake name and said he didn't know me even though he's been texting and calling me for the last year. I had to stand up for myself. He got what he deserved. Really, it's his fault."

"No," my dad insisted. "This is *your* fault."

"Of course you would say that." Typical. He'd choose any Royal snob over his own flesh and blood. Why did I expect anything different?

"Never mind. Don't even bother explaining. You've always been like this when it comes to Royals. If you had to save me or a Royal from drowning, you wouldn't even blink before pulling them out of the water," I said.

"That's irrelevant, Avery. The mistake is yours," he said simply, waiting several more heartbeats before dropping the hammer. "You didn't punch Lord Carlo Obelius Ferraro. You punched his twin brother, Lord *Domenico Aegeus* Ferraro."

Carlo had a twin? I was about to confirm this, when my mother piped in. "*Clearly* you didn't know Carlo as well as you thought you did. His parents split up long ago—Domenico lived with his mother in Sybaris while Carlo moved to Seattle with his dad. The boys were estranged." My mother looked over at my father. "Although in the wake of what's happened to Carlo, I'm sure the whole family will come together."

"What's happened to Carlo? Has he arrived at Court yet?" My mind leapt to his voice-mail message, which I hadn't had the chance to check.

Dad shook his head, his jaw clenched slightly, which made me feel anxious about what he was about to say. "He's . . . gone."

"What do you mean, *gone*?" I pulled my chair as close as I could get to the glass. "Did he take off?"

Was he angry with me for punching his brother? Had he already left because of me? My chest hurt knowing how much he had wanted to find his soul mate—how he had never skipped a Gathering since going to his first one.

Mom's face was filled with sadness. Her eyes lost their fury as she cast her gaze to the floor. The lines between Dad's eyebrows gave more years to his actual age. "He's gone as in . . . we've just heard the news that he died en route to Court, Avery," he finally said. "A car accident."

My parents exchanged a look—a conversation passing between them. In a normal situation, I would've asked what it was, but my mind was blank. Carlo was gone. I had the same feeling I had the day Bryan told me he was on his way to tell me something. Carlo was gone now, too, and there was nothing I could do to bring him back.

Ω

I don't know how I got back to the cell. Carlo was dead. Standing in the middle of the empty cell, I did nothing but exist. I was shutting down. How could he be dead? My mind couldn't accept it. I kept replaying the conversation with my parents—they could be cruel, but they would never lie about something like this. I lay back down on the hard bed, numb to its discomfort. A tidal wave of grief washed over me and I let myself be taken away by it.

First Bryan. Now Carlo. I wished I could have a face-to-face conversation with the Fates because there was one question I was dying to ask: Was everyone I cared for doomed to die?

CHAPTER TEN

For the first time in my life I had trouble eating. Judging by the number of meals they'd brought me, I'd been here a full two days by now. The lights had abruptly gone out for the night a few hours after a dinner tray had been delivered to me, the food going cold and untouched—the sight of it alone made my stomach turn. My appetite had not returned this morning, and now a guard took away my breakfast tray and replaced it with a lunch tray. I greedily drank the water, but after trying one bite of the dry sandwich, I pushed it away and curled back up on the bed.

I blotted my eyes with the sleeves of the uniform they had given me. They felt bruised and sore.

If Carlo was my soul mate, then I would never have a click in this lifetime. But if he wasn't, that meant they were still out there. I could have a click as soon as I turned eighteen. I was an Awakened—had drunk from the Golden Chalice. Even if I wanted to stay true to my original plan—which was to avoid next year's Gathering, like Adrian had done—there was still a chance I'd be in the same place as my soul mate and make physical contact with them. Maybe we'd accidentally brush shoulders at the beach, or there would be an introductory handshake—any skin-to-skin touch and a click would be triggered.

There had to be a way to break it. Some kind of ancient way of undoing what had been done. What had we learned about our Awakening? My annoying selective memory came up with nothing. All I desperately wanted now was freedom. Freedom from this cell so I could find a way to free myself from the possibility of getting stuck with my soul mate for life.

There was no way my Hellenic textbooks had the answers I was looking for. I would have remembered *something* if it had come up in my lessons. Wait. Maybe the Court had stored information about this. Maybe this was the kind of information Royals were privy to. Kris hadn't lived at Court since she was ten years old, so I'd have better luck asking either Vlad or Adrian. Both of them had grown up here and had gone to the Royal High Court Academy, and Adrian still lived here.

Yes. I would start with them.

Noise came from the entrance of my tiny cell. The door slid open and a woman in a dress the color of pomegranates stood there. She was older than my mom, maybe around fifty years old. Her dark-blond hair was gathered into a simple ponytail at the nape of her neck, and she wore a brooch of a diadem with lilies on either side of it. It was so unique and beautiful. I was mesmerized, at least until her head tilted eerily as she regarded me with unrestrained curiosity.

I scrambled up off the bed and stood in the corner of the room, my eyes never leaving her.

She hit a button on the keypad outside the room and the door closed. The two of us were now alone in the claustrophobic cell. My anxiety grew as she paced around the secluded area, pausing every now and then to eye me warily. I asked bravely, "What do you want?"

"Not what *I* want. What *the Faction* wants," she answered.

"What Faction?"

To my horror, she burst into hysterical laughter. I wasn't sure this woman was in her right mind. I gazed wistfully at the door, wondering if the guards had heard her and would come to take her away. "Oh, you really are clueless, aren't you, little Awakened one? Never safe, no chance to run." She paused, her twisted smile fading. "I'll die here."

"We're safe here," I spat out, trying to reassure her and curb her insanity. "The Court Guards won't let anything happen to you."

"No place is safe." The woman fiddled with her fingers anxiously, cold sweat dripping off her forehead. "Once those stupid Myrmidons learn that the inevitable cannot be avoided, that keeping the secret child alive and hidden all these years was for nothing, it will cause a distraction. Enough to grab the file from the archives and run." She let out a lamenting sigh, "Oh! It was supposed to be easy. You weren't supposed to be in here!" She raised her hand and I cowered, thinking she was going to hit me. Instead, she slapped her own face, hard.

She raised her hand to do it again, and I jumped in front of her, catching her wrist. "Stop! Hitting yourself won't do anything."

Terror overtook her eyes. "She will find me," the woman croaked. "She will find me, for I have failed her. She will have me tortured."

"Hey, hey." I inched closer to her, maintaining a safe distance while calming her down by rubbing her shoulder. "Listen, I get that it sucks to be in jail, but they follow the law here. Torture is illegal. Not even the queen could hurt you."

"Oh, poor child." She barked, "I am not scared of the queen. She's nothing compared to *her.* I can't be like Lamia. I can't let her touch Petros and Iosif. I can't." She backed away from me, crying into her hands as she crumpled to the floor. At least now she didn't look like she was about to murder me.

I crouched down next to her. "Listen," I said, knowing that my words were meaningless, "no one's going to hurt you."

The second I let my guard down she moved with lightning speed and lunged at me, her hands wrapping around my neck. I released an ear-splitting scream as I tried to escape her, hitting and kicking wildly, but she was determined to choke the life out of me.

I punched at her again, but my fist hit something else—a boot? Two guards came into the cell. They yanked her off me, restraining her violently and dragging her away. I scurried back into the far corner, curling my knees up into my chest, crying with relief.

"What the hell just happened?" Officer Warwick asked me.

"I should be the one asking that," I choked out.

Officer Warwick barked orders to the three guards behind him to secure the perimeter. He then kneeled down and put a reassuring hand on my shoulder. "You're going to be okay."

He picked me up like I weighed nothing and brought me to the medical room located at the back of the building. The nurse stood almost immediately when Officer Warwick slid the door open using only his elbow. The doctor, who was in the middle of reading something, set her papers down and adjusted her glasses, nestling them on the bridge of her nose. The doctor pointed to a bed attached to the wall and told me to make myself comfortable. Even in the best of conditions this would have been difficult because the blanket on top of the thin mattress was made out of a scratchy, puke-yellow fabric.

Officer Warwick put me down on the bed. "I'll wait outside," he said with a nod.

In addition to the physical checkup, the doctor also asked me how I was feeling. In all honesty, I was in shock. It was not every day a woman spewed nonsense at me before trying to kill me. Yet, if I was honest with the doctor, the examination would take much longer. It was funny how just yesterday I had been so desperate to leave my cell that I had been willing to have a visit from my parents. Now, all I wanted was to get back to my cell so I could be alone. After convincing her that there was nothing wrong with me, I was given permission to leave. I thanked her before getting up to go.

Officer Warwick, who had been leaning against the wall adjacent to the door, took two long strides to meet me. "Commander Hudson would like to have a word with you."

When would this endless cycle end? We got to the end of the hall and Officer Warwick swung open the door to Commander Hudson's office. I stepped into the dated office. Commander Hudson was waiting for me behind his desk. "Ms. Montgomery, please have a seat."

He spent the next twenty minutes quizzing me about everything the strange woman had said to me. Once he ran out of questions, his all-business façade dropped. He looked at me with genuine compassion and said, "I am so sorry, Avery, that you went through that."

My eyes widened a little. It was the first time he had used my first name, and from his voice, it seemed that he was actually genuine.

"She shouldn't have been able to get in here." His brow furrowed. "I'm going to get to work on your release papers right away. Then you'll be free to go."

Apparently almost getting strangled to death is a get-out-of-jail-free card, and I wasn't about to argue with that.

CHAPTER ELEVEN

It had only been two days since I'd sat in the waiting room with Vlad and Adrian waiting to hear about my punishment. But now I was getting out, and I couldn't wait any longer. I was still shaken from this afternoon's events but the freedom that I longed for was within my grasp—just as soon as Commander Hudson finished dealing with the documentation needed for my release.

Heavy footsteps echoed down the hallway, and I looked up from my trembling hands to see Hudson appear from the hall. "Ms. Montgomery."

He knew that I didn't want any trouble that might delay my release. "Commander Hudson."

"There are a few conditions of your release," he said succinctly, brows ascending. "Upon signing this,"—he passed me an official-looking document, complete with a Court seal—"you are not allowed to discuss what has happened here today with anyone."

A nondisclosure agreement. As I skimmed through the page, he handed me a pen, then I quickly signed my name at the bottom.

"Am I good to go now?" I asked.

"Not quite. There's one further condition." Seeming to find

amusement in his sentence, he chuckled, and for the first time since I had met him, he did not seem so stiff.

"What is it?" I asked warily.

"You aren't allowed to join any activities of the Gathering until further notice, and you have to avoid any confrontation, verbal and physical, with Lord Domenico Aegeus Ferraro."

Relief flooded over me. I could have hugged him—Hudson had just given me exactly what I needed the most: a reason to stay away from Carlo's twin brother. And an excuse not to participate in any Court-sanctioned activities. Domenico and Carlo were identical. It would be difficult to see Kris and Domenico together and not think about Carlo.

At last, Commander Hudson said the words I had been dying to hear: "You may go." He handed my phone and other possessions to me. "You should probably call someone to come pick you up."

There was no way I was calling my parents to come get me, so I texted Kris instead. I only had to wait ten minutes before I spied her coming through the glass door of the Court Guard Headquarters. She signed the administrative paper and I was good to go. I thanked Hudson, reached for the front door, then broke into a run toward freedom as soon as we stepped outside.

Kris folded her arms around me. "Ave! I'm so glad you're out!"

I squeezed her back and, smelling the sweet floral scent of her hair, I realized I must be pretty rank after my time in jail.

"That place is horrible. Never get arrested, okay?"

"That's an easy promise to keep. Listen." Kris's eyes glassed over as they filled with tears. "I'm so sorry about Carlo. And about the whole mix-up with Domenico—"

"It's okay, Kris." I interrupted her. "Neither of us could have known. Is he—did you click with Domenico?" I already knew the answer in my heart, but I needed to hear her say it.

"Yes! And it's as intense and wonderful as everyone said it is." The excitement abruptly washed off her face. "But I could also feel his pain. Even though Domenico and Carlo barely saw each other after their parents split, they had a strong connection. You know, being twins and all. I felt all of his grief as soon as he found out about Carlo's accident and—oh, Avery!" She stopped short and hugged me again as she saw the tears falling from my eyes.

I held on to her, feeling slightly light-headed as an emotional storm passed through me. Every part of me went completely still while my thoughts tried to catch up. I stood there, feeling my breath, inhaling and exhaling, as she held on to me. When I finally regained my composure, I pulled out of her embrace and said, "I'm okay."

Domenico walked toward us. He had one black eye—proof of what I'd done to him—and I couldn't help but cringe. With my temper getting the better of me, I had punched him without giving either of them time to explain.

"Ave." Kris reached out and grabbed Domenico's hand, her other holding mine. "I'd like to introduce you to Domenico *properly*."

"I'm so sorry." I didn't know what I was apologizing for—him losing Carlo or me leaving him with a black eye. To my surprise, Domenico hugged me. For a moment I let myself imagine I was hugging Carlo—a moment to say good-bye. We pulled apart, and I could see it written on Kris's face how much it meant to her for Domenico and me to be at peace.

"I hate to cut this short, but Kris, we really have to get going. My family is waiting." Domenico's voice was so similar to Carlo's it broke my heart again to hear it. "There's a kind of makeshift service for Carlo; you're welcome to come, of course."

My brain stuttered for a moment. It was as if hearing this piece of information had knocked every wisp of air from my lungs, and I stood there, struggling to breathe. My tongue was tied.

"Do you want to come with us to the service?" asked Domenico. By now, Kris had probably told him how close his brother and I had been. If he hadn't been able to read it in her thoughts, that was.

"No!" Dang. That came out too harsh. I faked a cough, rubbing my still-tender neck with one hand. "I mean, no, thank you. I don't think I could handle . . . I think I'm just going to go home and sleep for the rest of the day. It's been a rough couple of days."

Kris stepped forward and placed a comforting hand on my shoulder. "Do you want me to come with you?"

"No, I'll be fine. Domenico and his family need you."

Kris gave me a sympathetic nod. "Okay, but call me if you need anything."

The world's most perfect couple walked away together. My eyes lingered on them for a while before I forced myself to turn and head back home. The Court Guard Headquarters, where I had been held, was quite near the Hyped, so it only took me ten minutes to walk back.

There were times when I needed to be left alone, when I didn't want anyone to witness how miserable I was feeling. It was a miracle that I found the strength to get back to the Hyped and up to my floor. My whole body felt exhausted, as if I'd been running a marathon for days, and I was numb.

My grief was like the ocean: it came in waves—overwhelming me, crashing into me. I didn't shed another tear but not because I wasn't sad. I was *too* sad. The ache in my chest held a greater power. My legs buckled and I sank to my knees once I was inside my room and all alone.

Carlo. A shiver bolted down my spine. All I could think about was how he had been so excited about this Gathering. How he had promised me that he would see me as soon as he arrived. I had been deeply hurt when I had thought he'd pretended not to know me, completely deceived when Domenico cozied up to Kris. But those feelings were nothing compared to what I was feeling right now.

I don't know how long I sat sagged on the floor, nor did I care. My mind drove me into despair as it kept on swimming through what-ifs. Two amazing guys had been robbed from me because of stupid car accidents: Bryan and now Carlo. I wasn't just crying over Carlo but for Bryan too. I hadn't gotten much sleep while in my jail cell, and it finally all caught up to me. My eyesight blurred and everything became fuzzy. Still, I couldn't be bothered to get into bed or change. The darkness took hold of me as I succumbed to a deep slumber. Right before my last string of consciousness was taken away, I heard someone yelling, "Holy Zeus, Montgomery!"

Ω

Waking up, I smelled something burning. My eyes fluttered open and I could see the last of the sunset through the window.

How had I gotten into bed? And what was that smell?

I took the fact that there was no smoke surrounding me as a good sign.

Carlo. I pushed up into a sitting position as I took a deep breath before grief overtook me again.

"You're finally awake." A voice scattered my thoughts. Vlad was sitting on a dark-purple velvet couch in the corner of the quiet room. There was compassion mixed with worry in his expression. I wondered if he knew what had happened to Carlo.

"Wide awake. Do I have you to thank for getting me from there"—I pointed at the spot near the door—"to here?"

"Adrian carried you to bed," Vlad said, yet his voice didn't sound happy.

"Adrian? Wait, why are you guys even here?"

"Kris called. She doesn't want you to be alone."

Something was clearly wrong with me. I kept passing out and then there was this constant nausea. Maybe I should go to the Court Hospital to get checked out. A loud voice interrupted my train of thought.

"Sleeping Beauty's awake!"

Adrian stood in my bedroom doorway with a tray in his hands.

"Geez, Zeus!" I couldn't believe what I was seeing: Adrian Ambrosia was wearing an apron! My mom's pink apron to be precise. She always wore it around the house and evidently, had even brought it to Court.

"You're the one burning down the kitchen."

Adrian put the tray on the bed. "There was just a small incident, that's all." He pinched his thumb and index finger to show me how small.

"And these are the results from your incident?"

"Perfectly cooked bacon, toast from heaven, two splendidly hard-boiled eggs, and a glass of freshly squeezed orange juice. Specially made by Chef Adrian Ambrosia." He kissed the tips of his fingers before releasing them in the air.

"All right, all right, let me try it before I change my mind."

The toast seemed like the safest option. I inspected it—to be honest, it looked okay, but it wasn't in my nature to miss out on a chance to tease Adrian. I took a tiny bite using my front teeth, causing him to groan in frustration. "Oh come on, Montgomery! Give it a good bite."

Seemingly wanting to prove that his food was edible, Adrian grabbed the other piece of toast and took a huge bite. "See, yummy."

I finally gave into starvation and gobbled down the rest of the toast before grabbing one of the "splendidly boiled" eggs. I broke the shell and liquid poured out all over my hands. "Ew! I thought you said it was hard boiled!"

Adrian nervously scratched his neck. He pointed at the egg in my hand and stated the obvious: "That's not supposed to happen."

"Clearly." I got out of bed and headed to the bathroom, not willing to have gooey egg all over my hand for another second.

My reflection in the mirror revealed puffy eyes and a bright red nose. My hair looked like I was Dorothy and a tornado had just hit me. The boys were talking on the other side of the door.

"—so sad, it's heartbreaking seeing her like that," Adrian said.

"Don't worry," replied Vlad. "She'll get through this."

"I know, man, but I wish there was something I could do. I feel useless." Adrian sounded helpless and desperate.

"She's been through something like this before. She'll heal with time, I promise."

I never expected I'd be leaning on Adrian and Vlad of all people, but they were proving to be better guys than I'd ever given either of them credit for being. I looked at myself in the mirror again, grabbed a hair elastic, and pulled my curls up into a messy top bun. I counted to three before coming back into the room.

"I'm not sure that bacon is edible," I said. Adrian raised his hands in defeat. "But I'm famished. Do you guys know any good places to eat?"

Adrian and Vlad exchanged a knowing glance. Vlad nodded and stood. "We know a place that will blow your mind."

"Lead the way, General."

He sighed upon hearing the nickname but obliged anyway.

CHAPTER TWELVE

We arrived at a restaurant called Verona Ti Amo, which was nestled in the little maze of streets filled with shops and restaurants tucked away on the other side of the main Court buildings, a place I hadn't realized even existed.

The warm interior made me feel like I was inside a fairy-tale castle. A dazzling chandelier hung above our heads. The tables and chairs no doubt were antiques. Vases bursting with roses, the symbol of royalty, were placed in the middle of each table.

"This is Vlad's favorite place. Sometimes I wonder if he is the reincarnation of a duke or countess, with his love for antiques and all this"—Adrian gestured at the surroundings—"old, fancy stuff."

It was possible. As Hellenicus we were reincarnated over and over again, taking different vessels and genders. One thing would remain the same for me, though: I would always be born a Regular. A Regular could never be reincarnated as someone with royal blood. The Royals and Pure Royals, however, could be born as anyone. It depended on what they had done in their previous lives.

If a Royal had done good deeds in their former life, they could come back as a Pure Royal. Similarly, a Pure Royal who had done terrible things might become a Royal, or even a Regular, in their next life. This was one of the reasons why royal bloods kept their distance from the Regulars. It was almost impossible to track the original lineage of a Regular, so they couldn't trust that we hadn't been terrible people in our past lives.

There was quite a large number of Regulars, since the Great Massacre—one of the most gruesome events in our history. Our textbooks told us that some Royals had used Apollo's arrow to cease the Stavroses' existence, destroying their souls. The remaining Stavroses then met the same fate throughout the generations until there were none left. The murderers received one of the worst punishments for a Hellenicus: they were doomed to be Regulars forever.

"Avy, are you okay?" Vlad asked. "You were seriously lost in thought."

"Sure, General."

"I wish you would give the nickname a rest, Avy."

"If you want me to stop, maybe you should stop calling me Avy."

The hostess led us to a table. Adrian nodded toward a towering display of cakes and desserts. "Montgomery, you are going to be stuffing in the calories."

"We'll see. I'm not easily satisfied," I said, always ready for a challenge when it came to sweets.

Maybe this was exactly what I needed to help lessen the pain.

Ω

The grim reality of Carlo's death was fading from my mind because I was enjoying the company of Adrian and Vlad. We'd never hung out like this before. They were my seniors by four and six years, so I guess it wasn't cool for them to hang out with me when we were younger. But we were older now, and Vlad was proving to be more tolerable to be around. Adrian had no shame in recounting his own past misbehaviors, and I'd learned a lot more about them while we sat there talking over copious amounts of dessert.

"Goodness, Montgomery," muttered Adrian as he ran his eyes over the piles of empty plates on the table. "I never thought of you as a glutton."

"Hey! No fair. I was *starving*." I reached for the panna cotta and paused. "This was Carlo's favorite dessert. He said he used to help his grandma . . ." I trailed off.

Adrian looked like he was about to try to comfort me, but Vlad leaned forward. There was a playfulness in his expression that I wasn't used to seeing in him. I used to think he only had two manners: stern and smug. But he was proving me wrong. "So, do you prefer the term gourmand, Avy?"

It was like he knew I didn't want to get upset again, not here in the restaurant while we were otherwise having a good time.

"Gour-what?" Adrian said. I was as clueless as him, but there was no way I would let them know that, so I kept my poker face on.

"Gourmand. Someone who eats too much," Vlad answered.

I gulped nervously. Why did he have to look that good? I was secretly hoping they didn't notice my silence. The god of luck shone upon me as Adrian kept talking. "Wait, I thought that's a glutton?"

Finally averting his gaze from me, Vlad turned to Adrian. "A glutton is someone who eats more than what they need."

I was finally able to form a sentence and blurted out, "A walking dictionary is what you are."

I shook my head and reached for my cup of precious hot chocolate. Holding it with two hands, I raised the mug and took a sip. We'd ordered two slices of cheesecake, one tiramisu, two panna cottas, three cannoli, one pavlova, and two slices of pie. The boys only ate one *cannolo* each, and then Adrian grabbed two pieces of the panna cotta while Vlad took one slice of apple pie. I had eaten the rest.

"Hot chocolate is far superior to those coffees," I said.

Vlad put his Caffè Americano down. "After that much sweetness? You need something bitter to balance it out."

I was hoping Adrian would back me up but instead found him looking at Vlad with admiration. Kris had told me that when they were kids, Adrian used to look up to Vlad as a kind of big brother figure, a role model. Clearly he still did.

What was happening? Over the past few days, Vlad was becoming *Vladimir*, and not just my best friend's annoying older brother.

"Where to after this?" I asked coolly. Feeling Vlad's gaze still on me, I chose to look at Adrian instead.

"Depends on you, Montgomery."

"Where would you guys have gone back in the days of your rebellious youth? If you can remember back that far."

Vlad raised his mug, locking his eyes with mine as he took his time to drink. When he finally put the cup down, he said, "Royal Bar."

"Oh man. You almost got me excited for a moment there, but mingling with a bunch of snobby assholes is the last thing I want to do tonight."

Adrian leaned close to me. "Don't worry, Montgomery. I'll keep those assholes away from you." He gave me a cheeky wink as he leaned back in his seat. "We've got a tiny little problem if I'm going to play your loyal bodyguard."

"What?"

"You're not going to Royal Bar looking like that, right?"

Ω

Back in my room at the Hyped, I looked in the full-length mirror. I hated to admit it, but Adrian was right. My face was still puffy from all the crying I had done last night, and I could see faint bruises blooming on my neck. I could still feel the pressure of the woman's hands around my neck and closed my eyes, trying to pull my thoughts away from reliving it. A shower would help.

Adrian had gone back to his family's suite to see his sister, while Vlad said he'd wait here. It was obvious that he was reluctant to leave me alone. Another thing I hated to admit: I was grateful he had stayed without me having to ask. I knew that the bizarre woman was in Court Guard custody, but I felt safer and was able to relax knowing Vlad was in the next room.

Showered and dressed, with the tiniest bit of makeup on, I came out of my room to find the suite empty. Sitting on the couch where I'd left my phone, I was in the middle of texting Kris when Vlad came into the room buttoning up his shirt. A small towel hung around his neck, and his dark hair was slicked down and wet.

"You're still here," I said breathily.

"Of course," Vlad said. "I wouldn't leave you alone. I hope you don't mind that I used the other bathroom—I needed a shower."

The warmth from his body bled over to mine as he sat down beside me, and he squeezed my hand lightly, not realizing the impact that small gesture had on me.

It was an utterly foreign sensation; a strange and somewhat unpleasant feeling began to flutter in my chest. I quickly realized it was panic. When was the last time anyone had held my hand like this? Had my father? My mother? Kris always went for a hug.

"You are going to be okay," Vlad said.

The way he spoke made it seem like he *knew* I would be okay. And for some reason, I believed him. My panic subsided, and instead, calm washed over me. We stayed quiet for a long while, my mind combing over the events and emotions I'd experienced since arriving at Court, which seemed like eons ago now. It was almost as if my brain had rebooted.

"Vlad," I said. "Do you know if it's possible not to have a soul-mate bond?"

He looked at me with a funny expression, like I'd just asked the strangest question in the universe, and perhaps I had. In the Hellenicus's universe, anyway.

He chose his words carefully. "We're all taught about how special the bond is." He tried not to sound patronizing. "How magical the experience is and how we should be grateful for this gift that the gods have given us."

"There isn't a way." I sounded dejected.

"I didn't say that. There's this—"

His phone rang, keeping him from going any further. He answered the call and quickly ended it with, "We'll be there soon." He slid his phone into his pocket and stood. "That was Adrian. We should get going. They're already there."

Vlad walked back to the bathroom to put his towel away. I tried my best to stifle a groan. I was so damn close to the answers that I needed. What bad timing! Now I was back to square one.

But a second later my annoyance turned to delight as I realized that he had confirmed one thing: there *really* was a way to avoid having a soul mate. I just had to find out how.

CHAPTER THIRTEEN

The second we got out of the Hyped and into the street, I jumped back to our unfinished conversation. I was grateful that we walked to Royal Bar. I wasn't sure if I was ready to be in any vehicles without being reminded of both Bryan and Carlo. "What were you saying about the soul-mate bond?" The frustration was apparent in my voice. I wasn't sure if I would get another chance to speak to Vlad alone again this evening once we were at Royal Bar.

"What?" Averting his eyes to the road, he continued walking along the busy Ermou Street—in English, Hermes Street. It was particularly cold outside tonight, and Vlad tugged the collar of his jacket closed to keep out the night breeze.

"You didn't answer my question from earlier. You were in the middle of saying that there's a way to break a soul-mate bond, but Adrian interrupted you."

He kept his mouth shut as we continued walking, our breath visible in puffs of air against the cold.

"Are you *really* not going to give me the answer?" I asked again.

Vlad came to a halt on the corner of the busy street. We were standing in front of Royal Bar now. "Look, Avy, it's not that I don't want to give you the answers, I just don't see the point. Why does it matter?"

"Because I'm curious. People like Adrian, maybe like me, I wonder if they're better off without the gift."

"I shouldn't be telling you any of this, but we learned at the Royal High Court Academy that in the past, someone—seeing the soul-mate bond as a curse—managed to find a way to return it to Apollo, the god who had given it," he said quietly, probing for my secret agenda.

"How?"

"No idea. We don't even know who this person was. We're supposed to cherish our gift of clairaudience. Why would they teach us anything about throwing it away?"

He was right. And I had assumed this would be the case. But that didn't mean the Court hadn't kept any files on the subject. And it didn't mean that I wasn't going to find out more about it.

"Let's head inside before Adrian calls again." Not even two seconds after he'd said that, his phone rang. "See. Told you."

Royal Bar turned out to be the actual name of the bar, not a supercilious nickname used to keep us Regulars away, like I'd assumed. Vlad and I met up with Adrian, who had been waiting for us at the entrance, and the three of us walked into the dimly lit space. It was simple and minimalist. Along the wall at the far back were inverted bottles of amber liquid in every hue. A sharp smell of alcohol wafted toward me, like black plumes billowing from the windows of a burning house. A faint smell of vomit rose from the crowd of drunk and mingling Hellenicus, which tainted the fragrance of the room.

Standing so close to Adrian was overwhelming and dangerous; heat radiated from his arm on mine. There was this static, a crackling in the air, that always seemed to happen whenever the two of us got close. The baby hairs on the back of my neck stood up, and it surprised me that my skin longed to make contact with his. I dared to glance at Adrian, and judging by the look on his face, he felt it too.

"Did you see Kris and Domenico?" Vlad's presence broke the connection. All the yearning vanished into thin air. "I think we should find them."

Adrian picked up on the real reason for Vlad's concern. "You just don't like the idea of them being alone inside a bar for too long," he teased.

Vlad's mouth turned into a straight line, confirming Adrian's words.

I looked up at the two tall figures in front of me. "I can't see them from down here. You guys are tall—if you can't see them, why not call Kris?"

Adrian took his phone out of his pocket. "Actually, it's still too early for a party. Perhaps they are still wandering Ermou Street. Don't worry, Dom won't do anything inappropriate in public places." Adrian paused. "Voice mail."

We scoured the bar and then made our way through the crowd to find Kris and Domenico near the back, sitting at a round table for ten. I greeted Kris with a tight hug; it felt like a long time since I had last seen her, although it had only been yesterday when she had picked me up from jail. She looked breathtaking in a shimmery blue dress with her hair up. Domenico stood behind her. I said, "Dude, you lucked out with this one for your soul mate."

"Thank you, Avery. I agree entirely," Domenico said with a strange formality.

Kris gave me a look, and I realized that this would be the first time Vlad would meet his sister's soul mate. I took the hint. I nudged Adrian, motioning him back toward the bar. "Let's get some drinks. I think I'm going to die of thirst if I don't get some water ASAP."

And I wanted to talk to him alone. Adrian called to the bartender and ordered our drinks while I scoped out a place for us to sit.

We found a spot at the bar proper, and I looked around, making sure no one could overhear what I was about to say. It was taboo to talk about breaking the soul-mate bond, but I somehow felt like Adrian might agree with me, considering the heartbreak he'd experienced.

Adrian passed me a glass of water before downing one of a number of shots he'd ordered. Maybe if he was a bit tipsy he'd be more forthcoming about any secret documents the Hellenicus might have stored somewhere.

"How are you feeling?" I asked once the bartender had left us in our corner, away from prying ears.

He grabbed another shot off the sleek surface of the bar and tipped his head back as he downed it. A devilish grin spread across his face. "I'm awesome."

"I'm serious. We haven't had a chance to really talk after that encounter with Marsela."

"It sucked," Adrian admitted. "But I'll live. How about you, Montgomery? Are you okay? You know, after hearing about Carlo, and everything else that's been going on."

"No. And I don't think I will ever be."

"Hey, don't say that." Adrian slid one of his shots to me. "Here. Have a drink."

I slid it back to him. "I'm not eighteen yet, remember." Even if I was of age, I wouldn't be drinking tonight. I had to keep my wits about me. I needed to focus on figuring out a way to avoid ever having a click.

"Suit yourself." Adrian downed the shot.

"I'm not going to have a click," I blurted.

He said nothing for one full minute, then reached for another shot and said, "Everyone will have a click eventually. It's our fate. If not in this lifetime then the next one."

"But what if we can change it?"

"We don't have the power." He shook his head and stared at the dark-brown liquor in his glass. "Look, Montgomery, I don't want it to happen, either, but there's nothing I can do."

"If there was a way to break the bond, would you do it?"

His face turned serious. "After all the pain and suffering and heartbreak I've been through?" His brow wrinkled and the corners of his emerald eyes pinched. "Hell yeah."

I had found my new partner in crime.

Ω

Adrian went out for a smoke, leaving me at the bar, and when he came back in, a group of Royal girls stole him away. Not surprising at all. Kris and Domenico seemed to be letting loose and shaking off all the mourning. I sat alone at the bar until Vlad found me. He pointed to my glass of water. "Responsible teenager, huh?"

"Yep. That's what I am." I took a sip, letting the cool water with a hint of freshly squeezed lemon quench my thirst. "What about you? No alcohol before midnight?"

"Someone has to make sure everyone gets home safely."

Vlad seemed different tonight, and I wondered if this was the real him or if he was putting on an act because he knew I was mourning Carlo.

"What's with that look?"

"I'm just thinking about how nice you are." I didn't know who was more surprised. Him or me. "Okay. Let's not get carried away. What I mean is, it was not right for me to call you an asshole the other night. We haven't seen each other in two years, and people change. You aren't as bad as I once thought."

"I don't recall you calling me that."

"Maybe I didn't actually say it out loud, but I've lost count how many times I've called you that in my head. Anyway, I'm only going to say this once, and I will deny it until my last breath." I inhaled deeply before continuing. "You are a good person, Vladimir Ambrosia. And a good brother to Kris."

If someone had asked me last week to choose between praising Vlad and cliff diving, I would have chosen the latter without a blink, despite being afraid of heights.

"This is a one-time thing?"

"Yes, don't you know by now that I don't hand out compliments so easily?"

That got him laughing. "No, you don't."

We stood awkwardly at the bar, people milling around us, music blasting. Vlad didn't say anything, so I was the first to break the silence.

"How's work?"

"Stressful. There are some things that I don't agree with at the moment, but I'm doing my best."

"Now I'm intrigued. Tell me more."

He seemed hesitant, which only made me more curious. "Don't be so secretive. You can tell me. I won't judge, and my"—I zipped my lips—"are sealed."

"I can't. I can't disclose anything to anyone—it's illegal and against the code of ethics."

"Okay. Then why don't you tell me *generically* what it is that you do?"

"I think it will bore you."

"Try me."

He hesitated, and then said, "My work involves helping refugees get asylum, preserving human rights, fighting against irresponsible industrial waste—that kind of stuff. But I'm only an intern. Someday I'll be doing more than preparing files for trial."

Before I could form some sort of response, Kris came up behind us and linked her arms around our necks. "Hello, lovebirds, want to play a game?" Kris must have been well on her way to being drunk because she'd just called us lovebirds. She raised her hand to signal the bartender for another round, but I grabbed her wrist and pulled it down.

"Sure, let's play!" I wanted to be excited. Over the top of Kris's head, my eyes found Vlad's. I knew my best friend. If Vlad played the big brother and scolded her for drinking too much, Kris would drink even more. Distraction was the way to go.

"Yay!" Kris yelped in joy, clapping her hands like a kid who had just gotten an early Christmas present.

"If we play with her, she will forget about drinking," I whispered in Vlad's ear. He nodded and we followed Kris back to the table. Domenico smiled goofily at us, clearly also drunk.

"What game are we going to play, my love?" Domenico took Kris's hand as she scooted in close to him.

She pouted and scrunched her forehead, trying to align her thoughts. "I can't remember," she said as she slumped in her seat, and her shoulders hunched in defeat. Suddenly she sat back up and exclaimed, "Oh, I remember!" Kris clapped eagerly. "Basilinda."

"No, please, anything but that game," I groaned. Basilinda was a children's game and, just like everything else in the Hellenicus tradition, it was centuries old. To play, one person was appointed as the king, and everyone else became the servants who had to obey them. Adults played the more complex, mature version, which was a combination of Basilinda and *aporraxis*—a bouncing-ball game. The king would throw a ball on a flat surface, and when it bounced and landed in someone's lap, that person had to either swear on the River Styx to truthfully answer any question the king asked or do whatever the king requested of them. If they didn't obey, they had to spend one life cycle—one round of the game—in the Underworld. But if they obeyed, that person would become the next king and would have a chance to throw the ball. Some Hellenicus truly believed that they would have to spend one life cycle in the Underworld as a result of this game, so there was a lot at stake. Some even believed that if someone did not meet their soul mate in their lifetime, it could be because they had not abided by the rules of this game, and they were actually spending one additional life cycle in the Underworld.

Kris put her hand on my arm. "Please, please, please, Avery."

I was not fond of the game since it was a big deal to both swear on the River Styx and to spend one life cycle in the Underworld. No one could report back to let us all know whether this part of the game was true or not, so we did not know for sure. I wasn't the most superstitious person, but I also didn't want to take my chances when it came to spending any amount of time in the Underworld. Kris, on the other hand, looked like she wouldn't budge. I let out a weary sigh. Kris always acted like a five-year-old when she was drunk, and I figured agreeing to play would be the only way to stop her from being in a bad mood for the rest of the night, so I finally gave in. "Okay, okay. Basilinda it is."

Since this game was popular among the drunk, most bars had a few balls around, and Kris borrowed one from the bartender. We all appointed Kris as the first king. The ball bounced and landed in Domenico's lap. Kris smiled fondly at him. "Are you ready, pumpkin?"

I nearly choked on my water, hearing her say pumpkin. If Kris was sober, she would die from embarrassment to see herself acting like this.

"For you? Always, *mi amore.*" Domenico winked and she giggled. And I suddenly felt the need to throw up.

"Hmm, *alítheia í thárros?*" My best friend drummed her fingers lightly on her chin before finally coming to a decision. "How many girls have you been in love with?"

Domenico, looking at her with a stupid smile on his face, planted a kiss on her nose. "Just one. Unless you also count my *mamá,* then two." He drunkenly wiggled two fingers in the air.

"Moms don't count—you love your mom, but you aren't *in love* with your mom. There's a difference," I piped in.

"Okay, so one it is," Domenico replied as he bounced the ball and it landed on Vlad, who had to down three shots of tequila as requested. Classic. Vlad was about to throw the ball when Adrian and his fan club came to join us at the table. He sat between me and Vlad while the rest of the girls squished in where they could.

A blond girl, who somehow managed to squeeze between Domenico and Vlad, asked to take a turn. Without saying anything, Vlad held out the ball for her and she took it from the palm of his hand. She purposely bounced it in Adrian's direction and—surprise, surprise—she commanded him to kiss her. Realization dawned that this game would probably turn into a competition of how many girls could hook up with Lord Adrian Ambrosia by the end of this night.

As the girl leaned in, Adrian directed pensive eyes at me and I returned a questioning look. He gave me a rueful smile before he turned, putting his charm back on. "Come here." Adrian kissed the blond with a little more enthusiasm than was strictly necessary—at least in my opinion.

The ball kept bouncing here and there, mostly falling into Adrian's lap or one of the girls' laps. It was past midnight, and all I wanted was to be home in bed, finally getting to the resolution of *And Then There Were None*. Then the ball landed in my lap.

"Are you scared, Montgomery?" Adrian asked, his eyes playful.

"You wish."

"Swear on the River Styx, Montgomery, would you give me a hug now?"

"You sure you don't want to give me an order instead?"

"Nah, where's the fun in that? I want the truth."

I shrugged nonchalantly. "Of course, it's no big deal."

"Oh really?" A devilish smirk came to his face. His voice was silky as he laid out his challenge. "Prove it."

I thought for a moment.

"Fine." I stood up, grabbed his hand, and pulled him to his feet. "Come here, bud," I said in a sarcastic tone. Putting my arms around his middle, I squeezed him in a big bear hug. To my surprise, he reached around me and fastened his hands on my lower back. A delicious shiver ran down my spine, like a bolt of electricity, as he proceeded to hold me a little tighter, a little longer. I waited for him to let go, but he didn't. It took nearly everything in me to force my brain to work and my mouth to whisper to him, "I think that'll do."

He tensed up before dropping his hands and letting me go. I quickly scooted back to my seat and threw the ball, wanting to get my turn over with. It bounced and landed in Domenico's lap, and without putting any thought into my request, I ordered him to sing "Hey Jude" in Italian.

One of the girls jumped up and grabbed Adrian just as he was about to sit down. "Let's go dance! This is getting boring." Her girlfriends followed her lead, dragging Adrian away as he gave me a shrug that said *What can I say, girls like me, and I'm too much of a gentleman to turn them down.*

Vlad stood up and headed in the direction of the men's room. Domenico finished his rendition of the song. He looked a little sleepy, and I wasn't convinced he had given us an entirely correct translation. While still sitting, he took an awkward bow, nearly knocking his head on the table, then drooped his head down to rest on Kris's shoulder. Adrian was now dancing with the girls. "I'm glad Adrian's having fun," I said to Kris. "I didn't get a chance to tell you, but we ran into Marsela the other morning before the whole punching incident."

"Ouch." She cringed, then shook her head. "He tries to look

carefree and all, pretending that he doesn't give a damn, but he's hurting, and being back here only makes it worse."

The more I considered the soul-mate bond, the more I was persuaded that the ability to reconnect with our soul mates was more a curse than a gift. I really hoped Adrian and I would find the way to return the gift to the gods so that he would be free to fall in love with anyone he fancied without ever worrying that one day a soul mate would appear and ruin another relationship.

After a minute of silence, Kris suddenly exclaimed, "Hey! Why don't we keep playing?"

"It's just the two of us." I laughed. "Unless you want to wake Domenico up. It's his turn."

Kris looked down at Domenico, who was sleeping peacefully. "Vlad will be back in a sec, so we'll have company. I'll take Domenico's turn; I don't think he'll mind." Kris carefully took the red ball out of his grasp. He stirred in his sleep and she rubbed the side of his face affectionately before throwing the ball on the table. I wasn't surprised when it bounced and landed in my lap.

"Okay, bring it on, Kris. I don't have secrets to hide—you know them all, and there's nothing I am afraid of doing."

"I can't argue with that. Order, hmm? Thárros," Kris said, as if tasting the word in Greek would give her some ideas. Putting one finger on her chin, my best friend gave me a once-over as if hoping to get inspired. Then a glint of playfulness shone in her eyes. "I know exactly what I want you to do."

"Name it and it's done, Your Highness."

Kris leaned in, her large green eyes focused intensely on mine. "I want you to kiss Vladimir."

My cockiness ceased to exist in lightning speed. No amount of caffeine could have made me as wide awake as I was then. And right on cue, there was Vlad, walking to our table.

"You're crazy." I could feel my cheeks burning. *Kiss Vladimir Ambrosia?*

"Who's crazy?" asked Vlad as he claimed his seat next to me.

Creamy mashed potatoes!

"Kristen, for saying nachos and vanilla ice cream are a match made in heaven. Everyone knows that's just gross, but apparently not your beloved sister. I'm just trying to convince her that this combination would be a complete *disaster*." I was running out of breath by the time I finished concocting my false explanation. I gave Kris a look, hoping she had understood what I was trying to imply.

She did not. Or maybe she just chose to ignore it because she kept kicking me under the table while Vlad was distracted by his phone. "Disaster, Kris, it will end in a disaster," I hissed under my breath. There was no way on earth I would kiss her brother who, up until mere days ago, drove me absolutely nuts.

"Or you're just too chicken to try it." Drunk Kris was maybe even more stubborn than me. She continued kicking me until I was convinced I would be covered in bruises.

"Oh fine, I'll do it," I hissed at her.

I shifted to position myself so that I could just smack my lips on his cheek then make a quick getaway to the bathroom. I took a deep breath as I surveyed his dark hair and his sculpted body. A wave of nerves washed over me. I avoided looking at his lips. His forehead creased in serious lines as he read whatever it was he was looking at on his phone.

I could do this. It wasn't a big deal. I had watched tons of couples kissing on screen. I could just pretend I was an actress and this was just a movie—an act. I mean, it sort of was an act. It was an order. Something I had to tackle and be done with.

Bracing myself, I leaned toward him. My heart was beating faster and faster. I closed my eyes and my lips made contact with his warm skin. When I opened my eyes again, they were instantly locked with his.

"Sorry," I muttered quietly, ducking my head to avoid his eyes. "We're still playing the game and Kris ordered me to kiss you. I should've asked you first. I'm sorry." Maybe the floor would open up and swallow me whole.

"Game over." Kris giggled and then dropped her head on top of Domenico's, her eyes closed and mouth slightly open.

"Okay. Time for a bathroom break now." I tried to get up to make my escape, but my body refused to cooperate.

Vlad reached his hand out and gently tilted my head up, looking at me with such tenderness. He leaned forward and spoke with a playfulness in that deep voice of his. "Don't you think a kiss should be more like this?"

His eyes closed as his lips descended to mine. It was my first kiss and my body reacted before I even knew what it was doing. I couldn't stop myself from wrapping my arms around him. My heart pounded and the world around us dropped away. It felt good. Then it got better as my lips moved on their own and the kiss deepened. His lips were warm, like chocolate lava cake. Vlad seemed to know that he had made his point because after only a few seconds, he pulled away.

We stared at each other for what felt like a long time and I became afraid that he might see things that I didn't want anyone to see. He looked at me as if he could see through my walls and peek into my soul.

I faked a cough and grabbed my glass, emptying the remaining water, hoping that would cool my cheeks and distract me from the handsome man sitting beside me. The handsome man I had just *kissed*! Putting the glass down, I checked my watch. "It's almost two, we should get home. I think we better call the driver. There's no way they are going to be able to walk back to their suites."

Vlad bobbed his head and moved beside Kris, who had fallen asleep with her head still on Domenico's. I was relieved she had not seen what had just happened because I wasn't sure I was ready to talk about it—or be teased for it.

"Let's go, Krissy, we need to get you home." His voice was firm, but there was no mistaking the affection there.

Kris blinked a few times before finally focusing her sleepy eyes on her brother. "But it's not morning yet. I'm not leaving my bed, Vlady."

I tried my best to suppress my laughter at hearing the childish nickname.

Vlad managed to convince Kris that the seat she was in was, in fact, not her bed, and I helped her walk out of the bar and into the fresh night air while Vlad helped Domenico. The Ambrosias' driver was waiting outside. Vlad and I secured the couple in their seat belts in the back seat, and then he talked to the driver and gave him clear instructions to get both of them home safely. Their driver had been with the family for years, and we both knew Kris would be safe.

"Do you want shotgun?" Vlad asked.

I looked hesitantly at the car. Carlo's accident was still too raw for me to even think about getting into one. "Thanks, no, I'd rather walk. I could use the fresh air, and it's not far."

He seemed to understand my hesitation without me having to say anything. "I'll walk with you then."

He closed the car door and the driver waved as he went on his way.

Before we started walking back to the Hyped, I took one final look around behind me to see if I could spot Adrian. Maybe he had gone out for another cigarette. With no luck, I turned back to Vlad. "Shall we?"

He nodded.

Adrian had been missing for a few hours now, and I could only imagine where he had disappeared to—and with whom.

CHAPTER FOURTEEN

Vlad insisted on walking me to my door at the Hyped. My parents weren't there, but the note pinned to the fridge informed me that they were at Tiana's birthday party and would be back later. Wow, it was already past two o'clock in the morning. How much later did they mean? Seeing the note, Vlad offered to stay on the couch so I wouldn't be alone.

"You don't have to worry. They'll be back soon. Go home. Get some rest. I'm fine."

"Avy." His voice left no space for argument. I knew that I wanted him to stay. But I wasn't about to let him know that.

"Whatever you want." I shrugged. "But you're taking the couch."

With that decided, I went to grab a blanket and one of the pillows from my bedroom, then headed back. As I stepped into the living room, Vlad was taking his shirt off.

Holy piña colada! My eyes took in the thin, dark trail that ran down the middle of his eight-pack and circled his navel before disappearing beneath the waistband of his pants. I swallowed hard and did my best to look away. My eyes wouldn't cooperate. *Poseidon, help me.* I wanted to say something witty, something that indicated that his body on display had no effect whatsoever on me, but I couldn't think of anything. The blood had drained from my head.

He folded his shirt neatly and placed it on the table. He glanced up and saw me. "Are those for me?"

I washed off the dreamy look that no doubt had been on my face. "Yeah, here." I passed them to him and murmured, "Good night," before hurriedly going back to the bedroom.

"Good night, Avy." I heard his words as I closed the bedroom door.

Sleeping. Although the room was silent, my mind couldn't stop mulling over everything that had happened. Carlo's death, which endlessly reminded me of losing Bryan; Carlo's twin brother turning out to be my best friend's soul mate; the woman in the jail cell and how I had been strangely forbidden to ever speak about it; and of course, reliving the kiss with Vlad. It had been the weirdest forty-eight hours of my life.

Around five in the morning there was a huge crash outside my door. Panic-filled thoughts flew through my mind. What if the lady had escaped? Was she coming for me? I tried to calm myself down; it was probably just Vlad tripping on something on the way to the bathroom. I lay back down.

"Okay. I am calm. Calm is me. I find the calmness in me. I pull the calm energy from my surroundings." I breathed in and out, getting into my Zen zone.

Another noise followed and I jerked upward again. Silently crossing the room, I turned the doorknob slowly, careful not to make a sound. My hours awake in the dark meant I could see well without the lights on, and Vlad's figure lay still on the couch. My eyes darted to the kitchen. My breath hitched. I saw someone; their back was to me.

I wouldn't make the same mistake twice and try to chitchat with an intruder, as I had with the woman in the cell. I crept closer, until I was within swinging range, and could see that it was a man.

Now was my moment. I cleared my throat and as the man turned in surprise, I swung my fist, hitting him as hard as I could. He doubled over in pain.

"What the fuck!"

"Dad?"

Holy Hermes, please transport me elsewhere!

I found the lights and switched them on. Yep, the intruder was my dad.

"Avery Montgomery!" he growled. "What do you think you're doing?"

"I thought you were a robber or something! What are *you* doing?" I retorted.

Vlad scrambled up from the couch. *Shiitake mushroom!* I really didn't want him to see me get scolded by my dad. Oblivious to the tension building in the room, Vlad walked in, tugging his shirt down, which he'd clearly just thrown on. "Mr. Montgomery."

"Lord Ambrosia." The fact that my dad loved catering to the whims of the Royals could actually work in my favor for once. "Pardon me, I didn't realize you were here. My apologies for awakening you."

My dad shot *me* an icy glare, as if his banging and crashing and general robbery acting weren't what *actually* woke Vlad up.

"No, please don't apologize," said Vlad kindly. "I insisted on staying here—I didn't want Avery to be alone. Your couch is actually quite comfortable."

My dad's look was lethal. Vlad said quickly, "I'll just pop to the bathroom and then be on my way."

Once Vlad was out of earshot, my dad said, "Why did you let him sleep on the couch? He's a Royal. He should be in a *bed*."

"You're saying you'd rather I had invited *Lord Ambrosia* to sleep in my bed?"

The cold, hard stare, mastered over the years, had terrified me when I was small. But I was no longer a kid and I was in no mood to back down to his controlling nonsense.

I sighed. My eyes caught sight of a red purse on the counter, which could only belong to my mom. Only then did I realize that I had not seen her since she came to visit me in jail. "Dad, where's Mom?"

"She's staying at Tiana's," he said.

"Why? She was the one who chose what clothes I should wear and wanted to make sure I did okay at my first Gathering, but I've hardly seen her."

"She's going shopping with Tiana in the morning."

"Seriously?! It's her friend over her daughter. Again." I still found it dodgy. "But if Mom is going shopping tomorrow, won't she need her purse?"

My dad looked up at me then snatched the purse off the counter. "I came here to grab it for her. She accidentally left it. We'll finish this discussion another time."

And that was it, no further explanation. He left me standing there, furious. He hadn't even asked how I had gotten out of jail.

CHAPTER FIFTEEN

The only thing that was guaranteed to make me feel better when there were no Twinkies around was hot chocolate.

I filled the kettle with water, put it on top of the stove, and turned on the burner. I dumped two packets of hot chocolate into a mug as I waited for the water to boil. Vlad came out of the bathroom, but not before making sure the coast was clear.

"Please don't tease me about my sweet tooth. I'm so not in the mood," I said.

Vlad leaned against the counter, close to me. "I was just going to say that I wouldn't mind one myself."

"But you're a black coffee kind of guy."

"Sometimes I like sweet," he teased.

"I guess I'm dealing with Mr. Sunny Sunshine now."

I pulled out another mug from the cupboard, fixed him a cup of hot chocolate, and handed him the mug. He did not wait before taking his first sip. How were we simply getting along?

Vlad put his mug down. "Mr. Sunny who?"

"Nothing. I'm glad one of us is in a good mood."

His company was already making me feel better. It seemed like I wasn't going to be able to escape Vladimir Ambrosia during the rest of the Gathering. And it hit me like Zeus's lightning bolt: I wasn't sure I even wanted to.

Ω

Vlad ended up staying for the rest of the night. When I swung my bedroom door open in the morning, he sat reading the newspaper on the couch—already bathed and looking fresh despite wearing last night's clothes. Without even saying good morning, he jumped right in with, "I called Kristen—she won't be having breakfast with us. She wants to experience all the activities of her first Gathering, so she'll be following the official schedule. Should we call Adrian?"

We hadn't heard from Adrian since last night and it worried me a little. "Sure. Give me five minutes." I headed back into the bedroom to make myself look somewhat presentable.

Hey, you've reached the one and only Adrian Ambrosia. Unfortunately, today is not *your lucky day. I'm currently busy being awesome, so just leave your message at the beep!*

"He's probably still sleeping," I commented after we'd tried for the third time.

"Yeah. Maybe we should just pick him up along the way."

Fifteen minutes later, we knocked on the expansive, intimidating double doors of Adrian's family suite in the Royal Quarters, and their maid, Althea, let us in. Though Vlad had clearly been here many times before, the maid led the way up a beautiful spiral staircase to a far-reaching hallway lined with portraits of Ambrosia ancestors. She stopped in front of the third room on the left and, without knocking, opened the door.

Adrian was in bed with a girl. She had her back to us, but I could tell from her red hair that she wasn't the same girl who had kissed Adrian last night during our game of Basilinda. He certainly did get around. My eyes took in his hard pecs before I quickly turned around, not wanting to intrude any more than we had by barging into his room unannounced.

"You have guests, Lord Ambrosia," the maid announced before making her way back down the hallway to the stairs, not a care in the world. Who knew a maid could get away with that in a Royal household?

We followed suit, leaving Adrian sitting up in bed, looking dumbfounded as we headed back downstairs. Vlad led the way to a living room furnished with luxurious couches surrounding an antique table with intricate carvings. Next to the fireplace sat a white baby grand piano. A delicate green rug, interwoven with the kind of white that made you think of baby's breath flowers, was soft underfoot and warmer than the marbled tiles underneath it.

As if she had a sixth sense that could detect that we were now in the living room, the maid came in from the hallway carrying a tray of cookies, a pot of tea, two teacups, sugar, and milk. She placed the tray on the table and was about to pour the tea when Vlad stopped her. "Let me take care of it, Althea."

Althea smiled, placing the porcelain pot back on the tray, and took a step back. "You never let me do anything for you."

Vlad looked a little sheepish as he poured the English breakfast tea. He was about to hand the cup to me when he paused, then put in an extra spoonful of sugar. He knew how I took my tea. I couldn't believe he had even taken notice of these kinds of details about me. He passed the cup to me and I took it with both hands.

"Thanks," I said and sighed heavenly. Satisfied that we were content, Althea left the room.

Feeling the need to do something while we waited for Adrian, I took one of the delicious-looking chocolate chip cookies and stuffed it into my mouth. Once I had finished my third cookie and was reaching for the fourth, I heard Vlad say, "Don't think badly of him. He probably had a rough night. It's been tough for him, after Marsela that is."

"It's just typical Adrian," I said.

Vlad placed his cup on the saucer. "I don't think you understand Adrian as well as you think you do."

"Vlad, we both know his reputation. Let's not pretend that he's changed just because he's back here and—"

Rhythmic footsteps came from the spiral staircase as in walked Adrian, wearing a pair of jeans and a white T-shirt that fit him perfectly. He was rubbing the back of his neck with one hand while the other waved at Vlad and me. Vlad nodded in response; I grimaced.

"To what do I owe this honor?" Adrian stifled a yawn.

"Sorry about barging in." Vlad shot him an apologetic look. Perhaps guys had their own codes.

"Nah, man, it's okay. Althea can't seem to leave me alone lately. It's like she just can't accept that I'm no longer a teenage boy." Adrian smiled lazily. There was something in his eyes that bothered me. A lot. Like he looked guilty when he had no reason to.

"Do you want to go for breakfast with us?"

"Sure, give me a minute to clean up."

Before Adrian could turn to leave, Vlad cleared his throat. "Invite her, too, if you want."

Confusion crossed Adrian's face. "Who?"

"The girl."

Adrian looked like he wanted to say something, but swallowed whatever it was and gave Vlad a nod. One minute turned to five, and five to fifteen before we finally heard voices from the stairs.

"I don't have breakfast with guys I hook up with." The girl lowered her voice as if she was talking to herself. "Damn. I shouldn't have overslept. Look, just show me the way out and say that you'll call even though you won't. Because you don't have my number and I'm not about to give it to you."

Adrian chuckled and her protest was muffled. Maybe inviting her to have breakfast with us was not the best idea. Vlad looked unperturbed, as if he hadn't overheard her. He sipped his tea like it was any other day in the Ambrosia household.

I took a bite of the last cookie and nearly choked when Adrian came into the room with a girl I knew so well.

Renata Vidales. Nikki's twin sister, although she looked nothing like Nikki. Her lips curled into a mocking smile the second she caught sight of me. "Avery Montgomery, nice to see you again." She turned to Adrian. "I think I'll have that breakfast after all."

Ω

To my surprise, Renata acted nothing like her sister. No side-eye or snarky comments during breakfast. I knew she didn't get along that well with her sister, but I thought they would share some similarities, being twins and all. But she played the well-behaved Lady Vidales, daughter of a Royal family, the descendant of Aphrodite, goddess of love, beauty, and sexuality. She even managed to make polite conversation with Adrian and Vlad while I focused on my food.

"I didn't see you at the Awakening Ceremony," I mentioned to Renata once I had washed down the scrambled eggs with ice water.

"I arrived last night. I delayed my first Gathering for a year," she said, staring down at her plate and moving the food around with her fork. "Sharing special events with my twin sister gets old. This way, we each get our own time to celebrate becoming Awakened."

Renata was a wild card. No one really knew what she was going to do next. She had a reputation for being a rebel—not following our norm. We had two things in common: a tendency to rebel and a dislike of Nikki. But since she was Nikki's twin, I knew she was aware of my relationship with her sister and would side with her sister. Her coming to breakfast was obviously her way of torturing me. I could tell by the way she had accepted Adrian's invitation. But with everything else that had happened recently, I didn't have any spare energy for drama.

Scrambled eggs, bacon, sausages, and toast. Everything on this plate was all I cared about right now. Vlad seemed to pick up on my quiet mood and understood that I didn't want to be drawn into the conversation. I needed some space, and that was exactly what he gave me. Adrian kept our table far from quiet. Once in a while, I felt Vlad's eyes on me, but I only paid attention to my bacon.

After what felt like an eternity, our breakfast plates were taken away and our awkward meal came to an end. Now would be a good time to talk to Adrian and grill him about avoiding a click. If only I could get him away from Renata and shake Vlad's doting attention. Each day I got closer to being eighteen, the window I had for breaking the bond narrowed.

As we lingered outside the restaurant, I said, "Adrian, I have something to talk to you about. If you don't mind, perhaps we could—"

Before I could even finish my sentence, Renata turned to Adrian and locked her lips with his. Great. Another visual to haunt me. A weird lump stuck in my throat and I swallowed uncomfortably. I turned to Vlad, his eyes were already on me.

"Are you going to go check up on Kris?"

"Yeah, I'll pop over to the Awakeneds' event. And bring some aspirin."

"And lots of candy," I added. "She almost has a sweeter tooth than me when she's hungover."

"It's a good thing Mom and Dad are busy with the Council," he murmured.

"Lucky you," I replied.

I didn't bother asking about the Council business—he couldn't tell me anything. The Council consisted of two representatives from each Royal family and three from the Pure Royals. The queen called the shots, but her council took care of the lesser governmental concerns delegated to them, from mundane administrative things to crucial things, like maintaining the Hellenicus's secrecy from the Nescient and organizing the offerings to the gods and goddesses. Vlad and Kris's parents were both on the Council. It was unusual for a pair of soul mates to serve simultaneously, but the queen had bestowed them with the special honor. It was part of the reason why people tried to suck up so much to Kris and Vlad—both of their parents had the ear of the most powerful of the Hellenicus.

I hated all that nonsense, and a big part of me and Kris becoming fast friends was how much she appreciated me treating her like a regular kid, not one who was surrounded by prestige and power.

I turned to my left. Adrian and Renata were *still* kissing. I had no more patience or time to waste. Any decent person would have stopped, knowing it made others feel uncomfortable.

"Seriously, get a room!"

Adrian pulled away, earning me a glare from Renata—but her expression changed as she caught sight of something behind me. I turned to look, and there was Nikki, storming toward us.

One Vidales at a time, please! I was only a mortal being.

Nikki didn't even notice me. She stomped straight up to her sister and slapped her across the face. Adrian's jaw dropped in shock and there was a look of disgust on Vlad's face. No one had seen that coming—least of all Renata.

Renata's response was stormy, her auburn hair blazing like fire. I watched her hands curl into tight fists and her knuckles turn white.

Before hell could break loose, I stepped between them and looked at Renata. "Whatever you do, don't punch her. You'll wind up in jail and trust me, you'd rather *not.*"

Renata brushed me aside and spat out what I assumed to be some Spanish curse words.

"What the hell was that for?" Renata hissed at her sister. She somehow managed to keep her fists on both sides of her body as she held eyes with her dark-haired sister.

"Don't pretend you don't know! You slept with *Damian.* He's with me, you bitch!" Nikki flung her hand up to slap Renata again. This time Adrian stepped in front of Renata and grabbed Nikki's wrist. It did the trick; it was as if Nikki noticed for the first time that she and her sister were not alone. She dropped her hand and staggered backward.

Renata, who was not the type to hide behind a man, moved to position herself in front of Adrian. "Who's Damian?"

"Don't you dare pretend that you don't know! You left Royal Bar with him last night."

Renata was glowering at her sister so severely that it made me think she was going to explode. Instead, she raised her hands in defeat and said, "I have no idea who Damian is, and yes, I was at Royal Bar last night, but I left with him," she said, putting her hand on Adrian's shoulder.

Nikki opened her mouth and closed it, like a fish out of water. "Then who is this?" She pulled out her phone: someone had posted a video of what had gone down in Royal Bar last night, and she fast-forwarded to Damian and a redhead leaving the bar . . . and stopping to make out every other step. We all leaned in to have a better look.

Adrian looked like he was trying not to laugh. "Of course, it's Douchebag Tavoularis."

I shrugged. "It's not like Renata's the only redhead around here."

Nikki looked at Renata's reddened cheek and a glint of regret passed over her face before turning back to indignant anger as she shifted her glare to me. "It could be you!"

"Hold on right there, missy. I did *not* sleep with Damian. No way that would ever happen. If you don't believe me, you can ask him. He was with me last night." I pointed at Vlad.

Nikki seemed at a loss, but if she thought Renata was going to let it slide, she was mistaken. Renata put both of her hands on her hips and gave her sister a pointed look. "I'm waiting for an apology."

"I have nothing to apologize for," Nikki snapped.

"Oh really?" Renata grabbed her wrist and started dragging her sister away. "Let's not embarrass ourselves further, shall we?"

Just before they were out of earshot, Nikki turned back and called my name. "I heard Kris had a click the other day. Please pass her my congratulations. I'm really happy for her."

Her face betrayed a touch of envy, and I was caught off guard by her kind words. This was not the same Nikki who had slept with Kris's first boyfriend.

"What the heck was that?" I asked after the twins were safely out of earshot.

"That," Adrian said, "was an example of what happens during the Gathering after the Awakening Ceremony. Heightened emotions, extra intensity. All hell breaks loose."

Vlad laughed. "I'm going to go see how Kris is doing. Catch you guys later." He patted Adrian's shoulder and then walked away toward the Royal High Court.

"So . . ." Adrian inched closer to me once Vlad was out of sight. I held my breath.

He had always reminded me of a lion: fierce and predatory, filled with limitless energy. His hair, too, was tawny and hovered in that curious state between light brown and dark blond, and it was always styled in a messy way that made people assume he had just gotten laid. Being born with the Ambrosia family's famous green eyes—meaning that he had been an Ambrosia in all of his previous lives—did not help to curb his ego or the way he carried himself.

He had made me nervous when I was fourteen and crushing hard on him. Now, it was a different kind of feeling—the way he had paid attention to me since we'd arrived at Court, and how my body reacted to him, was more intense than four years ago.

"It's just you and me." Adrian leaned in so his face nearly brushed mine and he whispered in my ear, his voice as soft as silk against my skin. "I'm all yours, Montgomery. Tell me what you need."

Shivers raced down my spine. But I stepped back from Adrian and tried to control myself. It was true that I wanted to have a one-on-one talk with Adrian, but I knew what he was implying, and that wasn't what was on my mind.

"I only need to *talk* to you."

"If you say so, Montgomery." We walked toward the center of the Court, where the Whispering Oak of Dodona resided. "So, what is it you want to talk to me about?"

"Remember how I asked you if you would change your fate if you could?" My voice was pitched low as two Court Guards were patrolling the area.

"Wait, so I wasn't dreaming?" Adrian said.

"Of course not." I narrowed my eyes, wondering how much of our conversation last night he actually remembered. "Are you backing out now?"

"No," he said, shaking his head. "I can hardly remember what's real and what's not when I'm drunk, that's all. Remind me, why do you want to change your fate?"

"Because I want to be free, Adrian. Don't you want that too—to be able to make your own destiny and not just wait around here for your other half? Don't you want to have a shot at happiness? To love who you *want* to love?"

Adrian stared at me deeply, so many emotions reeling in his emerald eyes. "I do."

"Me too." I reached for his hand and gave it a comforting squeeze. "Anyway, Vlad implied that there *is* a way to do it—that it has happened in the past. Do you know anything at all about it? You went to the Royal High Court Academy, too, right? Vlad said he learned about it there."

"Montgomery, what happened? Why did you suddenly decide to do this? Was it because of that Carlo guy?" he asked tenderly.

"I've been thinking about this for a long time. The idea of being trapped in this predetermined destiny makes me sick. I'd been saving money with my friend Bryan to run away and avoid it altogether. Things changed when he died."

Adrian stopped and looked at me with concern.

"I loved him as a friend, Adrian, and maybe . . . maybe it could have been more. But we didn't have the time to find out. I was still determined to follow through with our plan, but—" I sighed, remembering the way Carlo had confidently walked over to me that first day we met. He had somehow managed to insert flecks of doubt in all my previous assumptions. "But then I met Carlo. I developed this huge crush on him, and even though I only knew him for a year, I learned so much about him during all our phone calls. Whenever we spoke, it felt like I was talking to an old friend. I can't explain it, but he got me, and it was so easy.

"For a moment I let myself think that having a soul mate—having him as my soul mate—might not be so bad. So I came here. Now?" Tears sprang to my eyes. "The last thing I need is to be forced into a deep connection with someone who can read my mind but can't ever truly understand me." I wiped a tear that had escaped. "But after everything, it also sort of terrifies me to think that I might have a click. I'm already a mess from losing Carlo *and* Bryan. What would it be like to lose your literal other half? I can't even imagine."

"Wow, Montgomery," Adrian said. "I didn't realize it ran that deep. But you're right. I think I know where we can get information like that."

"You do?" I said excitedly.

"They didn't exactly teach us anything about changing our fate or giving back the gift of clairaudience at the academy. But they did mention the consequences of doing so—bringing the gods' wrath and all that. I looked into it more at the Royal High Court Academy's library after what happened with Marsela."

"Great! Let's go there now!"

A breeze of wind tickled my neck and the sound echoed again, that whispering voice coming from the Oak of Dodona. I looked around, but everyone else was walking normally—enjoying the day and talking to their friends as if they didn't hear what I was hearing right now.

"We can't, it's not open to Regulars," Adrian said. "You know only Royals and Pure Royals can study at the Royal High Court Academy. Only they have access to the library."

"I won't be borrowing anything, and it's not like they require everyone to slide an access card to enter," I argued.

"It's exactly like that," Adrian said.

"Geez, Zeus!" I nearly went on to protest when I realized I had the solution at hand. "You have access, right?"

"I'm not worried about me. I'm worried about you."

"And can't you just pull some Pure Royal strings to get me in?"

Adrian responded with an apologetic shrug.

"Freaking mashed potatoes!"

There had to be a way to get in there. Maybe someone could make me a fake access card? Or I could borrow one? I had never wished Kris had gone to the Royal High Court Academy before, but if she had, I could've borrowed her card. There was no way I could borrow Vlad's—breaking the rules wasn't his thing, and he wouldn't hand it over to me without asking a million questions. Damn. If only there was someone I could— "Wait!" I grabbed Adrian's bicep. "Your sister! Caitlin went there, right? I could use hers."

Adrian leaned forward with a devilish smile. "Now that sounds like a legit plan. I'll get her access card for you. I'll text you when I have it."

With a plan in place, Adrian and I parted ways.

Ω

As I passed through the front doors of the Hyped, the three stern ladies sitting behind the reception desk eyed me up—perhaps they hadn't been informed that I was banned from participating in the activities and thought I was breaking the rules. I ignored them and dashed to the set of open elevator doors.

Entering my suite, I expected to have peace for a few hours, but I found my best friend waiting by my door, looking a little worse for wear. Still, she yelped in joy the instant she saw me.

"I thought Vlad was meeting up with you?" I said as I held open the door for Kris.

"Oh, he did. He brought me aspirin and candies," Kris replied with a yawn. She immediately headed for my bedroom, kicked off her shoes, and flopped onto the bed. "I figured it would be best to hide out here with you so my parents won't see me in this state when they get home from Council. I hope that's okay?"

I stared at the empty space. Two cups were still on the counter, chairs were pulled slightly away from the table, and the blanket Vlad had used was neatly folded on top of the sofa. Everything was exactly as I had left it that morning, which meant neither of my parents had come home. I always complained about their presence, how overprotective my dad was and how much of a nag my mom was, but now that I hadn't seen them lately, I had started missing them. Moreover, if this plan I had with Adrian was a success, I might never see them again.

"Ave?" Kris eyed me worriedly. "I can go if that's not okay."

"Of course it's okay!" Despite knowing I would have to figure out something to tell her when it was time to meet Adrian, I lay down next to her on the bed. It was so nice to feel like things were back to normal again.

Kris turned onto her side to face me and tucked her arm under the pillow, getting cozy. "How was breakfast?"

I relayed all the drama.

"Nikki slapped her sister?!" Kris gasped in disbelief. "In public? Did she get in trouble for that? And she congratulated me?" This time I cracked up while my best friend shook her head, her blond hair coming loose from the bun she had piled on top of her head.

"It's hard to believe, but that's what happened. And no, she didn't get in trouble. Renata probably didn't want to report her own sister, and it happened so fast that I doubt anyone except the three of us saw. She's lucky no guards were around either." I reached out for Kris's hand and held it. "Anyway, I don't care about Nikki or Renata. I care about you. How's your hangover?"

"The worst. I won't ever get drunk again."

I wrapped my arms around her and patted her back. "We both know that promise will be broken." Kris swatted my behind and I laughed.

"Damn! This means I can't join *phaininda*."

Phaininda, from the word *fenakidzo*, meant "to deceive." The game was simple: With the field being divided into three parts—one home field for each team on either side of the center part—two teams were set to play against each other. At the beginning of the game, each team started in their own territory and the referee would throw a small ball into center field. From this moment onward, the players were allowed to move freely in the field. If one team managed to throw a successful pass from the outfield to the center field, they scored a point, however, passes inside the center field did not count. After a point was recorded, the team who didn't score would hold the ball in their field while the scoring team occupied the center field in order to block passes in the area. The trick was to pretend to throw the ball to a particular player but then suddenly throw it to another—a small ball trick in the game of softball. Kris was a fan of sports, but with her hangover, there was no way she could play today.

"Vlad already informed them that I'm not in good condition to play, but I was hoping I could still show up and play a bit."

"Well, how about watching that new crime series everyone has been talking about instead?"

We spent the day in front of the TV, making our guesses of who the killer was. Yawning, Kris stretched out on the bed. "I feel so tired today and we didn't even do anything."

"I know, right? We're a lazy pair."

"Let's go get something to eat."

Twenty minutes later, we had managed to pull ourselves out of bed and were walking side by side, nestled in our winter coats. We found a diner called A Taste of Heaven, which reminded me of Adrian's failed attempt at making me eggs. I tried to stifle a laugh. My best friend eyed me inquisitively and nudged me, begging to know what was so funny. I told her all about Chef Adrian, and soon she was laughing along with me.

"Wow, you managed to get Adrian to cook?" Kris shook her head in disbelief. "That's a first. He always said that his hands don't do manual labor."

"And, honestly, it should probably stay that way." I grimaced, thinking of the gooey egg running down my hand.

We took the table in the corner beside the window. I ordered a cheeseburger and a root beer while Kris ordered a sausage platter and a strawberry milk shake. A comfortable silence fell between us as we watched the passersby through the window. A couple crossed the street, holding hands, then stopped by a street lamp, and the guy leaned down and planted a kiss on her lips. They looked like freshly clicked soul mates to me. But there was something about the intensity of the kiss that reminded me of last night's kiss with Vlad.

"Kris?"

"Hm?"

"What do you remember from last night?"

"What do you mean?" she asked.

I wasn't afraid to talk to Kris about anything—even when the matter involved her brother. "You ordered me to kiss your brother during Basilinda." I also knew when she was faking innocence. Kris was about to open her mouth when I raised one interrupting finger. "No, you don't get to say that you were too drunk to remember anything because I'm your best friend and I can just tell that you do remember *something*."

"Fine." Her scowl turned into a playful smile as she continued, "Since I am your best friend, that means I get to ask you any questions I like."

"Like what?"

"Like, did you actually kiss him?" There was a twinkle in her eyes.

"I did."

"Continuing with my best-friend-question-asking privileges . . ." Kris leaned forward, wiggling her eyebrows. "Was it a good first kiss?"

"Holy inventor of ketchup!" I pointed one finger at her, wide eyed. "You did that on purpose!"

She burst into laughter.

"*Why?* Why did you order me to do that? You know I hate your brother as much as cats hate water!"

"Some cats don't mind it," said Kris with a shrug. "And to answer your question, I did it because you two were acting like idiots all night long."

"Oh, your brother might have been, that's nothing out of the ordinary, but I certainly was not." I snorted.

"I'm an observer, you know. You were *looking* at him, and when you weren't, he was *looking* at you. It was really frustrating to watch, so I thought, why don't I do you both a favor."

Was he *looking* at me last night? He had kissed me, true, but did he enjoy it? Had he felt it? Had he felt the electricity spread through the rest of his body as I had? His green eyes had looked so tender when they were locked with mine. And then later in the night, when we had hot chocolate, there was a different kind of intimacy then.

"You *do* like him, don't you?" She grabbed my hand and squeezed.

"I—" I bit my lip and tried my best to come up with an answer but realized that I didn't have one. I knew my feelings for him had changed as I'd begun to see him in a different light these last few days. But did I *like* him? I had no answer to that. At least, not yet. "I don't know."

Kris understood the struggle going on inside my head as she let go of my hand and moved to the seat beside me. She reached her arms around me and held me tightly, knowing how much I needed it.

"I'm really sorry if what I did upset you. Maybe I shouldn't have done that." She paused, her hand rubbing up and down my arm. "You're my best friend and there's nothing I want more than for you to be happy. If you do like my brother, you should tell him. If you don't, well, you should tell him that, too, because I can assure you that he likes you very much. You are the first girl I've seen him treat so differently."

"Oh, you mean horribly? I still remember him calling me a flibbertigibbet short stack of pancakes."

My best friend laughed, neither confirming nor denying my statement. A small frown formed on her forehead. "What's up?"

Kris blinked a few times before turning to me. "It's Domenico. He just woke up." And just like that, her frown was gone and her smile returned. There was no mistaking the affection in her voice and eyes every time she mentioned his name. "He's complaining about his hangover." She broke a giggle and added, "Now he's complaining that I'm telling you about it."

"At one in the afternoon? He's even lazier than us. How does it feel? The click thing?"

"I don't feel like I'm myself," she said.

"What do you mean?" That was one of my worst fears besides losing any more people in my life: losing myself.

"Geez, Ave, why do you look so scared? It's not a bad thing."

"Care to explain?"

"From what I knew beforehand, even those who couldn't stand each other before the click became inseparable afterward." Kris's eyes sparkled as she spoke.

"*Okay.*" I uttered the word slowly, not connecting how that had anything to do with what she'd just said. "They didn't feel like themselves once they clicked?"

"No, it was even before the click happened."

"Wait, what?"

"After our clairaudience is awakened, it's like the gods are trying to send us a message, because everything—feelings, emotions, desires—is *intense.*"

"Sure, *that* kind of message, two halves impossibly destined to become one." Had I changed? Had my feelings for some people changed? All I felt was sick after my Awakening.

"And when you both finally have the click, everything becomes even more magical. It's like Domenico and I are one. He understands me, and I understand him. Completely, perfectly. Some people might say that it's because we can read each other's minds." Kris paused and shook her head before continuing. "But it's more than just clairaudience. It's this unbelievably strong connection. He can feel what I'm feeling, not just *hear* it from my inside head."

She put her hand on top of mine. "I'm not good at explaining things. You know how happy I am that you decided to come here. And now that I've experienced it, I want the same for you."

We hugged for what seemed like a long time. In the back of my mind I had always worried that our friendship would never be the same after the click. Now I knew better than to doubt our bond. There was always a place in her heart for me. I was genuinely happy for her. I truly was. But that didn't mean that I wanted the same for myself. If anything, her words gave me more validation that I would lose my freedom. My feelings, desires, and emotions would no longer be *mine*. Independence was rooted deep inside of me; I simply would not allow myself to be taken over.

"Domenico will be meeting my parents tomorrow at dinner. I'm kind of nervous. I really like his family and I want him to feel the same about mine," Kris said.

"Don't be nervous. Your parents are amazing! He's going to fit right in. Look, if he can get along with Vlad, he'll have no problem getting along with your parents."

Kris nudged my arm. "Admit it, you're finally coming around to Vladimir." She puckered her lips to make a kissing face in my direction.

I rolled my eyes and she giggled, knowing she had successfully gotten a rise out of me.

After our lunch, Kris headed back to her suite to get ready for *Laphria*—a ritual honoring Artemis, which everyone who participated in the Gathering must attend. Well, except those who were on probation and banned from joining. Kris told me she would video-call me so I could see what she was wearing, though I already knew she would look stunning.

Back at my suite, I sat in the living room, cross-legged on the couch with nothing but a mug of hot chocolate to keep me company. I could not stop thinking about how Kris had described her click with Domenico. I knew for her it was romantic and beautiful, but to me, it was anything but. It would change me. Perhaps not into a completely different person, but it *would* change me. Kris's explanation had confirmed that.

Yes, Kris did say that she knew it was true love because Domenico could understand her perfectly, but how could he not understand her when he could dig deep into her mind? That was cheating, right? The Hellenicus idea of normal was not the kind of normal I wanted. Was it truly worth it to have this so-called love at the cost of losing your freedom?

Realizing that I had just mocked something that Carlo had believed in all of his life, I suddenly felt bad.

My eyes flew open. Carlo's voice mail! There had been so many things going on these last few days that it had completely slipped my mind. Maybe a part of me couldn't bear to listen to it, hence why I had shoved the thought of this voice mail to the back of my mind. But I was now ready to hear what his final words to me were. I pulled out my phone, quickly unlocked it, and listened.

Avery, you have to run. The Court isn't safe. You are in grave danger. The Faction will find you and you won't stand a chance against them. There are things that you don't know—that I wouldn't know if I hadn't found your file in my father's safe. Come to Seattle and I'll show you. I'll explain everything. But now you have to ru—

I didn't understand. The urgency in his voice made me tremble. I replayed it over and over. His voice sounded breathy, almost as if he was running. The Faction—wasn't that what the woman who attacked me had said? The warning in his voice—had he died feeling as scared as he sounded in the voice message? Had he been driving recklessly because he was panicking about *me*—or was it something else?

I curled up into a ball, wrapping my arms around my legs as tightly as I could. I felt like if I let go, I would fall to pieces. I tucked my head down and squeezed my eyes shut tight, as if that would erase the thought of Carlo's final moments.

I told myself that I could have ten breaths like this and then I would get up. This was not the time to be weak.

I had to return my gift to the gods and leave this place. The sooner, the better. If I lived out the rest of my life as a Nescient, I wouldn't even have to bother with whatever this Faction was. I would be safe. More importantly, I would be free.

I uncurled from my fetal position and unlocked my phone. Feeling the sudden need to hasten our plan, I sent a message to Adrian.

Have you found it?

CHAPTER SIXTEEN

It had not even been a half hour when I received a disappointing reply from Adrian.

I can't find my sister's card—sorry, A.

I searched for my backpack and pulled out my laptop. The internet probably wouldn't yield any insider tips about the Hellenicus, but I figured it wouldn't hurt to give it a try.

I had learned about our origin myth back in Hellenic school, so all I needed was to dig deeper into the gods and goddesses. I started with Apollo since he had been the one tasked by Zeus to help the Hellenicus find their soul mates. I tried to find insight into the whole mind-reading thing but nada. After all, the Hellenicus are very secretive and would never allow the Nescient to have easy access to information.

I was moving the cursor to click on Eros when a high-pitched sound pierced my ears. The noise kept going as I searched for the source.

"Shiitake mushroom!" The source of the obnoxious sound was on the floor, half-hidden under the couch—my dad's cell phone. *Geez, Zeus! Could he have picked a more annoying ringtone?* "Hello?"

A deep, manly voice shouted back at me. "Hawke! Where are you? We've been waiting for more than an hour now! You were the one asking for an emergency meeting, at least have the decency to inform us if you want to call it off!"

Who?

I brought the phone closer once I knew for sure that the man had finished yelling. "There is no Hawke here, sir."

"Lincoln, is that you?"

"No, sir, there is no Lincoln either." I borrowed Domenico's polite formality and Kris's patience as I continued, "I think you may have dialed the wrong number."

There was a rattle, for which I couldn't distinguish the cause, and then the sound of a chair being dragged before I heard his voice again. "I am damn sure it's the right number, missy. Who the hell are you, and how on earth did you get a hold of this phone?"

"My name is none of your concern, and I know for sure that you dialed the wrong number because this phone belongs to my dad, whose name I won't disclose either."

It was quiet for what felt like a full minute; I thought the man had hung up. I glanced at the screen. The call was still connected. Maybe I should hang up. But before I could do anything, the man said something that led me to believe that he actually knew my dad after all. Or, to be more accurate, me.

"Shit! It's the girl!" He went on to spew a bunch of curse words.

There were more voices in the background, but none that I could understand. Then the call ended. As I put the phone on the table, the cogs in my brain started to turn. Three questions needed to be answered: One, the less important of the three, why had my dad chosen an ear-shattering sound as his ringtone? Two, what in Poseidon's name was that call about? Three, who the heck were Hawke and Lincoln?

Ω

After the disturbing phone call it was difficult to go back to focusing on what was proving to be fruitless research. Still, I aimlessly clicked on a number of Nescient websites about Greek mythology that led nowhere in terms of finding any answers. As the laptop battery drained, so did my energy, depleting to zero.

Then a typo in an ad at the bottom of one of the Nescient web pages caught my attention. The ad read:

Click here to get high-speed internet at a faction of the cost!

It should have said *fraction*, but instead said *faction*. Was this another cruel joke of the gods, taunting me with the fact that I was never going to find any of the answers I needed?

But right next to that ad was another one; one that sparked a memory:

Want to know more about your family history? Check out our internet archive with over ten million records.

Archive! During my odd encounter in the jail, the woman had mentioned something about taking a file from the archives. Maybe that was where we should be looking.

I reached for my phone to call Adrian.

"I told you, Montgomery, I couldn't find Caitlin's card."

"Have you ever heard of the archives?" I blurted.

His voice changed from slightly impatient to now slightly confused. "What's that?"

Aware that I couldn't tell him about the woman from jail, I simply offered, "Oh, I thought maybe the Court would have a place to keep their important files or something. Like an archive maybe?"

"I'm sure they do. But why would I know anything about that?"

"I don't know. I thought it was worth asking just in case."

"Admit it. You just wanted an excuse to hear my voice."

I didn't have time for Adrian's antics. "Good-bye, Adrian." I abruptly ended our call.

What I needed was a long, luxurious bath with expensive bath salts and lots of bubbles.

There was something relaxing about sitting in the hot, bubbly water while listening to my favorite playlist on my phone. The crick in the back of my neck loosened as I stretched and let my eyes rest, listening to Jimin's soulful voice singing in the background. The last song in my playlist came to an end, and there was peaceful silence afterward. My eyes fluttered open at the same time as my hands broke the water's surface. Pruney fingers made me realize how long I had been in the water. I grabbed the side of the bathtub and pulled myself up. I stood naked, scanning the room for my towel.

"Fu—" I caught myself before the swear word came out and quickly corrected myself. "Fruit salad!" Damn. It was hard to reform my drunken-sailor mouth sometimes.

I stepped outside of the bathroom to get a towel. The bedroom was quiet. Hell, the entire unit was dead. I moved around the bedroom, dripping water everywhere, until I found a clean towel in a drawer, pulled it out, and wrapped it around my body. Just then, I heard a soft click from the front door.

Who was that? Maybe it was Kris. Perhaps she had forgotten something from her earlier visit.

"Kris?" I called out. "Kris, are you there?" No reply. I called out again and waited. Still there was no reply. Just when I was about to head back to the bathroom, the bedroom door swung open and revealed the object of my distress: Vladimir.

"Avy! Are you all right?" he blurted, surprising me with the slight note of panic in his voice.

Our eyes met. He scratched the back of his neck, causing some of his dark locks to jut out. His lips parted as if he was about to say something, but he clamped them shut and hung his head. This was not a dream! I scurried back into the bathroom, and behind the closed door, I frantically pulled on my dark-grey hoodie and sweat-pants. I was so nervous that I almost inserted my head into the hole meant for my arm.

My hair was still wet, so I wrapped the towel around my head, twisted it, and tucked it in at the back. I tossed my dirty clothes into the laundry basket in the corner then headed to the living room.

Vlad was sitting on the couch, eyes focused on the newspaper. I plopped myself down on the couch across from him. "Um, hi?"

"Hey," he answered without looking up.

The long moment of disconcerting silence that passed made me wish I had something to read too. "Why are you here?"

He did not answer immediately, but when he did, I was shocked by what he had say. "I just got back from work—a trial actually. Kris asked me to come here and accompany you to dinner since she's eating with Domenico's mom."

I was surprised for two reasons: one, the realization that my best friend had no subtlety now that she knew that I felt something for Vlad, and two, the fact that he had actually followed her request.

Ah, you're nervous around him, aren't you? said a traitorous voice inside my head, and I ordered it to shut up. It didn't. *Admit it, you like him being here.*

"Are you ready?" he asked, followed by the crinkling sound of the newspaper flipping to the next page.

"For dinner? I ate a while ago."

He looked up from the newspaper and I caught a faint redness on his cheeks. "Check the time. It has been hours since you had your last meal."

"I suppose you're right," I said after consulting the clock. "Do you have anything in mind? I feel like I have tried nearly all the food at Court already." I paused, noticing that my dad's phone, which I had placed on the table, was gone.

Had he come back home while I was in the bath?

Vlad folded the newspaper and put it neatly on the table as he stood. His dark-green eyes twinkled in a way that made my breath hitch as he said, "I might. Grab your coat. Let's have a good dinner."

Surprisingly, the place he had in mind was outside the Court, so we would be driving. I stood frozen, staring at his car. Both Bryan and Carlo had died in car accidents, and I was wary of getting into the vehicle.

"You okay?" Vlad's voice broke through my thoughts as he opened the passenger-side door for me.

"Yeah. Fine, thanks."

"Get in, it'll be breakfast by the time we get there at this rate," Vlad teased.

"Oh, shut up." I pushed aside my hesitations and stepped into the car.

I didn't think that coming and going from the Court during the Gathering was possible—this whole place was heavily guarded, and the Court Guards didn't just open the gate on command to let people in and out as they pleased. But apparently I was wrong. Vlad handed one of the guards a letter and they let us out, no questions asked. "Whoa, how did you do that?"

"I have my ways."

Vlad handled the road better than anyone I knew. It made me feel less nervous about being in a car. Without speaking, we stared at the road as a classic tune filled the car. The low, throaty growl of the engine hummed in the background. I could only contain my curiosity for another twenty minutes before it got the better of me.

"Where are we going?" It was dark outside and I couldn't make out where we were. Not that I would be able to if it was broad daylight, either, considering this was my first time being here and I always had trouble with directions. Ferdinand Magellan could come back to life and teach me about circumnavigation and I would still get lost. I was *that* bad.

"It's a secret." He quickly looked back at the road.

"Oh come on!"

Something fluttered in my stomach, but I was completely sure it wasn't butterflies. A loud growl erupted from the depths of my belly and I wished I could crawl under the seat and disappear.

"Don't worry, we're almost there." As if my stomach had listened to him, it stopped embarrassing me further.

The road passed by outside the window. Hawke and Lincoln. Who were these people? Then there was *the Faction*, which Carlo and that woman in jail had mentioned.

"What's wrong?" Vlad's thumb reached out for the volume button on his steering wheel and turned the song down.

Not knowing how to answer, I remained quiet. Oddly, even in silence, I did not feel any awkwardness in the air.

Things were definitely changing. I had always considered him as a jerk, but lately I had seen a different side of him—a side that made me reconsider my earlier thought about him. I had thought he was selfish but he wasn't; he actually cared about other people, not just himself. He cared about me, and he cared about Adrian. He even cared about Althea, Adrian's maid, from what I had seen the other day.

I made the mistake of turning my head slightly to the right and risking my eyes meeting his. His moss-green eyes, wise and warm, and undeniably perceptive, were focused on mine. For one split second I had a bizarre thought that he somehow knew everything about me—every little bit. Things that not even Kris knew about me. That moment back in Verona Ti Amo, he knew I was trying not to have a breakdown and he swiftly changed the conversation. It seemed, in that moment, that he, more than anyone else in the world, truly knew me. Inside and out. No matter how many walls I had built to prevent that from happening.

It was thrilling.

But more than that, it was terrifying. So I did what I always did best: totally avoid the situation and talk about something entirely unrelated. "Do you know anyone named Hawke and Lincoln?"

"No," he replied. The good thing about Vlad was, unlike Adrian, he never asked why. He knew that if I wanted him to know more, I would tell him.

We had arrived at our destination and Vlad parallel parked with ease, turning off the engine as he undid his seat belt. With one hand on top of the steering wheel, he shifted to face me.

"What about the Faction?" I was desperate to find out *anything*. Because otherwise, today had been completely unproductive, and I was no closer to my end goal. And with my birthday looming time wasn't exactly on my side. He knew something, and from the expression on his face, I could tell that he was debating with himself whether to share this information with me or not.

I wasn't sure what came over me, but I placed my hand on top of his on the steering wheel. "What is it?"

Whether it was my touch or his own decision that changed his mind, I didn't know, but whatever it was, he unclasped his lips to say, "It's just, this afternoon I was tidying up Dad's desk—I've been using it to work. Anyway, earlier today, my parents were at another Council meeting, and he'd left a bunch of papers all over his desk. The word *Faction* was in bold, capital letters on one of his Council files."

"Did you read anything more?" I asked.

"No," he said, looking surprised that I would even think that he would pry like that. "But I did ask Dad about it."

"And? What did he say?"

"He said it's something to do with the Great Massacre and how it ruined the unity of our people. People taking sides, and the Faction was proof of that. He didn't explain further."

The silence returned. I was trying to remember everything I knew about the Great Massacre and how that could connect to what the woman in jail had said, when Vlad finally said, "Let's go." Acting like a gentleman, he walked to my side of the car to open the door for me, but I had already gotten out and closed it by the time he reached me.

The restaurant was called No. 5. An interesting choice of name. Maybe it was the property's address, but something told me it had a deeper meaning.

"Vlad!" The restauranteur greeted him with a warm hug. "It's been a while. We've missed you around here."

Vlad blushed slightly, somehow looking younger than usual. "I'm sorry, Lilly. I've been busy."

"Well, at least you're here now." Her gaze traveled to his left and locked on mine. "Is this your girlfriend?" she asked with a smile. "It's about time you brought a girl here, *Vovochka*." Turning to face me, she extended one hand. "Hello, dear."

"Hi." I greeted her and shook her hand. "I'm Avery." Once she let go of my hand, I pointed my finger at Vlad and me in a back-and-forth motion. "We're not dating."

The lady raised her brows as if asking, *Are you sure.* "Oh?"

"I'm his little sister's best friend."

"Oh, that's interesting," Lilly quipped. "No matter, dear. Come, sit down."

Soon Vlad and I found ourselves sitting face to face at a table in the corner of the restaurant. There was a baby grand piano at the front of the room, next to a medium-sized Christmas tree. Mistletoe hung from the top of the ceiling, right in the middle of the room. The whole place was clean and something about it made me feel like I was at home, despite it looking nothing like our house, which looked more like a bland corporate office, all cold glass and stainless steel and nothing like this place, with its warm wood and colors.

Since I had no clue what was good here, I let Vlad order the food for me. A moment later, Vlad stood with the menu and walked to the counter to let Lilly know our order. When he came back and was seated in his chair, I quickly asked, "Why did she call you Vovochka?"

For a second he looked slightly embarrassed, almost sheepish. "It is one of the diminutives for Vladimir. Lilly loves to use it, especially since it's closely associated with a long-running series of jokes featuring a naughty schoolboy."

I laughed. "Now that you mention it, I've always wondered why your name is Vladimir. Aren't you Greek?" He nodded. "Isn't Vladimir a Russian name?"

Lilly came back with a young boy who was carrying a tray. "I'm sorry. I interrupted something, didn't I?"

I felt the heat of a blush on my cheek as I heard the tone she'd used and the way her eyes sparkled as if she knew she was intruding on a special moment.

"No, you didn't. Don't get any ideas, Lilly." Vlad turned his attention to the boy. "Do you need a hand with that, Jake?"

"Nope," Jake said. "I'm good, thanks."

They served our drinks, and I thanked them before they left us on our own again.

"Why? Does my name not suit me?" Vlad asked.

"I did *not* say that."

"Most of us Hellenicus are doomed to have weird names, whether it's our first name or our middle name. The names our parents choose are supposed to represent a blessing or a hope." He shifted in his seat. "Actually, I was named after my great-great-great-grandfather. I don't think they cared whether the name sounded Greek or not, as long as it had a good meaning. But I think Kris lucked out while I got the short end of the stick."

"I'd have to agree there," I said. "But tell me, what's the meaning behind Vladimir?"

"Vladimir is formed from two words: *vladeti*, which means rule, combined with *miru*, which means peace or world. The name literally means one who rules the world."

"That's pretty cool."

"Every name has a meaning," he said.

"Oh yeah? Then what's mine?"

"Your name, Avery, is derived from the old French name Alfred," he explained, stroking his chin with his thumb and forefinger. "Alfred breaks down into the Old English words of *aelf*, which means elf, and *raed*, which means counsel. Avery means ruler of the elves."

"What the flying pigeon!" I shouted. "I'm going to strangle my parents."

"It's not that bad." He laughed

"My middle name is Zosime, in case you didn't know."

"I know." One corner of his lips tugged slightly upward. "Your parents chose your middle name to represent their hope for you. I think you're just as lucky as Kris."

"Uh-huh, so what's my parents' hope then?"

"Zosime means 'likely to survive.' Your parents must have hope for you to survive through any hard times in your life. Actually, I don't think either of your names is that bad."

"Okay, fine, the middle one is not that bad, but Avery's meaning, seriously? How is being named after a silly creature with pointy ears not that bad?"

"Some names have worse meaning than yours. Like Portia."

"How's Portia a bad name?" I protested.

Vlad said, "Portia is a Latin name that was derived from the word *porcus* or *porcius*, which,"—he leaned forward and smirked—"you can probably guess means pig."

"Okay," I said between peals of laughter. "I've changed my mind. I'm not going to strangle my parents after all. But I will definitely be careful when naming my future child. They certainly won't be Portia."

Vlad watched me with an odd expression, his head tilted at the slightest of angles. "Maybe you should name them Oliver."

"Why?"

Vlad looked pleased that I had asked. "Oliver comes from the Germanic name *Alfihar*, which breaks down into *alf*, meaning elf, and *hari*, meaning . . ." He trailed off as I saw a cheeky gleam in his smiling eyes.

"Meaning?" I refused to have an incomplete sentence.

"Meaning army. Elf army." He finished the sentence without hurry, clearly trying to wind me up.

"Yes, very funny. Thanks for the suggestion," I replied, sarcasm escaping my lips. "How do you know all this stuff, anyway?"

"When you grow up with Vladimir as your first name and Eneas as your middle name, you tend to do some research to reassure yourself that your name isn't *that* bad."

"Eneas?!" I laughed for a few seconds before abruptly pausing as I realized something. "But how'd you know about my name?"

He dropped his gaze to the white linen tablecloth, a slight pink warming his cheeks. "I looked it up."

Just in time, Lilly came back with our food.

I sank my fork and knife into the tender meat and stuffed my mouth with the delicious lamb steak. I was never the type to eat slowly, so within minutes, I stabbed the last piece on my plate and raised it to my mouth. I put the utensils down, and as I looked up, I caught Vlad staring at me. "What?" I asked curiously.

Whether I liked it or not, Kris's words came to mind.

You were looking at him and when you weren't, he was looking at you.

Not giving me an answer, Vlad pushed his chair back and stood.

"Where are you going?"

"I am not going anywhere." Standing to his full height of six foot two, he let his eyes bore into mine. "I'm going to show you what I usually do when I come here."

"Which is?"

Bending forward, he leaned in, his face inches away from mine, taking up too much of my personal space. The last time we had been this close, our lips were against each other's. My skin tingled and I could feel my heart beating, low and insistent in my chest. I was afraid he could hear the thumping—afraid that he could guess what was on my mind. I could feel his warm breath against my skin. The smell of soap and mint filled my senses with anticipation. Then he spoke, his lips intoxicatingly close to my ear, "So I could do this."

For a second I thought he was going to kiss me, right there in the middle of the restaurant, but he straightened up and walked away, leaving me puzzled.

Sitting here right now, I realized how much had changed between Vlad and me. The meal had been delicious, but more surprisingly, the company was enjoyable. We were getting along. He was caring, patient, and he could even crack a joke. I watched him saunter to the front of the restaurant to the piano.

At some point, Lilly and Jake had come out of the kitchen and were now sitting at the table in front of the Christmas tree. The expressions of anticipation on their faces made me curious. Vlad took a seat on the piano stool and carefully placed his fingers on the black and white keys. He nodded at Lilly and Jake before turning his attention to the instrument. A moment later, the music effortlessly filled the air, like waves filling holes in the sand.

It should not have come as a surprise to me that Vlad could play, considering all Royals and Pure Royals had to learn at least one musical instrument so that they could sing praises for the gods and goddesses, but I had never seen him do it before. Somehow this felt intimate, almost as if he was showing me a piece of himself that he usually concealed.

Closing my eyes, I let myself get lost in the melody, and only opened them when I heard cheers and claps from Lilly and Jake. Vlad rose to his feet and walked back to our table, not breaking our eye contact. He had a way of looking at a person, his dark-green eyes so focused and intent that you felt as if you must be the only two people in the entire world. I had used to flick that look away dismissively, immune to whatever charm he had, but right now, I could not find a way to detach my eyes from his.

"Are you all right?" he asked.

He moved his hand and grabbed the glass I was holding to refill it with water, his fingers brushing mine ever so lightly but enough to send an electric shot through my entire body. If he had not been holding the glass, I was sure it would have dropped on the table. "Are you feeling all right?" he reiterated. "You look kind of dazed all of a sudden."

"Yeah, I'm fine." If by fine I meant that my head suddenly felt like it was full of boiling water. He did not look convinced. "What was that you played?"

"Piano Concerto No. 5 in D Major, K. 175 by Wolfgang Amadeus Mozart."

I *needed* to google that once I got back to the suite. Something about what he said tickled my brain. Then it finally dawned on me. "Wait. Is that why this restaurant is called No. 5?"

"You're quick." Vlad brought his glass to his lips and took a large mouthful of water. "Lilly's husband, Rikkard, used to play this piece every Christmas. He played it better than I do." He continued, "Everyone would be on their feet, dancing with their partners, kids would be running around and crowding the Christmas tree. The whole village would come here every Christmas to celebrate, and I would escape from the Court to join them. He died three years ago. I offered to come here and play the piece in December whenever I am free." The way his jaw clenched told me that he had been close to Rikkard, and to Lilly and Jake as well.

"That is very kind of you," I commented.

Vlad shook his head. "It's just a little thing I could do for them." He turned his head toward Lilly, who was holding Jake in her arms. The boy's shoulders were shaking as he sobbed against his mother's chest. Losing someone was hard. I could only imagine how life shattering their sorrow and sadness were. Sure, I had lost Bryan and Carlo, and losing them was utterly heartbreaking, but I knew it was different than losing a family member.

My eyes wandered around the room as I tried to visualize what it would have been like during one of those Christmases. My heart pinched, realizing how those days could never return for them. At last, my gaze landed on the guy sitting across the table. I had learned so much about him tonight. He was not the snotty Pure Royal who majored in asshattery that I had once thought him to be. I started to see him in a new light . . . and it terrified the hell out of me.

This afternoon when Kris had asked me if I had feelings for her brother, I had told her that I didn't know. Because only a few days ago, there was one person in this entire universe I was sure I would never fall in love with: Vladimir Ambrosia. Now, I wasn't so sure.

CHAPTER SEVENTEEN

When I closed my eyes at night I usually drifted in and out of sleep, but tonight I was afraid I would fall into a sleep so deep that I'd never wake.

Everything was dark except for the torch at the end of a long, narrow hallway. I grabbed it from the hard, stone wall. I stumbled to the ground a few times but kept getting up. A figure walked toward me as my knees buckled once more, and I leaned against the damp wall to keep from dropping to the ground again. With each step the person took, my heart beat faster.

Only when I could see a familiar face did my heart beat steadily again. Bryan. I smiled, forcing myself to walk toward him. As soon as I was close to him, I realized that he was not alone. There was a taller, more muscular figure behind him.

"Carlo."

The two people I had lost were right in front of me, and the feeling was overwhelming. There were so many things that I wanted to tell them—things that I wished I had told them before they were gone. "Bryan." I continued to move toward him. When he was within reach, I hugged him tightly. "I'm so sorry. I know I didn't get a chance to say it before, but I do love you. I just wish we could've had the time to figure everything out. Maybe things would've been different."

He looked exactly like I remembered him. My cheeks were wet, and wiping the tears with the back of my hand, I continued, "I miss you so much. I've been so lost without you here. We would be on our way to New York, away from all this mess." I thought about all the nights we spent planning our escape from our first Gathering—tallying our savings and mapping out our options. All the good memories kept him alive in my heart. Being here suddenly felt like a betrayal. "I'm sorry, Bryan. You know me—I guess curiosity got the better of me."

I kissed his cheek then went over to Carlo. "Carlo. You have no idea how sorry I am for what happened to you. You deserved to find your soul mate, and I had hoped that it would have been me." He put a finger under my chin to lift my head back up to meet his gaze. The look on his face was the same look Domenico gave Kris. This was my chance to ask him about the odd voice mail that he had left me that had been plaguing my mind. "What did you mean when you said that the Faction is looking for me? What Faction—"

But before I could form another word, the two of them started screaming. Their eyes rolled to the back of their sockets and all that was left were the white, eerie sclera. With looks of utter terror on their faces, they continued screaming with all their might. At first, startled by their sudden change of expression and how loud their screams were, I could not grasp what they were saying.

Then I understood. They were asking for help. My help. Soon my skin looked like the surface of a boiling stew. Beneath the thin skin bubbled toxins, the pains of my past leaving my blood, seeking release. Then fog came out of nowhere, engulfing me, suffocating me. It felt as if I might die. I was desperately trying to free myself, screaming for help, yet nobody came. Then, just as quickly as it had come, the fog disappeared.

Suddenly, I was sitting in the passenger seat of a car—similar to the one Bryan and I had stolen from his parents that one time when he had tried teaching me how to drive. From the surroundings, I knew Bryan was the one driving without even having to check. I somehow could feel that this was it—this was the moment before he died.

"Bryan, please." He didn't seem to hear me. "Bryan, pull over! Slow down!"

As if he had not heard my warning, as if he had to follow the script fate had prepared for him, he continued driving, a steely look of determination on his face.

"Stop!"

No matter what I said, the car was still moving, getting faster with every second. My hand grabbed the seat tightly until my knuckles turned white.

Still speeding, he finally seemed to be aware of my presence as he turned to face me. A scary smile that I had never seen before formed on his face. "This is all your fault, Avery. You deserve this."

The fog came for the second time, like a dark void. A never-ending darkness that consumed me and left me with nothing. I was so empty that I couldn't even feel the pain as the fog continued to suffocate me. When the fog finally cleared, I was still in the dark, only this time, I could hear voices.

"Where is she?" The voice somehow felt familiar.

"I don't know," Carlo whimpered.

"Bullshit! You're supposed to meet her here. Where the fuck is she?" Again, the same domineering, rough voice asked.

Regardless of how many times Carlo expressed that he did not know, the other guy seemed to think he was lying. As he failed to answer their questions, all I could hear was Carlo screaming in agony. They must have been torturing him.

I screamed inside my head, frustrated that I couldn't do anything to help him. I couldn't see anything. I could only hear. Another scream from him and I felt my whole body go taut. "No, leave him alone," I cried to myself.

I felt so helpless. So useless, unable to save him. Them. The feeling of despair was a heady blackness. The weight of everything pressed down on my shoulders, and I struggled to take even a single step forward. Yet somehow, I kept moving. But every step cost me. The darkness grew darker; the pain became sharper; I began to wonder if things would get better. If things could ever get better.

And once again, I was pulled down and down, drowning in the feeling of helplessness and nothingness. I no longer struggled or tried to get back to the surface. I simply let myself sink deeper and deeper. I had caused them pain. I had cost them their lives. This suffering was nothing compared to theirs. Just like Bryan had said, I deserved this.

A loud sound shook me, and only when my eyes fluttered open did I realize it was only a dream. A terrifying dream, but it felt more real than my waking hours.

"For Hades's sake, stop it!" An alarm was ringing incessantly, so I reached my hand out to the nightstand, finding the alarm clock and throwing it across the room without opening my eyes. One loud thump and the noise died.

Peace and quiet.

"Touchdown!"

"Shut up!" I yelled. *Wait.* I quickly sat up and there, sitting on the chair in the corner of the room, was Adrian.

"How did you get in here?"

"You should know by now that we all have your passcode." He lifted his leg and placed his ankle on top of his other thigh. "A Pure Royal privilege: ask and you shall receive."

I made a mental note to request a change the next time I passed those creepy ladies at the reception. Of course, I would have to tell my parents, but I'd basically been orphaned since arriving here, and I doubted that they even remembered the current password. I was convinced my parents had forgotten that they even had a child.

I threw a pillow at Adrian, which he successfully dodged. "What are you doing here?" He doubled over laughing and I threw another pillow at him. This time, it hit him straight in the face. "Ha! Take that!"

Adrian took both pillows with one hand and threw them back on the bed. "I let you have that one," he said. "I figured it would make you smile." He snapped his fingers then pointed at my grin. "See, it worked."

"You just won't admit that you lost."

"*Pfft*, I've never lost anything, unless it was on purpose." Adrian stood and with long, easy strides, made his way to my bed, a charming yet sly smile on his handsome face.

My mouth went dry, and I was not sure whether my heart had sped up double-time, or if it had stopped. "Adrian?" My throat made an uncomfortable, awkward sort of sound. "What are you doing?"

"I'm hardly doing anything." A few seconds of utter silence passed as we stared at each other, me sitting on the bed, still half-asleep, and him standing at the edge of the bed looking down at me. Then he grabbed the nearest pillow and smacked the side of my body with it.

"Oh, the fight is on, Ambrosia!" I drawled, grabbing one pillow and hitting him.

He jumped on the bed and tackled me, angling his body to pin me down, my back flat on the bed, rustling the unmade bed into a messier state. My hands went to his sides and tickled his waist. Adrian wriggled and his grip on my wrists loosened. I took the moment of his lapse as a chance to turn the tables. Hooking my legs around his back, I rolled over and he ended up being the one looking up at me with me sitting on top of him. He tried to get up, but I grabbed both of his shoulders and pushed him down again. "Oh no, you don't." I grinned in victory when he, likely realizing that there was no point of struggling, relaxed.

"Okay, okay." Adrian's voice was low and his breath was uneven as he said, "I'm all yours, Montgomery."

I was excruciatingly aware of his nearness. The top button of his shirt was undone; only one small movement of my thumb and it would graze his collarbone. With a sweep of one hand, I could touch the little lock of his messy light-brown hair and figure out if it was as soft as it looked.

A tingling sensation shot through me, and I nearly gasped, my abdomen clenching. I suddenly felt hungry, but not for food. The secret place between my legs tightened with desire. I desired *him*. Adrian freaking Ambrosia. Even at the height of my crush on him years ago, I'd never felt this strongly for him. I was starting to understand what everyone said about how emotions and desires were heightened after being Awakened.

I let go of his shoulders and swung my legs to the side of the bed to get up. I couldn't stay in bed with his body pressed against mine like that. I grabbed fresh clothes from the drawer, making sure to stick my underwear between items so Adrian couldn't see it.

Walking to the bathroom, I tossed my crazy bedhead hair over one shoulder. "You haven't answered my question," I reminded Adrian. I stopped at the doorway and turned. "Why are you here? Shouldn't you be in bed at this early hour?" Without waiting for his reply, I turned around and faced the sink. I caught sight of my reflection in the mirror. As suspected. I looked like shit.

Adrian leaned against the door frame. He lifted one hand and pointed to my head before stating the obvious. "Your hair is a mess. What were you doing last night?"

"I'm not you, Adrian." I gave him a deadpan stare.

I turned on the taps and washed my face. The sleepiness was slowly leaving. Adrian handed me a small towel and I thanked him as I patted my face dry. I'd been up half the night, and the other half was spent having terrible nightmares about Bryan and Carlo. If it had not been for that stupid alarm, I would've still been in bed, trying to catch up on the sleep I'd missed during the night. I could've sworn I hadn't set the alarm last night.

I smacked Adrian's arm.

"What the hell was that for?" Adrian jerked back then rubbed his arm.

"You fucking set the alarm, didn't you?" I narrowed my eyes in suspicion. He did not need to answer because his face told me all there was to know. "Why the fuck did you do that?"

When I was overtired, my drunken-sailor mouth returned easily.

"Geez, Montgomery, so many fucks today." With a cheeky quirk of his brows, he leaned forward and murmured, "Or does that only happen when I'm around?"

I shoved him out of the bathroom, closed the door, and turned the lock. His laugh was still audible through the locked door between us. I hastily showered and got dressed. Water dripped from my recently washed hair onto the floor as I towel dried my hair. I grimaced. If my mom was around, she wouldn't be too pleased with me.

Adrian had left the bedroom and the door was closed tightly shut. I sat on the bed, toweling my hair dry, a comb resting on my thigh, waiting for its turn. After combing my hair quite violently—since there was no other way of doing it to make it look less dreadful—I placed the comb on the nightstand.

There was a knock on the door and I lifted one brow. So now he'd decided to knock after letting himself in twenty minutes ago while I had been sleeping, huh.

"Come in."

Adrian popped his head, grinning. "Now that's more like it."

I folded my arms in front of my chest and shot him an annoyed look. "Seriously, you have five seconds to tell me why you're here or you've got to go."

"Chill, Montgomery. You texted, so here I am." When I said nothing, he drawled, "*Seriously*."

"I did not ask you to come here. I only asked you about—" He reached into his pocket and pulled out a card. "Is that—"

"Yes, Montgomery." Adrian smiled triumphantly. "I got it."

Caitlin's access card, which meant that we could finally start our investigation. My lips curled into a smile that mirrored his.

CHAPTER EIGHTEEN

The Royal Quarters was not just a building; it served as a gateway to an entirely different universe. A gigantic, steel-blue gate kept the area hidden from the Regulars. The entrance was protected by Palace Guards, who wore uniforms with a golden emblem placed on the left side of their chest to distinguish them from the Court Guards. To get to the academy, we had to first go through the Royal Quarters and make it past the gate. Adrian, being an Ambrosia, didn't even glance at the Palace Guards, let alone need to show his ID before one of them opened the gate for us. My jaw dropped as what laid behind the gate was revealed.

So far, all I had seen at the Court was modern, but this area was vastly different. I no longer felt like I was inside the Court; I wasn't even sure I was in the same time period. Had the Hellenicus here been wearing medieval outfits, I would've been convinced that I had been transported back in time. The buildings were made of cream-colored stones, built to last thousands of years, generation after generation, and had no doubt had been stacked centuries ago. The novelty of them had worn off, yet everything still reflected the golden rays of the sun. It was like something out of a children's fairy-tale book.

"That's the Michelakoses' residence." Adrian pointed to a mansion on my left. There was a family emblem showing a laurel tree enveloping a sun, a lyre, a raven, and a silver bow and arrow on their wall. "You know, Apollo's descendants. There aren't that many of them around the world now. About two hundred, I think."

"You could probably fit them all inside that place for a giant family reunion," I joked. Even though the building was majestic, it looked pretty much abandoned. I followed Adrian closely, knowing full well I would get lost in here if I was on my own.

"That's Douchebag Tavoularis's family mansion. Hera's descendants. You can tell the type of person who lives there just by looking at their home."

From the golden window frames to the dome-shaped roof to the red double doors at the front, the mansion was the most eye-stabbing thing inside the entire Court Grounds. "They must've really loved red," I commented as I squinted to get a better look at their family emblem, a diadem and scepter in the middle with flowers and what looked like pomegranates surrounding them. It seemed familiar, but I couldn't pinpoint where I had seen it. I probably saw Damian wearing the emblem on that first night at the after-party.

"What about that one?" I pointed at the building on our right and watched Adrian's face turn reluctant to answer.

"The Costas."

"Oh."

We continued to pass many extraordinary buildings until Adrian paused. "This is the Ambrosias." His gaze raked from the front door up to the tower, which was arched toward the sky. "My grandparents still live here with my parents. I prefer the family suite at the Royal Quarters. If the brat wasn't there, it would be my bachelor pad."

I snorted. With girls coming in and out as they liked, it was more like a den. Then, I dared myself to ask a question I had always been too shy to ask Kris. "Adrian, why doesn't Kris's family live at the Court?"

"I know I probably shouldn't tell you this, but since I know your inquisitive self will only be satisfied with the truth, I'll spare you the extra effort. You have to promise not to tell anyone, though."

"I promise."

"Including and especially Kris."

I did not hide anything from Kris; we shared practically everything from the lightest truth to the hardest one, like my view on soul mates. Keeping the details of the woman from the jail and my quest with Adrian from her already made me feel guilty. I chewed the inside of my cheek, trying to decide. In the end, I concluded that this could be one more exception to our no-secret policy. "Okay." I added, "Do I have to pinky swear or what?"

His body relaxed a little as he rolled his eyes at me. "It's just that what I'm about to tell you is the other side of the Ambrosia family, the dark and twisted part."

"Now you're just playing with me. Spill the beans already."

"Fine." Adrian huffed. "There's a love triangle in our family. My dad—" His eye twitched and I sensed something bad coming. Kris had told me before that Adrian and his father, Norman Ambrosia, had a tense relationship. Yet it seemed that despite this, he was not comfortable speaking ill of him. "He loves Aunt Jane."

"Aunt Jane? As in Kris and Vlad's mom?!" I gasped.

"Yeah. Back when we all got along, we used to have a big family feast every December. I was fourteen and I remember asking him about how soul mates really worked. He told me that a soul-mate bond does not guarantee love or happiness and that those who find both love and happiness through the bond are the few lucky ones. He told me never to give up on love, to fight for it—regardless of the bond." For a flashing moment, I saw hurt engraved on Adrian's expression as he proceeded with the story. "I thought he was referring to Mom, so I asked him if he had to fight for her. He didn't answer right away, but when he did, he wasn't looking at Mom. He was staring at Aunt Jane as he said that he was still fighting."

I was not sure what to say in a situation like this, so I settled on, "Adrian, I'm so sorry."

He brushed it off as if he didn't care. I knew he did. "A week later, Uncle Kristov told Nana that they would leave the Court Grounds and live in the outside world. Both he and my father have not been on speaking terms since. I bet on Zeus's bolt that my father did something." Adrian gave me a bitter smile. "That was the last time we had a family feast with everyone present."

"According to Hellenicus law, isn't the eldest son supposed to live in the family's mansion?"

"Yeah, but apparently Hellenicus law didn't stop Uncle Kristov. I think he knew about my dad's feelings for Aunt Jane for a long time, but something happened at that feast and he was not going to let it continue to drag on." He turned to look at the Ambrosia mansion in front of us. "That's my mom's bedroom." He pointed at a balcony on the third floor. "She cried for months after that. I could hear her sobbing at night as I walked past her door to my room down the corridor." Adrian sighed, trying to compose himself. "Sometimes I hate coming back here. This place holds so many memories, some I don't want to revisit."

"I'm so sorry." I knew I should stop saying that, but what else could I say? I gave his arm a gentle squeeze.

"Just another reason why I agreed to help you with this." He lifted one hand, revealing the library card.

"Damn, so it wasn't my superb marketing skills!" I joked, trying to lighten the mood. It seemed to work.

"It's not just because of what happened with me and Marsela. It's because I know that the bond does not guarantee us happiness."

"Yeah, and at least if things don't work out, you don't have to live the rest of your life hearing every passing thought they have in their mind."

Adrian nodded. "At least they can move on."

We walked along the narrow road, passing a fountain in the middle of what looked like a town square, Adrian happy to leave his family's mansion behind. We turned left and I came to an abrupt halt, gaping in awe at the breathtaking sight in front of me. "Is that what I think it is?"

"That depends," Adrian said with a grand flourish of his arm. "If you think it's Queen Rhea's palace, then you are right."

The palace looked more primeval than any bone left in the soil. Trees surrounded it like great armies defending their citadel, their armored trunks reached out protectively in the air. The vast expanse of green enhanced the palace's eeriness and beauty as an iron portcullis guarded the passage. There were Palace Guards everywhere, from high up on the circular towers to in front of the enormous gate blocking the entrance.

"Enough sightseeing." Adrian chortled. "We have a mission, remember?"

At last we arrived at the building that had brought us here. The Royal High Court Academy was built to look like the Parthenon. I'd only seen the replica in Nashville, not the original in Athens, but this place was a sight to behold. In a courtyard to the side of the building was a giant statue of Apollo in front of a small temple, which was fitting since, on top of being the god of the sun, he was also the god of knowledge—among other things.

Fully aware that we had no time to waste, Adrian grabbed my hand and hurried me to the side of the building to a service entrance.

Unlike at the palace, no guards were watching over the school. All I had to do was follow Adrian. Despite the fact that the school was empty for the December festivities, the feeling that we would be caught washed over me. I knew it was a bad omen to say it, so I didn't utter a word, keeping my mouth tightly shut. I assured myself that if I did get caught, at least I had Adrian. Being a Pure Royal had its advantages, one of them being wiggling out of trouble—including trespassing, I hoped.

"Here," Adrian handed me the access card as we made a left at the intersection and soon faced a gigantic door. A girl was standing in front of it. "Oh shit."

"What?" I looked at his worried face and back at the harmless-looking girl standing there, her head ducked down, focused on the book in her hands. Judging from Adrian's reaction, you'd have thought a three-headed dog was guarding the library's door. "It's just a girl."

"Dear Poseidon, help us." Adrian groaned exasperatedly then looked at me. "It's not just a girl, Montgomery. She's Eulabeia."

"Yew-la-what?"

"Eulabeia." He regarded the girl, then shook his head, clearly thinking of aborting this mission. "She's the spirit and personification of fear, caution, avoidance, heedfulness, and vigilance."

"What?" I repeated, this time with more shock than amusement. "That girl is a spirit?! How do you know? She looks like a normal girl to me."

"There are things that only Royals and the Royal High Court residents are privy to." His head nudged in the direction of the girl who paid no mind to us. "And that's one of them."

"Okay, so what? Is she going to stop us even if we have the access cards?" I asked. I had no clue who this Yew-la Bew-la Banana was, but I saw no reason why we couldn't just carry on.

"She's not going to stop me, but she will stop you. She can tell that you're not—" Adrian paused, as if looking for the correct word. "Of royal blood."

"I didn't come this far to be stopped." I ignored Adrian's warning and marched straight up to the girl. Even when I stood right in front of her, she did not tear her eyes from the book. "I have to get inside there." I simply stated my intention, throwing it out in the open and hoping she would just scoot her little behind a bit to the left so I could get past her.

"It's been a long time," the girl replied, her eyes still glued to the pages of her book, which I could now see was written in Greek.

"What's been a long time?" I dared to ask, unable to squash my curiosity.

"Your kind." The girl flipped the page and her eyes skimmed across the curvy letters written there. "It certainly has been a long while since the last one." With no further explanation, she walked away, never looking up from her book as she did so.

What did she mean? My kind? What kind was that? The Regulars?

"If we were allowed to enter the Royal High Court, I'm sure more of my kind would come and visit your precious library," I mumbled.

Adrian caught up to me and watched the girl leave with a look of incertitude on his face. "What just happened?"

I shrugged, pretending not to care. "No clue. Let's go in."

There was something deeply sacred about the library in the Royal High Court Academy, something that I had never felt in any other place. It was full of our history, which was well hidden from the Nescient, and to some extent, the Regulars. There were statues all over the cavernous hall. Perseus holding a sword in his right hand and Medusa's head in the other, completely nude save for the useless drape he had on his arm to cover—what? His asymmetrical left arm? It certainly wasn't covering anything else. Not far from Perseus and his nudity was Hades, who had the decency to at least cover half of his body. One hand was carrying a staff while the other held the chain to Cerberus. Then there was Poseidon, carrying his infamous trident and riding what looked like a seahorse-dragon hybrid.

"This way, Montgomery," said Adrian, whisking me away from checking out Dionysus's abs, which were still intact despite the copious amount of wine displayed around him. Adrian took me to a secluded area in the corner of the room. "Take out your access card. This time you're going to need it."

This place was the epitome of a medieval library. High wooden arches and stained-glass windows almost made it look like a church—except for the long rows of floor-to-ceiling bookshelves that were lined with dusty, old tomes. The steel and glass door in front of me, which had a card scanner attached to the handle, indicated that this part of the library was very different. Adrian tapped his card on the reader and pushed the door open. I was about to follow suit when he raised one hand, telling me to stay where I was. Only after the door closed did he give me a nod to do what he had just done.

I felt slightly guilty when the monitor showed Caitlin's name and photo. I could only hope that this little visit wouldn't get her in trouble somehow. Inside the room there was only one thick book, laying open on top of a green velvet surface. Adrian and I exchanged a look before we approached it and dug our noses deep into it.

Unfortunately, it was in Greek, a language with an alphabet I had failed to remember. But Adrian, being a Pure Royal, knew Greek. While all the Hellenicus learned Greek at school, it was mandatory for Royals to master the language. I pulled out my phone to take photos of the pages, as Adrian did his best to speed-read them.

He had skimmed through not even one-fifth of the book when a guard walked into the library. He hadn't seen us yet, but it was only a matter of time—we were enclosed in a glass room after all. "Adrian,"

I hissed, and when his eyes didn't look up from the pages, I nudged his ribs hard. My left hand immediately shot up, covering his mouth, while the right one tore out the page he had been reading. His eyes opened wide in disbelief of what I had just done.

"No time." I dragged him out of the glassed-in room, where we were easily seen, and into the main part of the library.

He quickly grasped the situation and signaled me to follow him. We moved farther and farther away from the voices. Once we felt we were at a safe distance, we stopped against the back wall, the statue of Dionysus beside us. I leaned my hand on the statue's thigh, wanting to rest for a moment to steady myself. But we heard a soft click and the bookcase behind us swung open to reveal a hidden room. The voices gained on us. Without thinking, I grabbed Adrian and shoved him inside before getting in myself and pulling the bookcase closed.

The hidden room turned out to be nothing more than an empty broom closet. Or so it seemed, anyway. I wondered what warranted the need for this room to be here. Moreover, why the hell was the hidden button on Dionysus's thigh?

I was trying to distract myself from how hyperaware my body was that, for the second time today, there was so little space separating me from Adrian. Even without looking up, I could feel him watching me. The only thing that kept me standing there and not pooling on the floor as my knees weakened were those voices outside. They sounded so close, almost as if they were just on the other side of the door. What would we do if we were caught? What if Adrian's Pure Royal pass did not include smuggling a Regular into sacred places after all?

I felt Adrian's hand on the small of my back, the pressure was slow but inexorable, and suddenly it was all I could think about. I grew hot as our bodies inched even closer. I felt his soft breathing in my hair. His lips were inches away from my skin.

I stood perfectly still and didn't dare look up into his emerald eyes. I knew if I did, I would drown in them and there would be no turning back. I would keep drowning and drowning. Even with the closeness of Adrian clouding my judgment, I knew our purpose here was more important than satisfying this burning desire rising from the pit of my stomach.

"Montgomery." He whispered my name ever so slightly, as if he was scared of ruining whatever moment we were currently having. "If this works out, do you think we could—"

"I think they're gone." I cut him off from asking something that I knew he would ask. I was not so clueless as to think he did not feel the electricity between us. I pushed the door again, but it wouldn't budge. "Oh no. I think we're locked here."

"It's not the worst thing ever to be locked here." He added, "I mean, you're here, so it's not that bad."

"Oh, it's bad if we're locked here for days and one of us has to eat the other to survive."

"I'd probably let you devour my body," he answered in a low whisper. He laughed. "Not in a gory way, Montgomery."

I leaned my head back against the wall behind me and felt it press against a knob of some kind. As if by magic, the door opened. "They seriously need to work on the keys to this secret door," I complained to myself as Adrian stuck his head out to double-check if the guards were still around. Satisfied that the coast was clear, he held out one arm and said, "Ladies first."

We cautiously retraced our steps back to the entrance and stopped behind the door. The guards were nowhere to be seen inside the library, but it was possible that they were waiting for us outside. "How do we get out now?"

Before Adrian had a chance to answer, the girl from earlier walked through the door—not just walked in, but *through*—like a ghost.

Still immersed in the same book, she pointed with her free hand to a statue. "You can go through there. There's a tunnel."

"Go through where, exactly?" I dared to ask. All that was in front of us was a white-bricked wall, and unlike her, we couldn't go through solid objects.

The girl sighed, as if answering my question drew too much energy out of her. "Grip Charon's staff; the path will be opened." She turned the page, murmuring just above whispering level, "How can you be *his* kid and be *this* foolish?"

I would have inquired further if Adrian hadn't been waving his hand and pointing at a dark tunnel that had somehow emerged behind the statue. The guards outside reported to their leader that they couldn't find the intruders and that it was highly likely they'd still be inside the library. I rushed toward Adrian, and right before the brick wall swung closed, I heard the girl say under her breath, "kalí týchi" Growing up with a mom who insisted we were the descendants of Tyche, I knew what that meant: good luck. But it was the way she said it that made me wonder why on earth I would need luck.

I followed close behind Adrian as he held up his phone to light the path ahead of us. The cold, damp air wrapped around us as we descended the tight spiral staircase to only the gods knew where.

Ω

The path led us down a long dingy tunnel to a wooden door at the end. Once through the door, we found ourselves at the back of the Royal High Court Academy. Safely standing outside the building, with no scratches and no handcuffs around my wrists, I let the crisp December breeze fill my nostrils. I glanced back at the skyward-bound walls of the library. I didn't know if I would ever have the opportunity to feel this close to history again, and I wanted to savor the moment. Adrian tapped my shoulder, returning my attention to him, and I fell in step beside him as he effortlessly navigated the way back to the Hyped. Every few steps I checked over my shoulder to ensure nobody was following us.

Once we were back in the safety of the Court, blending into the crowd of people outside the Hyped, Adrian stretched out his arm and took my hand. He caught me off guard, and before I could even retract my hand from his grasp, our fingers entwined. My skin tingled. There was something about the way his skin pressed against mine that spread warmth throughout my whole body. It was a cold December day, yet I somehow felt warm.

I indulged the feeling for a second longer before untangling my hand from his. I found it frustrating not to be able to control my body's response to him. Perhaps the emotion showed on my face.

"Hey, are you okay?" Adrian asked.

"Yeah." There was no way I was going to tell him what had actually been in my head. Under his scrutinizing gaze, I found myself struggling to change the topic. Nothing came to mind except our mission. "What did it say?" I blurted. There must have been something that caught his attention when he had been reading those pages.

"It kept mentioning the Great Massacre, Zeus, and Hades."

"Okay . . . but what else is in there?"

Adrian shook his head, then his face changed and he looked slightly embarrassed. "Actually, I am not that good in Greek." His cheeks turned a darker shade of pink. "Okay, I suck at it," he admitted. "I only understood bits and pieces. And I think—" he halted, seemingly unsure about something.

"What?" I encouraged. "You think, what?"

"I think we should ask Vlad."

"I think it'll be easier for me to learn Greek from scratch than to convince him to help us."

Adrian went quiet. He simply stood there, unmoving. "What is it, Adrian?"

Without looking at me, he lifted his hand and pointed at the spot between two tall pine trees. From the scared look on his face, I expected to see a zombie or something sinister, but when I turned, I didn't see anything. I turned back to Adrian. "What's the problem?"

His voice was somewhat shaky. "I thought I saw a bald man standing there, watching us."

"Now you're just being narcissistic. Not everyone's looking at you, Adrian."

My joke seemed to shake his concern. He threw up his hands, palms facing forward in resignation. "Look, Montgomery. I'm a good sight. How can you blame them?"

"Whatever. Come on." I grabbed Adrian's arm and dragged him forward. "Our mission isn't over yet! Also, we haven't eaten yet today and it's already two thirty! I need food to function!"

Although I could see a hint of worry lingering in his expression, he nodded. "We can try the diner on the corner."

Across the table from each other, Adrian and I only talked about things that could be safely discussed in public—as in, anything but breaking the soul-mate bond. When our conversation ebbed for a moment, I decided to turn the tables on him. "Let's talk about you for a minute."

Adrian laughed, full and throaty. "Why? Are we at the stage where you want to get to know me better, Montgomery?"

"How was your date?"

"Date?" Adrian quirked a brow.

"With Renata. Have you fallen in love with her yet?"

He looked over at me with a strange expression, clearly taken aback that I had asked such a question. "Nah, it was nothing like that."

Adrian shook his head, his jaw clenched. "You know me. I don't easily fall in love."

"Everyone says that before they fall."

"I'm not just everyone."

"Oh yeah!" I tapped my forehead lightly with my palm. "That's right, I also forgot that you have a gigantic ego while the rest of us have normal-sized ones."

Adrian's phone dinged. Concern crossed his face as he looked down at the screen. "Caitlin is sick," he explained to me. "She claims it's the flu, but she has these small red bumps all over her body; I've told her the flu doesn't cause that. Althea has been sending me updates."

I gasped. "Maybe she has chicken pox!"

"Yeah." Adrian gave a nod. "That's what I think too. Anyway, I've called a doctor to stop by our place later."

"Wait, have you told your parents?"

"Why would I tell them?" Disdain danced on his face as he answered me. "They wouldn't want to be bothered with something like this."

Truthfully, I didn't know which surprised me more: Adrian acting like a responsible adult or the fact that he hadn't informed his parents.

That was when it hit me. Adrian and Caitlin were not like Vladimir and Kristen. They were like me. They also had to put up with crappy parents. I didn't know why it had taken me so long to notice. Perhaps because Adrian never showed any discomfort, and Caitlin, well, I had only met her once years ago.

"You know, if you need anything, don't hesitate to ask me." I squeezed his hand.

"Now that you've said it, I do get a little bit chilly at night, so if you don't mind maybe you could—"

"Not that kind of need!" I cut him off, letting his hand go and giving it a good smack.

"Can't say I didn't try."

My body relaxed for a moment before both of his hands caught mine. He kept his eyes locked with mine as he leaned in and brought my hands to his lips. I was transfixed by the severe edge to his voice as he whispered softly so that only I could hear, "Thank you."

The smell of the food being delivered to our table was enough to break the melancholic moment. I basically stuffed everything in my mouth, acting like someone who had not eaten for forty days. Adrian, on the other hand, ate gracefully. Once we finished our meal, the desserts arrived; I went for a slice of New York cheesecake while Adrian just had a cappuccino—which was a pitiful choice for dessert, in my opinion.

"Hail Zeus! This is to die for!" I licked some leftover cream cheese off of the small fork then set it down on the now empty plate. Adrian laughed.

"Hey! Cut me some slack. I'm technically on vacation here. Everyone indulges while on vacation. I'm a Regular, remember? I don't get to go on lavish vacations like you, so my sweet tooth and I have to take advantage."

"You Montgomerys seem to all have good metabolisms. I mean, your dad is still jacked at his age!" Adrian shook his head in slow disbelief. "Isn't he, like, fifty?"

"Forty-five," I corrected. "Yeah, I don't know what his secret is."

Adrian gave it a thought. "Maybe he secretly hired a trainer and goes to the gym all the time."

"*Pfft!*" I choked a laugh. "No way. He's too damn stingy."

Adrian bobbed his head then took a sip of his cappuccino. "I haven't seen him around the Court. I suppose he's been busy, huh?"

"Busy pretending he doesn't have a daughter, that's for sure,"

I replied. It was rather odd how I had gotten so used to it that I could even joke about it. Sure, at first it had been a pain to grow up feeling alone most of the time, but slowly I became numb to it. I buried myself in books, reading crime novels to escape real life and pretending that I was the characters in the stories, whether it was Miss Marple or Hercule Poirot or even Dr. Watson.

"You know, Montgomery," he said, placing his now half-empty cup back on the table, "I'm here, too, if you need anything."

The moment passed and he delicately shifted to a lighter subject. "Kris told me she was staying at Domenico's. I was out partying last night . . . if I knew you were feeling lonely, I would have asked you to go with me." He leaned forward. "Whenever there is a damsel in distress, Lord Ambrosia to the rescue."

"I don't do damsel in distress. I look after myself, thanks."

Adrian shrugged and lifted his cup to his lips and emptied the remaining contents. "What did you do? Pull a movie night?"

"I went to dinner with Vlad." I reached for my drink and looked at the children at the next table. Adrian's silence made me channel my attention back to him. He was frowning.

"How was that? Where did you two go?"

"It was nice. We went to No. 5, and I got to meet Lilly and Jake. They're lovely people, and the food there was great."

His eyes lit up. "Jake!" There were affection and fondness in the way he said the boy's name. "How is he? Is he still reluctant to help out his mom?"

"No. He seemed to enjoy it."

"Then it must've grown on him. He used to complain about helping out at the restaurant." Adrian paused. "Vlad told him that a real man helps his mother, especially since his dad has passed away."

"His talk seemed to have done the trick then." I turned the spotlight back on him. "What about you? How was your night of partying?"

Adrian gave me a sheepish smile. "I wasn't really partying. I spent the night playing poker with Jet, the bartender at Royal Bar. Instead of winning five glasses of whiskey, apparently I now owe him two hundred bucks."

"We all know you suck at poker, Adrian."

"Damn, Montgomery. I've told you—I let you win that time so you could experience beginner's luck."

"Yeah, yeah. Whatever." It felt like such a long time ago even though it was really only four years ago.

We reminisced like this for a while longer, until the bill came. No matter how much I insisted on paying, Adrian took care of it. We sat there chatting until around four o'clock when Adrian's cell phone rang. "Hello. Yep. Okay. Tell her I'll be there soon." He hung up as quickly as he had answered. "Sorry, Montgomery. I've got to go. It's the doctor—he's arrived at the suite. I better go see what's up." He stood up and slid his phone into his front pocket.

"Of course. I hope everything turns out okay." I put my coat on in preparation once again for the chill of the Alaskan winter air.

"Thanks, Montgomery." We crossed the diner and he held the door open for me before following me outside, the bell on the door ringing as we left. "Listen, I'm sorry I can't walk you back to the Hyped."

"I'm pretty sure I can manage on my own, thanks. I don't even need a map anymore. Besides, you bought me lunch so you're forgiven. I guess next time it's my turn to pay."

"You're promising a next time, huh?"

"Get over yourself already. Go see your sister, she needs you." As I said this, a wave of sadness flooded over me. I wished I knew what it felt like to have a family member who cared about me. Someone who checked up on me when I was unwell. Adrian might've regularly referred to his sister as the brat, but when it really mattered, he was there for her.

He must have seen my thoughts on my face because his expression softened and he placed his hand on my shoulder. "Hey, try to relax, okay?"

"The only thing that'll make me relax is finding a way to break free of all this."

"Yeah," he whispered as he pulled me into a hug. "That's all I want too." He kissed the top of my head.

Adrian held me for a little while longer before finally letting me go. "Catch you later, Montgomery." He bid his farewell and then walked away while I headed in the direction of the Hyped. I could still feel the spot on the top of my head where he had kissed me. It was like his touch had released all of the tension I had been feeling.

How did he know just what to do to make me feel lighter? I stuffed my hand inside my pocket to grab the paper I had tucked inside earlier, making sure that it was still there. This piece of paper could be the key.

I suddenly felt a tinge of excitement. I couldn't wait to get to my room and find a way to translate this. One of the beauties of the internet was that it provided a free translator.

CHAPTER NINETEEN

The lobby of the Hyped was busy as usual. A few more people had arrived and were waiting to be checked in. As I made my way through the crowd, I noticed a refreshment table had been set up in the corner of the room. Might as well make a pit stop. I was only a few steps away when I heard a familiar voice.

"Yeah, I know. We have to inform the queen immediately, before it's too late. No, we can't risk that." I could see a large man in a blue shirt and black pants; he didn't have a single hair on his head. "Okay. All right. You're right."

As I got closer to him and was able to hear his voice more clearly, a realization hit me. It was him! It was the man who had called my dad's phone. I needed to get a better look at him. I walked past him—not too slow, but not too fast either—and waited until I was a few feet in front of him before I "accidentally" dropped my wallet and pretended not to notice. It worked. He picked up my wallet and I soon felt a tap on my shoulder.

He moved his phone away from his ear and said, "I think you dropped this, miss."

I turned to him, quickly scribbling a mental note of his overall appearance in my head: long oval face, square jaw, tan skin, thick eyebrows, very muscular. Most importantly, I noticed an odd-looking tattoo on his wrist. It looked like someone wearing a helmet that had a mohawk. I quickly thanked him and walked off. I tried my best to keep my pace steady to avoid looking suspicious.

As soon as there was some distance between us, and it was clear he had no interest in following me, I let out a relieved sigh, only to follow up with a gasp as I recalled what Adrian had said a few hours ago.

I thought I saw a bald man standing there, watching us.

No. No. It couldn't be. No matter how hard I tried to deny it, it did not erase the fact that this could be the same guy. Had he been following me? I realized the hand that was holding my wallet was shaking. I had to go. I couldn't stay here.

I tightened my grip to cease the shaking as I turned around and headed through the front doors. I needed to get out of the Hyped. To get away from this strange bald man. There was only one person I needed to see right now: my best friend. She was the only person I could count on for advice. With each step I took toward the Royal Quarters, I felt determination rush through my whole body. Kris would know what to do.

Ω

"Kristen, I need you."

Maybe it was the urgency in my voice or the way I called her Kristen instead of my usual Kris, but whatever it was, my best friend nodded and quickly followed me to the corner of the living room in her family's suite.

"What is it, Ave?" Kris put one hand on my arm and rubbed her thumb up and down, her way of telling me that no matter how dire the situation was, she would be there for me.

Before I could continue, Kris's parents, Kristov and Jane Ambrosia, walked in. I gave Kris a nudge. I whispered, "Did I come at the wrong time?"

"Not really," she whispered back. "Domenico's having dinner with us, that's all."

I *had* come at the wrong time. I had totally forgotten Kris had mentioned that Domenico would be meeting her parents tonight.

"Avery, dear, Kristen told us you were coming. I had Augusta cook an extra portion," Jane said, motioning for both of us to join them. "Come. Dinner's ready." Jane moved to the dining room, closely followed by her husband.

"We can talk after." Domenico trailed after Kris's parents, looking far too eager to win over his future in-laws. My chest grew tight; he looked every bit like Carlo. My nightmare came flooding back to me and I wondered if I would ever get used to seeing Domenico without thinking about Carlo.

"Are you sure it can wait?"

I wasn't sure, but I also didn't have the heart to ruin this important dinner. "Yeah. I'm sorry; I totally forgot."

"No need to apologize! I'm glad you're here. It makes me less nervous about the whole situation."

Once settled next to Kris at the table, I noticed Vlad wasn't here. The dinner wasn't formal, but it wasn't normal either. Jane and Kristov spent more time asking Domenico questions than they did paying attention to the food in front of them. Frankly, I was convinced they were better interrogators than the Court Guards. But Domenico had made it through most of the parental interrogation by the time our second course was served, and Jane and Kristov were warming up to him.

"So, Domenico, tell me—" Kristov's millionth question was interrupted by the sound of the front door opening and closing, and footsteps approaching. Domenico seized the opportunity to take a large gulp of water.

A moment later, Vlad, wearing a dark-brown, nearly black trench coat, slid into the room. "My apologies for being late. The trial lasted longer than I thought. And I had to help out the lawyer." He moved next to Jane and planted a kiss on her cheek, causing her to smile instantly.

"No matter, dear, as long as you're here with us now. I really don't like how you have to travel back and forth. Can't you arrange to just work from here for the rest of December?"

Vlad squeezed Jane's shoulder to reassure her. "You've asked me that pretty much every day, Mom. I can only work from here on days when the trial isn't going on. They are already being very lenient with me. I can't risk losing this internship."

"We are very proud of you, Son." Kristov Ambrosia stood and the two of them walked toward each other to meet in the middle, right in front of me. His father patted his shoulder lightly. "How was the trial?"

"Tough." Vlad's voice dropped to a whisper. "But don't worry, we'll find a way."

"I know you will," Kristov said.

Naturally, Vlad took the only available seat left at the dining table—directly in front of me—and settled once he took off his coat. One of the younger maids came and offered to hang the coat up for him. She blushed when he thanked her.

With my encounter with the bald guy clouding my mind, I lost my appetite and found myself pushing my food around with my fork and knife. I had had a late lunch with Adrian, just a few hours ago, but that usually wouldn't have stopped me from eating. I hated how everything that was going on could influence my relationship with food. Augusta had made such a delicious meal and I felt guilty wasting it, but my stomach was not in the mood.

"Are you not fond of the fish, Avery dear?" Jane Ambrosia asked, her cutlery paused above her plate. "Do you perhaps wish to have something else instead?" She nodded at the maid standing behind her, indicating for her to come forward.

"No, Jane, please. I actually had a late lunch before I came here, so I'm not really that hungry."

"Very well then. Perhaps your appetite will return when the desserts are served." Jane winked.

I let out a small laugh and nodded. Jane Ambrosia was more of a mother than my own mom. I had had many meals at the Ambrosias' over the years, and she had paid attention to what my favorite foods and desserts were—something that my own mother didn't even bother with. Jane was also the only Pure Royal, besides my friends and Kristov, who had told me to call her by her given name and not by her title.

The maid took away my plate and I sat awkwardly as everyone else finished their food. Domenico seemed to be winning over Kris's parents. I was right, Kris had nothing to worry about. As I tried to focus on the details of Domenico's story about the time he lost his small dog only to find him in their neighbor's garden, eating their tomatoes, I felt Vlad's gaze on me. I looked over at him, then tore my eyes from Vlad's and shifted my focus back to Domenico, pretending to laugh along with the rest of the table. I felt that Vlad could sense my worry somehow.

Jane had been right; my appetite did return once the dessert was served. It was like they said: there was always room for dessert! Plus, I couldn't turn down my favorite chocolate soufflé. I sighed dreamily as the plate was placed in front of me. With just one spoonful, my mood lightened. "My treasure," I whispered quietly. Not that quiet apparently because I saw Vlad try not to smile.

After the maids cleared away our plates and everyone was sitting in the living room having a cup of tea or coffee, Kris and I excused ourselves to go to her room. Domenico was making comfortable conversation with Kris's parents by this point in the evening, and I could tell that Kris was much more at ease, so I didn't feel bad about pulling her away. Right before we left, Kris and Domenico shared a look and I knew there was a conversation going on between them.

"What was that?" I asked once we got to Kris's bedroom.

"Nothing. I told Domenico to keep my parents and Vlad occupied." Kris closed her bedroom door.

We sat cross-legged on her bed. I was happy to be alone with her—between me being banished from all the Gathering events and her commitments to Domenico and his family during their time of grief, I felt like we had barely spent any time with each other over the last few days.

"Tell me what's up," I said.

"You know you're my best friend, right?"

"Yes, of course." I didn't see where she was going with this.

"What I mean is, don't push me away. We're best friends, we don't turn away from each other."

Before I could say another word, we jumped as someone knocked at the door. Kris called for whoever it was to come in. The knob turned and the door opened to reveal Vlad on the other side. "Do Mom and Dad need something?" Kris asked him.

"No," Vlad answered, his eyes on me. "What's going on? I knew there was something wrong the second I saw you at dinner."

"Nothing," I said casually.

"Maybe it's best if he also knows," said Kris.

"Avy," Vlad said softly, his expression growing serious. "You might as well tell us what's bothering you."

"Why should I?"

"Because I want to help," Vlad said.

I looked at my best friend, who was nodding vigorously, then moved my gaze to Vlad, who practically looked like he was ready to slay a dragon for me. "Fine," I said.

All the secrets I had been keeping from my best friend were eating away at me, and there was no way for me to tell her all my fears without breaching the nondisclosure agreement that I had signed. I decided to take my chances. I told them about the incident with the scary woman in the jail, then the troubling phone call I had answered for my dad, and finally about the weird encounter I had had with the caller with the strange tattoo. Kris gasped every now and then while Vlad listened intently as I went on, the lines on his forehead seeming to deepen with every passing minute.

"I don't know if it is a coincidence, but Adrian said he thought he saw a bald man watching us earlier." I shuddered. "This man referred to me as 'the girl,' and now he might be following me. He probably knows I'm here. I'm really getting freaked out."

Worry flashed across Vlad's face. "You shouldn't be alone at any time," he said.

As much as the situation was bothering me, I wasn't about to let Vlad swoop in and take charge. "I think I've proven I can handle being alone."

Vlad let out an exasperated sigh. He probably already knew that I wouldn't agree with him so easily. "I'm serious."

"Well, me too."

His voice was stern as he said, "It's not about proving that you can handle being alone. It's about you being safe. I'll accompany you around Court from now on and make sure this guy keeps his distance."

"Look, General, I'm not a damsel in distress, so you can put your shining armor away, okay."

He gritted his teeth, and by the way his hands curled into fists, I could tell he was close to the edge. "What is wrong with you? Stop being so stubborn."

"What's wrong with me? Not much. My mom had me tested." I shrugged nonchalantly. I wasn't trying to antagonize him, but he was acting like it was his decision to make, and it made me feel like he thought of me as a weak little girl who knew nothing. I understood how potentially dangerous this situation was, but that didn't mean I would let him go back to his patronizing ways.

"Your life could be at stake!" His voice was getting louder and I was worried his parents might hear us.

"And I told you, I can take care of myself," I said.

Our bodies were close to each other by this point. We both refused to lose the argument. Kris came between us, putting her hands on our shoulders in an attempt to calm us down. "Don't fight, guys. Ave, I know you're tough. But Vlad is right—it is dangerous. You don't know who they are or what they want. I just—" My best friend's voice broke. "I just don't want to risk losing you."

I knew that if I were in her shoes and she were in mine, I would want at least a half dozen Court Guards to accompany her everywhere, twenty-four seven, so I understood her concern. For that reason alone, I was willing to swallow my pride—a little, not too much, though. "Fine. If it'll make you feel better, I'll take the babysitter." I pointed my finger at Vlad. "Looks like you'll be my nanny now, General."

My best friend smiled gratefully and hugged me. I was just hoping this wouldn't interfere with my mission.

Vlad interrupted our hug. "Do you remember what the tattoo looked like?"

"Why?" Hope started building inside me that this could be a legitimate lead that Vlad had picked up on. "Do you think it could mean something?"

"Yeah. Could you describe it to me?" Vlad pressed.

"It was jet black. The whole thing was round, like some sort of emblem." I closed my eyes as I tried to recall the details of the image. "It was like one of those fringed helmets worn by the armies in any movie about the Spartans. And the guy had it on his inner wrist."

"I think I know what you're referring to." Vlad fished out his phone and tapped his screen rapidly before showing it to me and Kris. "Just to be sure, did it look more or less like this?"

"Yeah. Except there was gold lining here. Not just yellow, gold."

Vlad and Kris shared a look before he turned to me. "The Myrmidons."

"Wait! That creepy woman mentioned the Myrmidons. I swear I've read about them somewhere. Was it in Homer's *Illiad*? I think they're Achilles's soldiers, right?"

Vlad was more than happy to elaborate. "The name comes from the Greek *murmedon*, derived from the Greek word for ant, *myrmex*, meaning 'ant bed' or 'ant's nest,'" Vlad slid his phone back into his pocket. "A long time ago, a princess of Phthiotis called Eurymedousa was seduced by Zeus. He transformed both of them into ants so they could carry on their affair without his wife, Hera, being able to catch them."

"I've never heard that version," I murmured to myself.

"There are lots of versions, but this one's what we Hellenicus believe to be true." He saw my face scrunch up and chuckled. "I know. It sounds bizarre, but that's what happened. It led to them having a demigod son, King Myrmidon. Eventually, Hera found out about the affair and cursed the land. Everyone suffered from a great plague and died."

"That's awful!" I had always known that Hera was insanely jealous—who could blame her; Zeus was such a man-whore—but I never thought she would do something as drastic as punishing an entire nation.

"The gods can be unkind." Kris chimed in. "And Hera, well, she can be ruthless when she gets jealous."

"What happened then?"

"Myrmidon lived, but what's a king without his people. So he prayed to Zeus to fix what Hera had done. Bringing people back from the dead is taboo because it imbalances nature." Vlad took a brief pause. "In response, Zeus turned the ants who resided in his sacred tree into people. The small insects rose up from the ant bed on the oak to become strong, brave, and diligent people."

"Wait." I held up one hand. "Did you just say his sacred tree? Are you referring to—"

Vlad nodded, seemingly knowing where my thought was headed. "The Whispering Oak of Dodona, yes."

"The people who have this tattoo are actually in a cult that worships the oak tree?"

My best friend shook her head. "I don't think that's how it works, Ave."

"I don't think it's a cult. Myrmidons are more like soldiers, militaristic people. They are disciplined and focused. They obey orders without question—quickly and efficiently—doing whatever they are told. Myrmidons have an innate understanding of weapons, fighting, and tactics. They can also resist mind manipulation. They're trained to be immune to any kind of mind control that would compromise their moral integrity. Moreover, they are very loyal and will choose to die over disobeying an order or breaking a promise."

"They sound like a badass army." He hadn't answered my question, though. "But what are they doing at the Court?"

"No clue. But the fact that he's here on Court Grounds means he has permission to be here."

"Do you guys think—" I swallowed hard, unsure if my theory held any value. "Do you guys think the Myrmidons are here because the queen allowed them to be?"

Kris bit her bottom lip, looking uncomfortable with the whole thing, but Vlad gave me confirmation via a curt nod. "That seems likely."

"That creepy woman mentioned the Faction. Do you think the Faction is actually the Myrmidons?"

"That's why you asked the other night at dinner?" Vlad asked.

"Did you get any more info from your dad?" I asked.

He shook his head dejectedly. One look at my best friend and I knew she had no clue either.

Meeting a temporary dead end, we decided to hold our discussion for another time. Kris had to get back to her parents and Domenico, and, with even more things weighing on my mind now, all I wanted was to go home and get some rest.

Kris gave me a tight hug then walked us to the front door. "Call me if you need anything, Ave. Even if you can't sleep, just pick up the phone and I'll rush to you with chocolate chip cookies and warm milk, okay?"

"I might take you up on the offer."

As we stepped out of the indigo-blue door, I noticed the red door across the hall; it was the same as the one in my dream from my first night of the Gathering. Turning to Vlad, I pointed to it and asked, "Where does that door lead?"

"The queen's residence."

Now that the door was in front of me, and very much real—not just a dream—I couldn't help but wonder how many other parts of the dream were also real. "Is there another set of doors beyond it—for each Pure Royal family?"

That got his full attention. "How did you know?" He knitted his brows as he asked.

"Just a guess." I paused and chose my words carefully. I was sure it would freak him out if I told him about the dream. "Tell me about them."

Vlad looked at me a little curiously but obliged. "There's a door to represent each of the Pure Royal families: Christoulakis, Ambrosia, and Stavros."

"Zeus, Poseidon, Hades."

"Exactly. Legend has it that each door accesses each god's realm. One to the sky realm, one to the sea, and the third to the Underworld. Practically speaking, it's where Pure Royal families keep their artifacts and sacred offerings to the gods. Well, where the Ambrosia and Christoulakis families do. Of course, the Stavros door hasn't been used in a long time."

I could see them perfectly, the doors from my dream—the doors that actually existed. How had I known?

Soon, we arrived back in front of my door at the Hyped, where I punched in the code on the keypad and started to swing the door open. Vlad put one hand on my shoulder and let the door close again. "What is it?"

"I don't mean to babysit you. It's not that I don't think you can take care of yourself. I know you can. I've seen how strong you can be over the last few days. But I could never forgive myself if anything happened to you. And I don't want to take any chances. You can hate me for being ridiculously stubborn. I'd rather be hated than see you hurt."

I snaked my arms around his waist and pulled him into a hug. "Thank you," I muttered against his coat as I took in his usual scent of mint and soap.

We were still holding each other when the door opened, revealing my dad's stunned face. His eyes shot to the tall figure who had his arms around me. "Lord Ambrosia."

Well, this was awkward.

Vlad bid his farewell. Before he turned to leave, I saw a tint of redness in his cheeks. I followed my dad inside, knowing full well that he would chastise me. Luckily, he was absorbed in the fact that his daughter had been wrapped in the arms of a Pure Royal, so he let it slide. I took his speechlessness as a chance to go straight to my room. It had been a tiring day and I longed to curl up under the duvet.

Ω

The next day, I woke up feeling much better. My dad had left early—I saw his note on the fridge, reminding me that today was the day that I was supposed to drop by the Court Guard Headquarters to sign a few more papers before I could officially be released from probation. Next to his note was another note from Mom saying that she would be staying at Tiana's.

It took me fifteen minutes to shower and twenty minutes to get to the Court Guard Headquarters. I was on my way in when I bumped into Officer Brad Warwick.

"Hey, pretty redhead!"

"I have a name, you know."

"Avery." He grinned boyishly, lifting a few years off his face. "You've come to sign the papers, right? Just head to the front desk and find Dawn. She will get you sorted."

"Thanks."

Officer Warwick held the door open, and only then did I notice he had a familiar tattoo on his inner wrist. I wondered if it meant he knew the bald guy. Were they both apart of some weird Myrmidon cult? "Hey, are you okay?" he asked.

"Yeah. Just can't wait to get this over with," I said.

"Don't let me keep you then."

It didn't take longer than five minutes to sign the document—actually, it only took a few seconds to literally sign it, but Dawn made sure I had read the whole document, especially the part that mentioned that the punishment would be doubled if I misbehaved again.

I was about to leave when someone called my name. It was Commander Hudson. He offered me a smile and his hand. I shook it, feeling a bit awkward. "Are you excited to rejoin the Gathering?"

No. Because now I had less time to work on my investigation and it seemed like I was only adding to my list of things I needed to figure it. "Yes. I can't wait."

"You're lucky today is the first day you are free to rejoin the events," he said.

"Why is that?"

"There's the Panhellenic Festival this year," he explained. "It's held here every four years. There are a lot of athletic competitions, so it's usually very crowded at Court. Haven't you noticed how packed the Hyped lobby is? There's a welcoming party there in two hours."

With everything going on, I clearly hadn't been paying attention. "That's awesome." I tried my best to sound enthusiastic. "Thanks for letting me know. Now I have something to look forward to."

"Have fun!" Hudson waved as I pushed through the door and stepped outside.

Ω

Standing on the pavement in front of the Court Guard Headquarters, I texted Kris to find out where she was, then pulled up the photo I took of the schedule on the first day. Hudson had been right about the Panhellenic Festival. The welcoming party and opening ceremony would be held later today, but the competitions would take place throughout the rest of December, finishing with a closing ceremony before Christmas. Attending the athletic competitions wasn't mandatory, so I skipped over the details to go through the list of other Gathering activities. Tonight there would be a beach party outside of the Court. "That sounds like fun," I scoffed, not being able to conceal my sarcasm. Tomorrow was the *Symposium*—a huge dinner party. But since today was a free day, there wasn't really anything I had to do until the beach party; I wasn't sure if I felt relief or disappointment.

The lobby of the Hyped was packed—filled with swarms of Hellenicus. It would take twice as long as normal to get from the entrance to the elevator.

"Excuse me." I lost count how many times I had said it.

A hand caught my wrist and saved me from being mashed between two tall guys. To my surprise—and horror—it was Damian. "Blond surfer boy," I blurted automatically.

"Hey, you remember that I love surfing." He mistook my jeer.

After listening to him mention it over and over again during the after-party on the first night, I wouldn't be able to forget even if I wanted to. Not wanting to acknowledge him, I simply moved past him.

"Wait." His hand grabbed my arm and I gave it a murdering glance. He let go, raising both hands. "Sorry. Look, I just want to get to know you better. You left the after-party before I had a chance to."

"Oh, so I exist now? Because I remember you treating me like I didn't at the after-party. We're not friends, not even acquaintances, so save me the trouble and keep it that way."

Before he had another chance to grab me, I slipped through the crowd. Knowing that he had slept with a redhead the other night, which was the catalyst for Nikki slapping Renata, I had no intention of being the next redhead in line. After all, I had other things I needed to focus on. Things like figuring out ways to escape my destiny.

CHAPTER TWENTY

Apart from the weird encounter with Damian, the day turned out to be—as I'd initially predicted—uneventful. I had gone back to my room and tried to translate the torn page using the online translator, but I didn't get any new information. It was just a continuation of what Adrian had said—the Great Massacre, Zeus, and Hades. However, I discovered one thing of interest: at the corner where the paper was torn there were three Greek letters: τιμ, which was part of the Greek word for *price*. Perhaps it was talking about the price of angering the gods or something along those lines. I texted Adrian to let him know I was making some progress but that I needed his help. He replied soon after to say that he was at the Court Hospital—it seemed that Caitlin's condition required her to be admitted—but he could meet up with me this evening. Before I typed my reply to Adrian, a text from Kris came in:

I'm bored. Domenico is going to the Panhellenic archery competition. Are you up for shopping? Then the beach party later?

I'll meet you in fifteen on Ermou Street!

I sent another text to Adrian to let him know where I'd be tonight. He replied,

I'll stop by for a bit. Don't forget to bring that paper,
I need to see it again in person.

I was putting my coat on when I heard the sound of the keypad and my mom burst in, hugging a paper bag of groceries with one hand.

"Are you going out?" She put the bag on the counter.

"I am." I straightened the collar of my dark-grey coat and grabbed my purse.

"Where? With who?"

"I'm going shopping with Kris, Mom." I sighed.

"Oh, perfect. I need to do some shopping too," she said. "Wait until I sort these first."

As my mom put away the groceries, I sent Kris another text to let her know that my mom had invited herself.

"Are we going or what?" My mom asked, as if she had been the one waiting on me.

I begrudgingly accompanied Mom to Ermou Street to meet Kris. A wide variety of shops lined the busy street, from antique and art stalls to jewelry shops and luxury boutiques. Kris and my mom were determined to browse in each of the small shops. I was happy to be roaming places at Court that I'd never been to before. It was nice to see the Royal Bar area in the daytime when the long, twisting street was filled with shoppers and not drunkards.

When we got closer to the end of the street, my mom and Kris squealed at the sight of what they both declared to be the best boutique on the Court grounds. I had had about enough of shopping at this stage, but Kris persuaded me to follow them inside. "One more store, Ave. Promise."

It was wedged between two taller buildings. Despite the old sign with some letters that had rubbed off and become illegible over the years, it was clean and all the clothing was arranged neatly. Kris and my mom basked in the attention of the sales staff and pawed over different fabrics and textures.

"Ave, do you have a dress for the Symposium?"

A Symposium is a party usually led by a feast master. In the old days, the guests wore garlands, but in today's world, you could wear whatever you wanted. There would be musical performances, acrobats, and dancers who played the kithara.

"She doesn't." My mom, who had incredible hearing, answered from across the shop. "I'm trying to find one for her. Do you want to help, Kristen?"

"I would love to, Kath."

"No, no." Knowing full well that this meant I would have to spend at least an hour in the fitting room trying on dresses, I shook my head adamantly. "I already have a dress."

Annoyingly, my mom answered once again, "No, you don't."

"Yes, I have."

"What about this purple one, Kristen? Do you think she would look good in it? Or maybe this pink one?" My mom had clearly decided that ignoring me was the best solution. She roamed the aisles and came back with a bunch of dresses draped over her arm.

"Mom, I'm not buying a new dress."

Kris looked at me and asked softly, "Do you actually have a dress to wear?"

"Yeah. I think I'll wear that—" I paused and tried to recall the color of the dress my mom had forcefully packed for me. "The cerulean dress I wore on the first day."

"What?" My mom, who had been sweeping through the rack of

dresses, stood on her tiptoes and looked at us over the metal pole. "You're going to wear that dress again?"

"Yes."

"Are you sure you don't want to get something new? The Symposium is a big deal," my mom said.

"That dress is a big deal too. It was passed down from your grandmother to your mother, and then to you before you gave it to me, right?"

Then a miracle happened. It was happening in the form of glistening tears in my mother's eyes. "Right." She turned to Kris, smiling. "She doesn't need a dress. She has one."

I stood there, realizing that a second miracle had also just happened: my mom had agreed with me.

After that, my mom was in a good mood. She even allowed me to take her car to drive to the beach party with Kris that evening. After quickly showering, playing dress-up, and—most importantly—making sure I had the page from the book with me, I went to the Royal Quarters. Kris was waiting for me outside. "I think it's going to be so much fun, Ave! I'm so excited that you can participate in the Gathering events again."

It was unlikely that people would immediately think of beaches when they thought of Alaska, but believe it or not, there were about five thousand miles of coastline and several beaches. It was almost a three-hour drive to Wonder Lake, where the party was held, and by the time we got there, the bonfire had been set and the party was in full swing with music and dancing.

We walked toward the bonfire, glad that we had decided to wear our faux-fur coats because it was freezing. Despite the temperature being fifteen degrees Fahrenheit, the guys looked as if the cold did not bother them at all. Maybe they were just playing it cool, or perhaps the heat radiating from the bonfire was enough to keep them warm while dancing. Kris clicked Domenico, who was among the guys crowded around the bonfire. Unlike the others, he wore what people normally wore during the winter season in Alaska: a scarf, a beanie hat, some gloves, and a long navy-blue coat. Domenico ran to meet us and took Kris's hand, raising it to his lips as he said, "Buonasera, *amore.*"

My best friend giggled as she wrapped her arms around his neck and he pulled her closer. They went to dance while I stood by the bonfire to warm up, counting the minutes until Adrian arrived. Being the third wheel was never enjoyable.

As I walked aimlessly around the party, I could hear familiar voices shouting back and forth. I quickly pushed through the crowd that had gathered around the source of the commotion. In the middle of the circle of nosey people, Damian and Adrian stood a few feet away from each other. Two or three people were holding their arms to separate them. It was a good thing they were being held back because I saw venom in Adrian's eyes, and he looked ready to strike. How did I not notice him arrive?

"Walk away, Tavoularis, or there'll be hell to pay."

"Wait till we get back to the Court, Ambrosia. I'm going to report this right away."

"Oh yeah? And I suppose you are going to leave out the part about you harassing a female, right? Because I certainly won't."

Damian seemed hesitant. He slid his gaze over to me then back to Adrian before pulling himself out of the grips of the people surrounding him and stalking off without another word.

I ran over to Adrian as he was also released from the grips around his arms. "What happened?" I asked him, baffled.

"Douchebag Tavoularis happened," Adrian grunted, and sat on the ground. "He just keeps pursuing her even though she's said no."

"Her?" I took the spot next to him.

"Renata."

"I thought you said you're a lover and not a fighter, yet here you are, ready to square up against Damian for Renata," Kris said when she reached us, Domenico and Renata in tow.

"Tonight's an exception." His eyes were fixed on Renata. I wondered how long Adrian had been here. He had obviously been hanging out with Renata before getting into an argument with Damian. Had he already lost interest in our mission?

Renata sat on the cold ground to face Adrian as Kris, Domenico, and I took a step back to give them space. "Hey, thanks for sticking up for me. You know you didn't have to do that. I know how to deal with a jackass like Damian."

Adrian leaned forward, his face only a few inches away from hers as his lips curled into a devilish smirk. "I have to admit, it's kind of cute when you act all tough."

"Don't get cocky. This doesn't mean you're getting into my pants again."

"Hey. That's not why I did that. I was just—"

Renata interrupted him by putting one finger under Adrian's chin and guiding his face to hers to kiss him. Kris and I exchanged a dumbfounded look.

A few seconds later, Adrian pulled away from Renata's kiss and stared at her through heavy-lidded eyes. "What was that, then?"

"A token of thanks," Renata quipped.

"Well, Miss Tough Girl, I have to get back to my sister now, but if that idiot bothers you again, message me, okay? I mean it." He gave her a stern look. "I won't let him get away with that behavior." Adrian stood, helped Renata back to her feet, and then turned to me. "Hey, Montgomery, do you have a second before I go? Caitlin wanted me to ask you something."

"Wha—" Then I remembered the reason why he had agreed to

meet me in the first place. I reached inside the pocket of my coat and felt the page from the library book. "Oh yeah. Sure."

Adrian and I walked side by side along the beach, away from the partygoers, minding our steps so as not to slip on the layer of snow. When we were out of eyesight, I reached inside the pocket of my coat and withdrew the page, handing it to him. "Here you go. Tell Caitlin I say hi."

"Hey. Don't kick me out just yet. It took almost three hours to get here and all that's happened so far is an argument. I want to make the trip worth it." Adrian smiled, then his face grew serious. "Can we talk?"

I nodded, then followed him over to a large, flat rock. We were far enough away from the party now that the sounds of nature were able to reach our ears over the music. He sat down on the rock and I sat next to him. The surface was cold on my behind through my jacket. "What is it?"

"I just want to know. After you get your freedom, what are you going to do?"

"I planned on leaving the Court and never coming back."

"And go where?"

"Anywhere but here. Someplace where I can pretend I'm not a Hellenicus," I said. "I will forget the Hellenicus. I will forget this place. I will live as a Nescient."

"Will you forget me?" There was a sadness in his question.

"Adrian—"

"Can I come with you?"

"What?"

"Can I come with you when you leave all this Hellenicus stuff behind?" he asked.

"Adrian, I—" I thought of the kiss he'd shared with Renata and how he had defended her. Clearly he had some feelings for her, and it made me doubt that he sincerely meant what he'd said.

Adrian seemed to notice the doubts dancing through my mind. "You know I like you, right?" When I said nothing, he continued, "Well, I do. And if you'll have me, I want to come with you."

"I don't know if that's a good idea," I said.

We sat there for a while, watching the moon before he finally rose to his feet. "Think about it, Montgomery. You don't have to do this alone."

Adrian left and took with him his warmth, the cold stinging in his absence.

Ω

And I did what he'd asked. I thought about it during the party. The thought of Adrian coming with me was a relief. After all, my intention had been to leave with Bryan, and a part of me still wondered if the true reason why I was at Court was because I had been too afraid to leave on my own. I had convinced myself I came here for Carlo, but there was still a niggling in the back of my mind that told me I was making excuses for being a coward.

But I was worried. Adrian had just admitted to liking me as more than a friend. What if I could not return his feelings? What if I hurt him? I had gone through this already with Bryan. And Adrian had been hurt so much already; I didn't want to be added to his list.

I spent the rest of the night consumed by my newest dilemma, and yet I still couldn't make up my mind.

Ω

The Symposium was finally here, and it was going to be a good day. Since it was held in the Hyped, I only had to take the elevator downstairs, so I had a bath instead of a shower, and took my time drying my hair and getting dressed. I was walking into the lobby when I spotted three people standing facing each other near the couch.

"Kris!" I hugged my best friend the second I saw her. "You look absolutely gorgeous!"

She was wearing a pale-green dress, which she'd bought the other day when we went shopping on Ermou Street. Domenico was on her right, and Vlad on her left. I greeted them both.

"Are you excited?" I asked Domenico, seeing how cheery he looked.

"Yes! Where I come from in Sybaris, we usually have wine piped directly from the vineyards during a Symposium. Do they do the same here?"

To Domenico's disappointment, Vlad indicated that the Court didn't have the facilities to do that.

"That's too bad. That's too bad," Domenico said.

Any disappointment he might have felt disappeared less than an hour later. The feast master had done a great job organizing and hosting the Symposium. The schedule was packed with everything from acrobatic stunts to kithara players. The whole room gasped simultaneously as a girl performed a stunt through a hoop rimmed with knives. Then there was a cheesy play retelling the tragic love story of Eros.

Of course, for me, the real star was the food. The tables were long and solid wood, laden with every kind of food I could think of when I thought of Italy, and even dishes I had no idea existed. Platters filled with countless cheeses, loaves of bread, vegetables, and pastas lined the tables. There were waterfalls of wine scattered around the room for Hellenicus who were of age. Against the far wall sat three dessert benches, showcasing all the classics: tiramisu, cannoli with generous creamy fillings, sweet panettone, moistened cassata from Sicily, and so much more.

The night ended with a group of musicians serenading the room of full-bellied Hellenicus. The combination of food and music coaxed everyone into sleepiness. Decidedly too exhausted to walk back to the Royal Quarters, Domenico, Kris, and Vlad ended up back at my place for an impromptu sleepover. Both boys slept in the living room while Kris and I slept in my bed.

The food coma was real! I didn't wake up until around eleven the next morning, still wearing the cerulean dress and my makeup, Kris asleep still beside me. Letting her continue to sleep off last night's feast, I dragged myself to the kitchen to make up for missing breakfast. I might have been full last night, but I was hungry as hell this morning.

"You're awake." Vlad was in the kitchen already, cooking.

"I didn't know you could cook."

"I can." His brow quirked up as he folded an omelette over in the pan.

I saw groceries on the counter. "Wait, I thought my mom brought in some food yesterday."

"There weren't any eggs, so I went to get them this morning." He pointed at the grocery bags. "And I bought you something."

"Really?" I climbed up on one of the kitchen stools and began ransacking the groceries. Aside from the usual ingredients for cooking, there were cheesecakes, bags of potato chips, some fruit, and then my hands stopped. "You bought Twinkies!"

"I did." He paused cutting the onions. "It's still your favorite snack, right?"

Even though it was embarrassing, Twinkies had been my favorite food since childhood. Whenever I was in a bad mood or feeling down, Twinkies provided a healing balm to my troubled heart. I would instantly feel better after I had one.

"Are you okay?" he asked.

"How did you know about Twinkies?"

"Oh." He scratched the side of his head and ducked his face, but

I could still see that he was blushing. "I don't think you remember this, but when we were kids—you were about six or seven—some kid named Axel tackled me in soccer. Our team ended up losing, and I had a sprained ankle." He shrugged, shaking his head. "Anyway, you gave me a Twinkie."

"I gave you a Twinkie?"

"And you said it was your favorite food in the world. You said you always ate them whenever you were sad because they made you feel better. Actually, I found your chatter rather annoying, but I knew you were just trying to cheer me up—to make me feel better the only way you knew how to."

How on earth had Vlad remembered that?

As Vlad transferred the omelette to a plate, I pulled my hair back in a ponytail. "It smells so good." I rested my hands on the counter.

His hand covered one of mine, and warmth spread through my whole body. There was a part of me that wanted to pull my hand away. A part that wanted me to run, to remove myself from this situation. But before I could do anything, I suddenly felt his arms wrap around me.

I turned and spread my hand against his chest, intending to push him away, but I couldn't. Instead, I left it there for a moment before I snaked both of my arms around him. I held on to him as if my life depended on it, absorbing his warmth. Vlad tugged on my hair and drew me to rest on his chest as I listened to his heart beat. Pulling back slightly, he put his hand under my chin and tilted my head so our eyes met. "It will be all right, Avy." He took a sharp breath then reiterated it with more force this time. "Everything will be all right. I will make damn sure of it."

If I ended up in New York or another part of the world, I wanted to remember this moment: the first time the nickname Avy hadn't bothered me.

After a while, he let me go. As I turned to avoid having to look at him after our tender moment, I could see Domenico was still sleeping on the couch, his mouth hanging slightly open. "I think you should wake him up. I'll get Kris."

Ω

Halfway through the meal, Adrian texted, urging me to meet him outside the Court Hospital. I confirmed I'd be there in twenty minutes.

Laphria, the sacrificial event, would take place later today and, after waking up so late, Kris was anxious to start getting ready for it as soon as possible. We said our good-byes and the three of them headed back to the Royal Quarters as I rushed off to meet Adrian. I found him outside the building, leaning against one of the wide pillars with his eyes closed. "Adrian." I spoke softly to avoid startling him.

"Montgomery." He smiled.

"Hey, how's your sister?"

His smile morphed into a grin. "She's getting better."

"That's great! I hope she can get back home soon."

"Yeah."

"So, why did you call me here? Did you figure out what was written on that page?"

"Yes," he said. "You're not going to like it, though."

"Try me."

"I went back to the library and found the rest of the letters." Adrian pulled out his phone and showed me a photo of the torn page next to the remaining page that was still left in the book. Together they formed the word *τιμωρία*.

"You know I don't speak Greek, right? This photo doesn't help me."

"It means punishment, Montgomery. The only way to get rid of the gift is by forcing the gods to take it back."

"I figured that. But how exactly are we going to get them to do that?"

Adrian shook his head. "That's the part you're not going to like."

And he was right. I didn't.

CHAPTER TWENTY-ONE

I hated the answer because we still didn't have one. My birthday was drawing nearer, and we were no closer to figuring this mess out. I told Adrian not to worry about it for now and to focus on his sister's recuperation. He seemed sleep deprived and I didn't want to add more to his plate. He promised me he would try to get some sleep and I rushed back to my suite to get ready for Laphria. Kris, Domenico, and Vlad already had a head start on me, and none of them had a bird's nest on their heads to tame.

I spent the rest of the afternoon trying on practically every single item of clothing my mom had packed for me. I finally settled on an outfit—a short dress, some extra-thick tights, and a long, heavy coat to keep me warm during the outdoor event. I didn't know exactly what happened at a sacrificial festival, so I hoped my choice was appropriate.

By the time I had finished making myself look presentable, I needed to head down to the garden to meet Kris, Domenico, and Vlad. The garden was even more crowded than the Hyped lobby had been the other day; it seemed like I was the last Hellenicus to arrive. I caught sight of Kris, Domenico, and Vlad and headed toward them. As we stood waiting for the event to begin, I took in the setup. There was a circular altar sitting in front of the Oak of Dodona. Large logs had been placed carefully on top of the altar and steps had been constructed for a smooth ascent to the pyre. None of this had been here the other day.

Within minutes, the festival was kicked off with a splendid procession honoring Artemis, the goddess of the hunt, wilderness, wild animals, the moon, and chastity. Trumpets played as Hellenicus danced in front of the procession, leading golden chariots filled with fruit and flowers toward the altar. Some of the Hellenicus men carried large sacks over their shoulders. A group of maidens rode last upon a cart pulled by deer. Among them was Queen Rhea Christoulakis, although she took a back seat to the event while one of the other maidens officiated as priestess.

Since I had never been to a sacrificial event before, watching the people in the procession make their way up the steps was intriguing. Any excitement I had was quickly stifled when they opened the sacks and started throwing dead birds and other small animals on the altar.

"I think I might be sick." I covered my mouth with my palm, trying to suppress the urge to vomit.

The altar was set on fire and I had to look away as the animals burned. The smell wafting through the crowd was revolting. Right when I was sure I was going to be sick, a trumpeter sounded the signal for the next part of the ceremony: the feast. I wondered how anyone could even think about eating after witnessing that, but I was glad to have an excuse to get away from the sacrificial area.

Behind the oak tree a massive tent with long tables piled high with food and drinks had been set up. The tablecloths were Artemis's favorite design: white with a thick band of red lining the edge of the cloth. The fabric was stitched together with silver thread. There were moons in every phase drawn on the white surface of the cloth. Bows and arrows had been strung up along the sides of the tent. A statue of Artemis with her hunting dog was placed in the center with floral arrangements at her feet.

Everything from Western foods to Mexican cuisine was on display. I even saw sushi on one of the tables. The Hellenicus came from all over the world for the Gathering, and this feast seemed to honor the diversity among us. Everything looked delicious, but the burning smell still sat inside my nostrils.

We took our seats at the tables, happy to be out of the frigid evening air. Despite the extravagant feast we had had last night, everyone seemed to be in the mood to indulge in food. Everyone except me. After the sacrifice, I found that even taking a sip of water was too hard. I stuck it out for another hour, listening to the conversation between Kris, Domenico, and Vlad, but not participating. Finally, I decided it would be best for me to head back to my suite and crawl into bed.

It wasn't until around two in the afternoon the next day that I woke up to my stomach growling in protest. I had had terrible nightmares about the sacrifice and didn't feel rested despite how late I had slept in. I forced myself to sit up in bed and, leaning back against the pillow, scrolled through my messages and chats. My finger paused on the group chat that Adrian had created with Kris, Vlad, and me. He'd sent an invitation to a party that Renata was throwing tomorrow night at a place called Isles of the Blessed. According to Adrian, Renata was bored with official Gathering events. I couldn't blame her. After what I'd witnessed last night, I was also desperate for something more normal—preferably with no dead animals involved.

My stomach growled again, as if to let me know I was taking too long. I dragged myself out of bed, pulled on some jeans and a hoodie, and threw on my grey coat before heading out. Vlad had pretty much cleaned out our fridge yesterday while making lunch for everyone, so I wandered around the Court grounds to find somewhere to eat. I soon found myself outside a diner called Quickfood.

The front door of the restaurant opened as a couple wearing matching sweaters came out, and I caught a whiff of burgers and fries. My stomach let out another impatient growl.

Quickfood was the perfect name for the diner because within fifteen minutes of placing my order, a cheeseburger, fries, and one large chocolate milk shake were placed in front of me. I felt comfortably alone in the sparsely filled diner. I pulled out my phone and opened the Wattpad application, eager to finish the crime story I had found the other day. It was an odd time for a meal, which explained why the only other customers was a group of five Court Guards sitting at the back.

At least, I had thought they were all Court Guards until one of them leaned back and I could see it wasn't a guard at all, though she wore the same uniform as the others.

Mom?

I choked on my milk shake.

Before I could even rise to my feet, she stood and quickly left without seeming to notice me. Could that have really been my mom? The woman looked *just* like her. But why would she be here with Court Guards . . . and dressed like them too? Also, why had she ignored me? Surely she would have noticed me when I walked in. None of it made any sense.

My phone buzzed. There were at least four missed calls from my dad. "Seriously, Dad, what's going on?" I whispered to myself. After not hearing from him for days, now he was calling incessantly?

I texted my mom,

Where are you? Was that you?

She'd either think I had officially lost my marbles or she'd know exactly what I was talking about.

Totally unsettled, I sipped my shake and tried to collect myself. Just then, one of the guards stood and walked past my table on his way to the bathroom. My whole body froze. That weird tattoo! Was he part of the Myrmidons too?

I was *over* having so many unanswered questions. Maybe the best approach was the direct approach. Forget sneaking into libraries and doing research. That wasn't getting me anywhere. I pushed myself up and walked to the table of Court Guards. All of them looked at me as if a horn had suddenly sprouted from the middle of my forehead. I stared right back at them and that was when I noticed that all of them had the tattoo, albeit in different spots. One guy had it on the back of his neck, the guy sitting beside him had his behind his ear, and the guy who had just passed by my table had his in the same spot as the bald guy, on his wrist.

"So." I dragged the chair from a nearby table and sat. "Anyone here know a large, bald guard?" All of the guards had the same blank expression on their faces as they looked at me. I wondered if they had been trained to keep their faces so emotionless.

When they did not reply, I carried on with my questions, becoming more direct to see if I could get some reactions out of them. "What's up with the tattoo? Are you all in a cult? Is that it?"

Nothing. Not even a twitch of an eyebrow. Damn. They had been trained well. I decided to change the subject.

"What about the Faction?" I asked, searching each of their faces. I noticed two of them give each other a sideways glance and I knew I was on the right track now. "Don't you guys know anything? Some Court Guards you lot are," I scoffed, folding my arms and leaning back in my chair. I switched it up and asked a serious question now. "Am I being followed?" I swallowed the anxiety growing inside me.

The guy on my right clenched his fist. He finally opened his mouth, earning a disapproving look from his companions. "You don't know anything, kid."

"That's very true." I fixed my gaze on him. "So why don't you tell me?"

His Adam's apple bobbed up and down, and right when his lips parted—either to spill the beans or to tell me to eff off—I felt a familiar grip on my shoulder. "Hi, Mom."

"Outside. Now."

"How did you get changed so quick?" Her hair was loose and down, not in a bun like the female guard had had, and she was in her usual camel-colored winter coat. Had it really been her I had seen with the rest of the guards? When she didn't respond, I asked, "Were you here with them before?"

Out of the corner of my eye, I could see that the face of one of the guards was strained and his breathing appeared to be quick and shallow. But my mom was an entirely different case. She looked at me as if I had been sputtering absolute nonsense, making me feel like maybe I was going crazy after all. She shook her head in disappointment. "Let's get you home."

We didn't exchange a single word the whole walk to the Hyped. Back at the suite, I couldn't ignore it any longer. "Mom, where have you been?"

"What do you mean, Avery?" She answered with a heavy sigh. "You weren't here, so I went around trying to find you."

"No. I mean these last few days. I can count how many times you've actually been in this unit. Look, I know Tiana's your best friend, but—" I breathed out, trying to force my eyes to cooperate. This was not the right time to cry, and having never cried in front of her, I didn't want to start now. "But I'm your daughter." Despite my efforts, when I finished that sentence, my heart ached and the dam broke.

My mom opened her mouth then closed it again. She looked like she had no idea what to do. In the end, she opened her arms and held me. "Oh, Avery." Her hand caressed the back of my head while she continued to whisper my name as if it was a mantra—one that she hoped would calm me down. And surprisingly, it did. She had never comforted me like this before and I clung to the moment, not knowing if I would ever have this kind of affection from her again.

She seemed to also be relishing our rare moment of tenderness.

For the first time in the seventeen years, eleven months, and twenty-three days of my life, my mom and I watched TV together without bickering. We even laughed at the same scenes in the romantic comedy she had put on. As we waited for the credits to be over and the next movie to start, she offered to make hot chocolates for us. My mom's sudden displays of affection made me forget about what had happened that afternoon in Quickfood.

When it was time for bed, my mom followed me into my room and curled up beside me. At first, I thought that maybe she felt guilty for leaving me alone so much during the Gathering, but when I asked her why she wanted to sleep in my bedroom, she responded, "Because your father is working. His office called a few days ago. And I can't sleep alone."

She was being selfish after all. I should've known.

I found it awkward at first sleeping next to my detached mother, but I eventually managed to dive into dreamland. At least for thirty minutes, before her phone rang. I kept my eyelids glued shut as I heard her get out of bed and answer the phone.

"False alarm." I heard my mom speaking in a hushed voice. "She's with me. Yes, Hawke, she is *here*, I'm literally watching her with my own two eyes. No. She's sleeping. Okay. Bye."

With my back to my mom, I tried my best to breathe normally. Had she said *Hawke*?

My mom crawled back into bed and soon she was snoring beside me. I managed to fall asleep again after a few hours of replaying what she had said during that phone call. I still woke up early the next morning.

My mom had woken up even earlier and had left my room without a trace that she had been here. As I sat crossed-legged on my bed, my phone blipped, indicating that I had just received a new text message. It was Adrian.

Are you naked?

"Eww, what the fruit—"

Before I could complete my sentence, the door creaked opened. "I'll take that as a no." With both of his hands inside the back pockets of his jeans, he let a slow, dangerous smile curve his lips. "Montgomery, I think I know how to make the gods take the gift back."

"What?"

"The photos of the book I took when I went back to the library the other day, I had Caitlin help me translate. She has nothing better to do while she's stuck in the hospital, and she's fluent in Greek. Anyway, it was about Hades kidnapping Persephone. You know the story, right?"

I nodded, indicating for him to continue.

"It's linked with the Great Massacre. According to the page after the one you tore, Zeus and Demeter were angry at Hades. But because Hades is a god himself, it meant that they couldn't punish him. The Hellenicus at the time felt they needed to pick sides. Siding with the king of the gods seemed to be the better option, so that's exactly what they did. Some went to the extreme and decided if Hades could not be hurt, they would hurt his descendants instead. And the bloodbath began. First they killed the Stavroses, then they started killing anyone who had a click with a Stavros. To make sure no Stavros would ever be born again, they used Apollo's silver arrow. Killing a Hellenicus with this special weapon destroyed their soul. Eventually, all of the Stavroses were killed in this manner, rendering the bloodline extinct."

"*Okay*, our history books tell us all of this already, Adrian. How does this information help us?"

"I'm getting there." Adrian tutted at me before continuing, "The Hellenicus who committed these terrible crimes were punished severely—being reincarnated as Regulars in the next life and whatnot. But the Hellenicus who led the bloodbath received an additional punishment . . . they were punished—"

"—by losing the gift." I finished Adrian's sentence and earned a nod of approval from him. "Wow."

"Exactly! If we want the gods to take back this gift, we have to anger them."

"How?"

"I don't know, Montgomery. It has to be something major, though. Maybe steal the Golden Chalice or ruin a sacrificial ritual—I don't know."

What could possibly anger the gods enough that they would take back the gift? What would be worthy of a punishment *that* severe? As much as I wanted to be free of any clairaudient abilities, I wasn't about to become a murderer! I paced as I reeled on what Adrian had just said. Suddenly, an idea popped into my head. "Adrian, you're a genius!"

"Huh?"

"Ruining the sacrificial ritual!"

"But we don't have any more sacrificial rituals, Montgomery. The last one was two nights ago."

"Ah, but that's not true. There will be one during the closing ceremony for the Panhellenic Festival," I answered.

"You're right! The closing ceremony always includes sacrificial animals. What are we going to do? Steal the offerings?"

"No. That's not big enough." I stood and walked to the window then looked down at the garden where a huge tree stood, minding its own business as it reached toward the heavens. "We're going to burn down Zeus's tree."

"Damn. That's badass, Montgomery. I'm game!"

I was about to say something when a noise from outside the bedroom door startled me. It sounded like something dropping on the floor. "What was that?"

"Don't go getting paranoid already, Montgomery." Adrian waved his hand in front of me as if to shoo the thought away. "This mission is too ballsy to start getting jitters now."

He was right. I needed to keep it together if we were going to pull this off. But I swore I had heard something. Before I could dwell on it and waste any more time, Adrian pulled me out of my trance with his next question.

"Shall we get a plan together over breakfast?"

By now, he knew how much food motivated me. Besides, I wanted to get out of the suite in case my mom returned from wherever she had snuck off to. I wasn't ready to face her about the mysterious phone call she had taken last night when she thought I was sleeping.

It was still early enough that most people were still in bed. It was peaceful with the morning light streaming in through the tall windows as we made our way past the lobby and out into the cold. Not wanting to disturb the peace, Adrian and I stayed quiet, though, in my mind, I was feeling the pressure of time running out for me to break my soul-mate bond before my eighteenth birthday. I was so deep in my thoughts that I didn't even realize that we had cut through a narrow alley. Walking toward us from the other end was Officer Brad Warwick.

The last thing I wanted was trouble—not on an empty stomach. I was ready to fake some pleasantries, but then I saw that he wasn't alone. To my shock, he was with the bald guy with the tattoo—the man who had been on the phone call meant for my father! And they were both striding right toward us. The sparks in my brain desperately tried to connect the dots. I grabbed Adrian's arm. I wanted to run as fast as I could, but my legs turned to jelly and I was rooted in place. I could hear Adrian asking me what was wrong, but I could not utter an audible word. When the men were within reach, the bald guy stretched his arm out and grabbed my upper arm.

"Hey! What the fuck do you think you're doing?!" Adrian tried to brush off Warwick's hold, but the young Court Guard grabbed both of Adrian's arms from behind and pinned him in place. Struggling, Adrian tried his best to escape but failed miserably.

I was overwhelmed with fear. The bald guard looked at me with recognition and gave me an unnerving smile. "Avery Montgomery. We finally meet."

The guards separated us. The bald one took me into a building that looked like an out-of-business restaurant and sat me down in a chair in a windowless room. There was only one way out—the door behind him. He didn't tie me up or anything, but he made it damn clear—by resting his hand on his Court-issued weapon—that I would be foolish to try to get past him. He'd taken my phone. I had nothing on me, no tricks up my sleeve to get out of here.

A few minutes later Officer Warwick came back alone.

"Where is Adrian?" I yelled at him, trying to hide the slight note of desperation in my voice. Maybe I was too prideful, but I refused to be intimidated.

There was no reply. Neither guard would meet my gaze. The two exchanged a look and then a nod. Something was about to happen. I could feel my heart beating.

"Let's begin." The bald guard dragged a chair over in front of me and sat down. "My name is Commander Drake."

"How nice for you," I said. "Where is Adrian?! You better not hurt him—he's a Pure Royal and you'll have your asses handed to you by the queen, let alone what I'll do to you."

I got nothing but perfect calmness in response, which only made me angrier. "We're not here to hold you hostage or harm you or your friend." Leaning forward, Drake placed his elbows on top of his knees and added, "I am here because there's something I want to discuss with you. Something important."

"Hate to break it to you, buddy, but keeping someone against their will is kidnapping. If this is official Court business, take me to headquarters!"

Drake continued as if I hadn't said a word. "You've spent your entire life being a Regular."

"Thanks, Sherlock. Tell me something I don't already know."

"But you aren't. You are not a Regular."

Hope sparked inside of me; perhaps I was not a Hellenicus. Maybe this was all just a mistake and I didn't have a soul-mate bond to break after all! Maybe I was already free. "Are you saying I'm a Nescient?"

"No." My new hope was immediately crushed and the confusion returned. Officer Warwick passed Commander Drake a file, which immediately piqued my curiosity. But before he opened it, Drake dropped a bomb: "You're not a Nescient, and you're not a Regular. You are a Pure Royal."

"No, Drake, I'm most certainly not a Pure Royal. I can't be. You clearly haven't met my parents—they're as Regular as the sunrise."

"Avery, you are not a Montgomery," Drake said.

My face showed the complete and utter befuddlement I felt. I had seen my birth certificate; I knew who I was, but I decided to play along with his strange, elaborate prank. "Then who am I?"

"You are Camila Stavros."

I broke into a fit of giggles. Drake looked at me as if I had just lost my sanity, while I thought *he* was the insane one. "Impossible," I said. "The Stavroses are extinct."

Drake shook his head slowly as if he was trying to explain to a five-year-old that humans could not fly. "As you know, most of the Stavroses were killed during the Great Massacre, and the rest were slowing picked off in the generations afterward. But you are the last of the surviving Stavroses. The only one to survive the Faction." He opened the file and handed it to me. "This is your real birth certificate."

Camila Reanna Stavros was on the first paper of the file. There were more details about this Camila—all the usual data on a birth certificate. "Just because you show me a piece of paper and tell me that I'm this person, you think I'm going to believe you?" I said.

"I am telling the truth. It is up to you whether you choose to believe it or not."

"Well, I don't," I said. "Holy Poseidon, if my dad ever heard this, he'd have an absolute heart attack."

"Remember when you felt nauseated after you drank from the Golden Chalice?"

"What about it?"

"That's proof that you are a Pure Royal." Drake gave me a pointed look. When it finally dawned on me what he was referring to, a small smile crept on to his rough features.

As if in a trance, I whispered just slightly below hearing level, "Regulars can't drink the Royals' nectar or vice versa without getting sick."

"As for your dad, you don't have to worry about Jared Montgomery," Drake said.

At the mention of my father, I started having my earlier doubts again. Just because I had suddenly felt sick after drinking from the chalice didn't mean that I was a Pure Royal. Perhaps I had eaten something bad beforehand that could have caused a similar reaction. "What's the point of all this? Why are you two grown men, not to mention Court Guards, trying to prank me?"

"This is not a prank, and Jared Montgomery is not your father, Avery."

Sure, I looked nothing like my parents, and we had never gotten along, but that didn't mean I wasn't their child. There were many kids in the world who had no physical resemblance whatsoever to their parents.

He was silent for a moment then sighed irritably before turning to Officer Warwick. "Tell them to come in."

I had not believed a word he'd said until the moment I saw my parents walking in.

"Morning, Avery." My mom greeted me with a smile that I had never seen in my entire life. Then, as if she remembered something, she cringed a little and clarified, "I mean Camila."

My dad, always the more practical one, only gave me a formal nod. "Lady Stavros. My apologies for not calling you by your title before now."

Completely speechless, I turned to face Drake, beginning to wonder if I was the insane one after all.

"They are Special Court Guards, part of the Myrmidons, assigned to raise and protect you." Drake pulled a document from my file. There were my parents' faces and information. But their names were different: Nathan Hawke and Sera Lincoln.

Hawke and Lincoln! The names from the phone call. "I was right! You were the voice on the phone."

Drake's reply was a short bob of his head. The two people I had thought were my parents were not; it was shocking and unbelievable. I asked, "Why them?"

"They're the best teachers you can get."

"Teachers? You're kidding, right? They've basically abandoned me my whole life." Again, I avoided making eye contact with the two people I had spent my entire life believing to be my family.

"They taught you many lessons without you knowing it." Drake took a moment, as if thinking carefully about what he was going to say next. "And they've been monitoring you, even when you thought they weren't. They've been reporting back to the rest of the Myrmidons all these years. They've dedicated their lives to protecting you."

Anger rose up inside of me. This guy clearly had no idea what he was talking about. "I can assure you, Drake, they didn't teach me anything."

"Remember that time when you forgot to lock the door?" asked Hawke, his expression holding no emotion. "Well, you had actually locked the door."

Sweet roasted corn! I freaking knew it!

"I went to your school and yelled at you in front of your classmates to teach you humiliation."

"And why the fuck would I need to learn that lesson?" I spat the words at the face that I had spent nearly eighteen years searching for any resemblance. Jared Montgomery or Nathan whatever his name was.

He didn't flinch. In fact, he stared at me with a serious expression. "You're a Stavros. You need to handle being humiliated. Your bloodline is the most hated and feared."

"Do you know how many hours I cried in the bathroom because of what you did?" I marched up to him and shook him by the shoulders.

He took both of my hands from his shoulders and dropped them. "But you didn't show any hint of tears when you faced your friends. You held your head high. You handled it well, you learned the lesson."

"I have a question." I turned to Drake, who motioned for me to continue. "If you knew I was being targeted and these two"—I pointed at Hawke and Lincoln—"are working for you, then why have they been like ghosts? Since I've been at Court I've barely seen them." I just couldn't understand how they could have been monitoring me my whole life and still knew so little about me? They didn't even know that Bryan had lived in my bedroom for days. How could they have been protecting me when they didn't know anything about what was going on in my life?

"They were in fact still protecting you, but they were also investigating the Faction."

"That's another thing! What is the Faction? And who are my real parents if these two are fakes?" I was struggling to keep up with everything.

Drake shook his head. "I can't answer either of those questions until I get approval from the queen. The only reason we are having this conversation in the first place is because you drew attention to yourself when you questioned those Myrmidons in Quickfood. A Faction member must have overheard you; they know for sure you are their target. You might as well have just painted a bull's-eye on your forehead."

"But there was no one else in Quickfood to hear me." As I said this, I tried to picture the restaurant again. I was certain the group of Myrmidons were the only ones there. Had I been so distracted by the sight of my mom in a Guard's uniform that I had failed to notice someone else? "Are you sure one of the Myrmidons didn't let it slip to the Faction?"

"The Myrmidons are the queen's most trusted guards. Their job has always been to protect the Stavroses. To protect you."

The guards with the weird tattoos weren't part of the Faction after all, but they did work for the queen. My mind couldn't untangle it all.

"That woman in the jail cell, she wasn't some random criminal, Lady Stavros. She was sent by the Faction to kill you. Now that they have confirmation that you are the one they've been looking for, who knows what they will do next. You have to be more careful from now on."

"That woman said someone was going to kill her." I barely found my voice with all the revelations swirling in my mind. "Who?" Who on earth wanted me gone? As if my existence mattered to anyone but my closest friends.

Drake dropped his gaze to the floor and remained silent.

"What are you not telling me?" I asked again.

"It's none of your concern for the time being."

"Are you kidding me? That woman was trying to *kill* me. Someone sent her to kill me. And this was before they knew *for sure* that I was their target! At the very least I deserve to know who sent her."

"Yes. Someone sent that woman to kill you. She has spent every day since your attack crying and begging to be released. She's worried that her sons will be harmed. But that's really all I can tell you."

I opened my mouth, about to protest, when he held up one hand. "This concerns someone with greater power than all of us. Even the queen herself won't speak a word of it. I'm sure you have many questions still unanswered, Lady Stavros, but we can't tell you anything else right now."

There was no point in trying to get more out of him.

Drake went on to impress upon me that if I told anyone these secrets, not only would I be in danger, but they would be too. The only way to keep my friends safe was to lie to them.

I sat quietly for a moment as puzzle pieces fit together in my mind. So that's why I had been forced to sign a nondisclosure agreement before I was released from jail. I immediately recalled my conversation with Kris and Vlad when I told them about my encounter with the woman from the jail. Should I tell Drake that I had already let some information slip to my friends? What kind of danger were they in now because I couldn't keep my big mouth shut?

Before my thoughts could race any further, Drake handed me back my phone. I noticed there were numerous missed calls and texts from Vlad and Kris, as well as from Adrian—who was, thankfully, fine and had been released immediately after I'd been whisked away. I was forced to reply to all of them and tell them I was fine, not to worry, that it had been a misunderstanding about the terms of my release from jail.

I hated lying. But I had no other choice. The last thing I wanted was to put anyone's life in danger. Looking down at my phone as the messages of relief flooded in from Adrian, Vlad, and Kris, I saw another name farther down the screen. *Carlo.*

My dream. His voice mail. I had to know.

"What about Carlo?" I fixed my eyes on Drake and noticed that his expression faltered a little. "Was he killed because of me?" My voice barely sounded like my own; I could hardly spit out the question because I was so afraid of the answer, which I knew in my gut.

"Lord Ferraro—yes, he had discovered who you were when the Faction tried to get to you through him." Drake's voice leveled as he said this, making no effort to deliver the information less harshly. "He had hoped to escape with you, but they found out and killed him."

My stomach dropped. My worst fear was realized. I felt icy cold, but I had to press further. "What about Bryan? Was his death an accident—was it really a car accident, like it was in my dream?"

The look on Drake's face said it all. "We believe he was killed by the same people who killed Carlo. They had meant to kill you." Drake inclined his head to one side, a questioning look on his face. "But what do you mean 'like it was in my dream'?"

"I had a weird dream where I met both of them. I heard Carlo being tortured, but—" I swallowed hard. This was too much to handle, but I forced myself to get it out. "But with Bryan, I was there, riding shotgun, while he kept on driving faster, no matter how many times I told him to stop."

"And when was this?" His voice grew persistent, and when I told him, he let out several curse words. "This is what I've told Rhea about." He seemed to be talking to himself. I was surprised that he was calling our queen by her first name.

"Does that mean Bryan was sent to kill me and failed? Is that what got him killed?" I felt someone's hand on my shoulder, squeezing me as if trying to transfer energy. When I looked up, my eyes met Sera Lincoln's.

"No." Drake finally gave me a valid answer. "I don't know if I'm supposed to tell you, but, at the risk of you breaking into the library again and tearing another page out of a historical relic, I suppose it's better to inform you."

So he knew about my rendezvous with Adrian, but did he know what we were looking for? About our plan? I decided to keep my mouth tightly shut, and instead, I took a deep breath, preparing myself for what he was going to say.

"We were informed by the Moir"—Drake cleared his throat—"someone, that the spirits were coming here to disrupt the Gathering. One of them must have found you in your sleep."

"What happened to Bryan and Carlo in that dream wasn't real?"

"Maybe it was, maybe it wasn't. We mortals don't have the power to know for sure. All the deaths of non-Stavros that were caused by the Faction are considered collateral damage. We classify them as car accidents so as not to draw attention to the fact that the Faction still exists."

"Seriously? You don't think people are going to be suspicious if you just list the same cause of death over and over again?"

"Our goal here is to ensure that the Faction doesn't kill anybody else. Then we won't have to worry about people cluing into what's really going on." He opened the door, indicating our conversation was drawing to a close.

Fire and determination took me over. Burning rage hissed through my body like a deadly poison, demanding release. It was like a volcano ready to erupt; fury swept off me like ferocious waves. I did not care that I was a Stavros. I couldn't care less about the royal blood. All I could think about was the fact that two people died because of me.

They had died because of me.

I had to break all ties with the Hellenicus and the Court before anyone else got hurt.

Right before they let me leave, my father—or Hawke, I had to stop calling him Dad now—held my hand and, for a rare moment, his face showed parental concern. "I know it's tough, kiddo, but you're stronger than you think, and you will get through this."

His speech didn't work. A moment of kindness didn't erase the years of feeling unloved. And they had been lying to me the whole time. I didn't even have unloving parents—I had no family. I was truly alone—the last Stavros. How dare he try to tell me those horrible experiences growing up were to teach me lessons and then expect me to buy this act. Not going to happen.

Hawke started talking about how they intended to keep me safe, how he and Lincoln would take turns guarding me, and how we would continue to act like a family so no one would know the truth. He kept emphasizing how important it was to keep my identity secret, reiterating that I would put my friends in danger should they find out.

I barely listened. If they had been protecting my identity this whole time, how had that woman found out about me?

"Do you understand?" Hawke gave me that expectant look one more time. When I did not respond, he repeated himself. "You have to act normal, especially in front of your friends, and especially in front of Lady Ambrosia. It's best to keep them in the dark, that way they won't be harmed."

"Crystal clear. I need some time alone. I'll stay within the perimeter you're allowing me."

Without waiting for a response, I stormed past them. I couldn't stand to be there another second. I decided that I could not trust these people.

CHAPTER TWENTY-TWO

I couldn't face my friends just yet. No matter how much talking to them would help me process everything I had just learned, I simply could not risk anybody else getting hurt—not after finding out that what happened to Bryan and Carlo was essentially all my fault. I would never forgive myself if I put anyone else in danger.

I also wasn't ready to pretend like nothing had happened, which was what Drake, Hawke, and Lincoln were asking me to do. I had just been given a serious mental overload, so I spent the rest of the day alone in my room. As I paced my bedroom, pieces of the puzzle kept clicking into place. The very first night here I had been sick after taking one sip of wine from the Golden Chalice. Now it all made sense: Because I was a Pure Royal, I couldn't ingest the wine meant for the Regulars without feeling ill. No wonder I had passed out. And that time when Adrian and I had snuck into the library, that spirit Yew-la Bew-la or whatever her name was had let me in, and she even mentioned that it had been a while since my kind had been there. Had she meant Stavroses? Had she known all along? Then there was my dream about the Stavros door—had my subconscious somehow known the truth?

Eventually, I couldn't ignore the group texts any longer. Renata's party at Isles of the Blessed was apparently already in full swing. In Greek mythology, the Isles of the Blessed, or the Fortunate Isles, were a winterless earthly paradise. Only the heroes who had been reincarnated three times and were judged as being pure enough to gain entrance to Elysium (the afterlife) all three times could live there. At Court, Isles of the Blessed was a nightclub. I found it odd that the queen would allow such a prestigious name to be used for a nightclub. But, as I was discovering, not much seemed to make sense here at Court.

I pulled on a black T-shirt and black jeans and let my hair fall loose around my shoulders. I looked in the mirror and my fiery locks steeled me for the performance I would have to put on for my friends. I really hated this, but what choice did I have?

By the time I got to the club, it was already packed, nearly overcrowded with wall-to-wall people dancing to the music played by the DJ. Like a neon version of the northern lights, an array of blue, acid-green, hot-pink, and gold lights swirled beneath the dry-ice smoke in time with the music.

Kris and Domenico stood out in the crowd because, even though the rest of the crowd was jumping up and down, their hands in the air, the two of them were slow dancing, ignoring the loud music and everything going on around them. My heart dropped as I realized that getting rid of my soul-mate bond was more important than ever. Before finding out my true identity, I hadn't wanted a soul mate for selfish reasons. Mostly, I didn't want someone I barely knew inside my head at all hours of the day. But everything had changed now that I knew I was a Stavros. During the Great Massacre, even the Hellenicus who had a click with a Stavros were killed. I knew that I could never endanger someone by having that kind of connection with them.

I immediately pushed my way over to the sweethearts. "Ave! You made it!" Kris's heart-shaped face lit up with genuine happiness and my spirits lifted a little. Kris turned to Domenico, giving him a nod and a smile. Domenico returned her smile and left.

"Where is he going?" I asked my best friend once she turned back to face me.

"Oh, he asked if we wanted some drinks. I said yes."

I felt a pang. Another reason I could never tell Kris my secrets: Domenico would know too. My body was an empty shell. I'd have to distance myself from Kris if I was going to keep this huge secret from her—and Domenico.

It was a mistake to come here. I should have stayed in my room at the suite until I was able to come up with a proper escape plan.

"Ave, are you okay?"

Worry lines formed on Kris's forehead and I quickly gave her a reassuring smile. "I'm just a bit tired. Where's Adrian?" I had texted him numerous times before I left my suite, but he hadn't replied—calling his phone had only sent me to voice mail.

"I haven't seen Adrian, perhaps he's at the bar," she said.

Domenico returned and handed Kris her drink and then one to me. Their eyes met and there was that lovey-dovey look all over their faces. I knew to excuse myself from their moment. "Okay. I'm going to wander a bit. You guys have fun."

Kris's hand caught my arm as I was turning to leave. "Ave, you don't look okay. Do you want me to come with you?"

"No, I'm fine." I placed my hand on top of hers and squeezed a little to add more reassurance. "I'm going to find Adrian."

As I walked toward the bar, I downed the root beer Domenico had given me, letting the carbonated bubbles fizzle down my throat. I went up to the bar and ordered another one.

As I waited for my drink, I watched Kris and Domenico. I was glad they seemed to be enjoying the party. I nodded my thanks when the bartender came back with my order, and alone I watched the party as my muddled mind dulled a little with the noise.

Was I acting normal enough? Was I being watched by Court Guards or by a member of the Faction . . . or both?

I took the last big swig of my root beer and headed to the bathroom, which was at the end of a long, narrow hallway. And of course, the hallway was filled with couples making out, thinking somehow that this was more private than the dance floor. I squeezed my way through, trying my best to make my body as small as possible while ignoring various moans and groans. I couldn't help but cringe. As usual, the ladies' room had the longest line in history.

Twenty freaking minutes later, I walked out of the bathroom and pressed my way back through the crowded hallway. I was about to turn the corner when someone grabbed my wrists and pushed me up against the wall.

"Adrian—"

A pair of sensual lips pressed against mine with so much hunger. His hands wrapped around my waist, and he pulled my body toward his. As if in a trance, my lips responded to his kiss as my body responded to his touch. It was as if my brain had caught on fire and the warmth spread throughout my entire body. Just then, my senses came back to me and I put my hand on his chest, pushing him away with all my might. He stumbled back.

"What in Poseidon's name are you doing?" Wide eyed and full of anger, as well as confusion, I stared at him. My hand reached up to my lips.

"I was so worried about you. You're okay. Oh hail Zeus, you're okay!"

"Of course I am."

Adrian looked at me with desperation in his eyes. I could sense how nervous he was. "Do you want to know something, Montgomery?"

"If you promise not to kiss me again, *yes*."

"I'm afraid I might be falling in love with you." His words came tumbling out, and for a split second, I didn't register what he was saying until his words replayed in my mind in slow motion—one by one.

"What?"

Both of his hands, gentle and warm as ever, reached up. One brushed my hair back, then settled there while the other cupped my cheek. There was such an innate connection that even with a simple touch, he managed to pull all my thoughts to a stop. He held my gaze, stealing the passion from my eyes in a way that only magnified the spark. There was no smile on his lips, only the hot intensity of his gaze, and I somehow knew that this was a sign of an incoming storm. "I think I'm falling in love with you, Montgomery," he repeated.

The acceleration of my heart rate indicated what my body really wanted. What it craved.

"Adrian, I—"

A sudden movement caught the corner of my eye. And that was when I saw him. Vladimir. His dark-green eyes stared coldly at me and his jaw was tense. Before I could react, he walked away.

"Adrian, listen. You're drunk. Go home and drink lots of water, okay?"

"Yes, ma'am." He grinned goofily.

Then I followed Vlad—or at least tried to. There were too many people, and just when I caught his silhouette walking out the door with the exit sign on top, I felt a pair of big hands on my waist. I turned expecting to see Adrian again, though the hands felt different, and sweaty—it was Damian Tavoularis and his haughty smile. A low voice rumbled next to my throat. "We have to stop running into each other like this." His hands pulled me back against him and I elbowed backward at him.

"Eww, go away!" I rushed forward through the crowd and out the exit. Thankfully, I spotted Vlad walking back toward the Royal Quarters and I chased after him, my feet slipping on the sidewalk covered in fresh snow. I barreled into him and his arms caught me. We paused for a moment like that, feeling the warmth of each other, but then he let me go as I regained my footing.

"Look, please don't be angry. I don't know what's wrong with me. It's like my body just yearns for Adrian's."

"Thanks for letting me know," he said.

"No, listen. My body wants him, my heart's connected to you."

"Avery, it's okay. We're not in a relationship or anything. You can kiss whomever you want. We had a kiss, and you've had one with Adrian. I get it. If you want to kiss a bunch of guys, that's your prerogative. I really don't care, now run along will you?" he said.

It seemed like these last few days didn't matter. He turned back into the jerk he had been before. So I did what I have always done in the past: I shrugged off his words as if they didn't hurt and walked away.

CHAPTER TWENTY-THREE

I spent the night pushing the conversation I had had with Vlad out of my mind. Instead, I focused on what I needed to do to move forward with my plan. It didn't matter if I was a Stavros. The show must go on. If anything, I had even more drive now. I knew I couldn't lose sight of my mission.

With newfound determination, I raced to Adrian's suite. His maid, Althea, opened the door to let me in, and like before, I found him naked and sprawled on his king-sized bed—except today, he was alone. The morning sun filtered through a crack in the drapery and stretched a pillar of light onto the thick grey covers covering the bottom half of his body.

"Adrian." I tried waking him up. I tried again a little louder, but it still didn't work. I would've shaken him, but I wanted to avoid any physical contact. If I had learned anything this past month, it was that physical contact with Adrian was proving to be dangerous what with all of my newly Awakened feelings. Then an idea struck me. I pulled out my phone and set the alarm before putting it on the nightstand. It worked like magic: the second the alarm rang, he abruptly sat up on his bed, blinking rapidly as his eyes tried to adjust.

"Montgomery?"

"Yes, the one and only."

"What are you doing here?"

"I want to talk to you."

"Can this wait?"

"Nope," I said. "You've done this to me numerous times before. It's only fair for me to return the favor."

"But I'm naked."

"And I don't care." When he was about to doze off again, I clapped loudly to regain his attention. "Adrian, I'm going through with the plan. We're going to do it in three days. And you have to help me gather all the supplies we need to burn down the tree."

He yawned. "Okay."

"Also." I breathed in and out. "After we do it, I'm okay if you come with me."

"Are you serious?" He was awake now.

"Yes."

He opened his arms, about to wrap them around me, but I quickly stood up, and he fell into his bed instead. I tried hard not to be affected by his behind on display. "But we're going as friends. No trying to kiss me like you did last night. We'll wait to see what happens after we get rid of the gift. Maybe our feelings will change, maybe they won't. But we'll deal with that later."

Adrian had recovered and leaned back against the head of his bed with a smile on his face. I expected him to argue with me, but all he said was, "Okay."

Sometimes I forgot that with Adrian there was no need to complicate things. I smiled and copied him. "Okay."

Ω

I avoided leaving my room as much as possible after solidifying my plans with Adrian. Hawke and Lincoln checked on me every now and then, but I still needed time to process everything, so I kept our interactions short.

It was around five o'clock in the afternoon when I received a text from Kris telling me that Vlad would come get me for dinner. I quickly hit the call button. She seemed to be expecting that because she answered on the first tone. "What's up?"

"Do you seriously want to torture me or something?"

"What?" She sounded innocent, perhaps a little *too* innocent.

"Why are you asking your brother to take me to dinner? Please, for the love of your ancestor Poseidon, stop trying to set me up with your brother. It won't happen. Trust me."

"Ave, it's not like that. Maybe I should've been clearer—I mean he'll meet you at the Hyped and walk with you to the Royal Quarters so you can have dinner with my family. It's still not safe for you to be alone, Ave."

She had no idea how unsafe it really was.

"Of course, if you want to invite your mom and dad, they are more than welcome. And I'll tell Vlad he doesn't need to escort you after all."

I suddenly felt dumb. What was I thinking? How could I jump ahead and think Kris was still trying to set me up with her brother over a simple dinner invitation? Was it possible that I was secretly hoping—*Stop it, Avery!* I pushed away the thought and inhaled deeply. "Right. Of course. Sounds great. See you later, then."

Just as I hung up the phone, there was a firm knock on my bedroom door before it swung open and Lincoln stepped inside. "Hey, I'm sorry to bother you." She smiled nervously. "But do you need anything?"

If this was a month ago, back when I had no clue I was a Stavros, I would've done a backflip if my mom had knocked on the door instead of just letting herself in uninvited. Now, here she was knocking *and* apologizing for knocking.

"No." I shook my head. "Not unless you can give me answers about my real parents."

The look on Lincoln's face when I said the word *real* was almost as if I had stabbed her in the heart. I had spent all my life believing that she hadn't cared for me, and seeing her reaction made me wonder if she actually did care after all and had just pretended not to. I quickly brushed that thought away, though. If she cared, she wouldn't have made my life miserable by picking a fight every chance she could get.

Still, I felt bad for hurting her. Whatever happened in the past, Lincoln and Hawke had spent eighteen years of their life protecting me. They could've had their own lives instead of putting them on hold. A thought came up and I knew how I could make it up to her for now.

"Do you want to go to the Ambrosias' for dinner with me? Kris just called. They've invited us over to their place at the Royal Quarters."

Lincoln blinked. She had probably expected another harsh statement. "Sure. I'll let your father—I mean, I'll let Hawke know."

"Okay." Well, that wasn't difficult. At least I wouldn't have to spend alone time with Vlad now. I pushed myself up from the bed and texted Kris to let her know that I didn't need Vlad to babysit me after all.

Ω

I had been wrong. Even though I had come with my parents and didn't have to endure walking to the Royal Quarters with Vlad, I still had to try to ignore his presence once we got to the Ambrosias' suite.

That was hard to do when I could feel him watching me throughout dinner. Yet every time I looked up, his gaze was on his plate or anywhere else but on me.

Was I imagining it?

About the seventh time I felt his stare, I looked up and my eyes finally caught his. He was blatantly staring. Neither of us broke away until Kris nudged me, asking if I was all right.

"I need to use the restroom." Although it was a lie, I excused myself from the table anyway and made my way to the bathroom. I locked the door behind me and sat on the closed seat of the toilet for one full minute. I stood, hit the flush button, and washed my hands, dedicated to my white lie. When I opened the bathroom door, I found Vlad leaning against the wall by the door.

Without saying anything, I turned left, heading for the dining room when his words stopped me in my tracks. "I'm sorry."

I was convinced I had misheard him. "You're—what?"

"I'm sorry. I shouldn't have said the things I said to you the other night." He shook his head, looking both dejected and regretful. "I was out of line."

"It's fine."

His eyes searched mine for the truth. Before things got awkward, I spun on my heels and left him standing there. No one seemed to notice that Vlad and I had both been missing except Kris, who looked at me questioningly. I gave her a tiny head shake.

Later that evening, as Hawke and Lincoln were thanking Jane and Kristov for their hospitality, I pulled Kris into a tight hug. It was heavier than any hug we had ever had. I remained like that for a long while, knowing that this was probably the last time I would ever see her. Once the tree had been burned down, I would run away with Adrian as a fugitive, leaving this part of my life behind. There was no one I would miss more than my best friend. Kris seemed to pick up on how strangely I was acting. Her eyes questioned me once I let go. I didn't have an explanation for her, so I simply gave her a meek smile. Vlad was nowhere to be seen, probably in his father's office working on files, which was fine by me because somehow I felt that if he had seen that hug, he would've been able to guess that it was a good-bye.

Ω

I locked myself in my room for most of the next day, preparing myself mentally and physically for what Adrian and I were going to do tomorrow. Neither Lincoln nor Hawke pushed me to go to any other activities in the schedule; it seemed that they agreed that me being home was the best way to keep me safe for now. I wasn't sure what excuse they had given the officials, but I didn't really care. I had other things to focus on.

My partner in crime, however, had a different idea. He showed up at my door around seven o'clock in the evening with a crazy idea. "I think we should celebrate it."

"Celebrate what, exactly?" Both Lincoln and Hawke had received a phone call about an hour ago and left after telling me to stay put. Their words were less harsh than back when I had thought they were my real parents, but it was an order nonetheless.

"Our freedom."

I blew out a heavy, "Hmm," and walked to the kitchen to pour myself a glass of water. "Yeah, no. I don't want to celebrate anything when we have yet to accomplish it."

"Oh come on, Montgomery. Let's hit Royal Bar or Isles of the Blessed."

"Nope." I drank then put the glass on the kitchen island.

"Fine. Then let's do whatever you have in mind."

"Err, nope." I moved to the couch and sat with a sigh. "Adrian, why are you here?"

His expression turned serious as he took the empty seat beside me. "I heard you went to dinner with Vlad again."

He wasn't exactly wrong. "And?"

"I'm just—" He ran his hand through his hair and sighed loudly. "I'm just checking you don't have cold feet."

"My feet are toasty warm." When his face didn't look convinced, I continued, "Look, I don't know what you're thinking, but nothing's going on between me and Vlad. Yes, I had dinner with him, but it wasn't just the two of us. My parents were there, his parents were there, Kris was there."

Adrian's frown turned into a boyish smile. "Okay."

"Besides," I felt the need to remind him, "didn't I tell you that we would start slow? That we would be friends first."

"Yeah, I know. I was just worried when Domenico told me Vlad was picking you up for dinner last night that you were going to change your mind."

"You thought wrong." Suddenly I felt more exhausted than I'd ever felt before.

Adrian was about to say something when Lincoln and Hawke walked through the door. They were surprised to see him. Hawke lifted one brow, looking expectantly at me. I gave him a shrug.

Lincoln was the first to break the ice. "Lord Ambrosia, I didn't expect to see you here. Would you like a cup of tea or coffee?"

Player or not, Adrian suddenly looked very nervous in front of my "parents."

"No, thank you, Mrs. Montgomery. I'm about to leave, actually." He turned to me. "I'll see you tomorrow?"

"Yeah."

Adrian nodded at my reply, and after saying farewell to Lincoln and Hawke, he left.

"What is he doing here?" Lincoln muttered under her breath

without directing the question to anyone. I stood up and moved back to my bedroom, leaving the two of them with their questions. I was going to try to make it an early night.

Maybe it was the nervousness, but I found myself wide awake at two in the morning. And apparently claustrophobic as well, as I felt that it was getting hard to breathe inside my own unit. Perhaps I was starting to go stir crazy. After tossing and turning to no avail, I finally swung my legs out of the covers and got out of bed.

I tiptoed out and took my coat from the hanger with one hand while the other carried my boots. Once I was standing in the elevator and on my way down, I put my coat and boots on. I pulled my coat tight as I walked across the lobby and out the front sliding doors. My gaze fell to the oak tree in the garden at the center of the Court. Twinkling lights had been placed on each branch, like it was a makeshift Christmas tree. I found myself compelled to walk toward it just like the day I first arrived at Court.

Up close, I felt the peace I'd been longing for. My chest no longer felt tight, and I could breathe normally. I looked up to see that many flowers had bloomed; they looked like tiny ornaments.

I felt his presence before I heard his voice.

"You were called by Dodona, too, huh?" He walked closer until we were side by side.

"What do you mean?"

Vlad bobbed his chin toward the oak tree before us. "Legend has it that the tree whispers things to those who can hear it." The lights from the tree cast shadows and made him look mysterious. "Were you called?"

"No," I replied curtly. When he didn't say anything yet continued to stand there beside me, I couldn't help asking, "What are you doing here?"

"I was going to the fish pond, it's my favorite place. But then I saw you."

"And?" I sneered, still avoiding eye contact. "You saw me and you thought I wanted company?"

"No. I'm probably the last person you want to talk to."

"Then why are you here?"

"Because I keep my promises, and I promised my sister I would keep you safe, so here I am."

I replied, "That promise is null and void. You don't have to bother yourself with this anymore." When he didn't move, I added, "Just walk away, Vlad." I didn't see it coming until his hands were on my arms. "What are you doing?"

"You're so stupid." His low voice laced with desperation. In any other circumstance, I would've argued until his ears bled how he was more stupid than me. Yet something in his voice made me stay quiet. Then, with a voice filled with agony, as if it took everything in him to say it, he uttered three words I never thought I would hear from my nemesis, Vladimir Ambrosia. "I love you."

He leaned in, and our lips were mere breaths away, and my heart beat faster and faster as he inched closer. I felt the velvety brush of his lips on mine before he jerked upward as if he'd just kissed molten lava. "I can't."

"Why?" I asked, startled by the desperation in my voice that trounced the curiosity.

"It's complicated." He shook his head, frowning. Despite the chilly air, he was sweating. "Let's just leave it at that."

"Are you serious?" I threw my hands up in the air. "You just confessed your love for me, nearly kissed me before suddenly pushing me away, and all you have to offer as an explanation is 'it's complicated'? What is it? What is it that you're not telling me?"

"I can't, Avy. Just forget what I said."

"No," I stubbornly answered, holding my ground.

"Just drop it."

"No," I repeated, and inched closer, closing the distance between us. "Tell me."

"Damn it. Stop." He raised his hand to stop me, yet his feet did not move.

"Spill." I moved closer.

"Holy Poseidon, I've made a promise! I can't—" He closed his eyes for a brief moment, and when he opened them again, determination flared in them as he sighed. "I just can't."

"What promise?"

"It's nothing. None of your business," he said.

Damn. That hurt. "Fine." I lifted both of my hands, raising my white flag as I backed away a few steps. "Whatever."

Later today, once the sun was up and everyone was at the Panhellenic Festival's closing ceremony, Adrian and I were going to execute our plan. This was it. No turning back now. I told myself that Vlad was right. It was none of my goddamn business. I should let it go. Let him go.

CHAPTER TWENTY-FOUR

This was it. This would be the day I finally got what I'd been wanting for as long as I could remember. With only two days until my birthday, I had to act fast. Dressed in a black hoodie and jeans, I waited for Adrian under the Whispering Oak. As expected, everyone was at the closing ceremony of the Panhellenic Festival, and most of the Court Guards were patrolling the stadium.

Where was Adrian? My fingers fought against the cold as I sent him another text.

I heard a rustle coming from the tree, then a voice brought by the wind. Just like the first day, it felt as if the tree was speaking to me. I thought back to what Vlad had said to me early this the morning while the rest of the Court was sleeping. *Legend has it that the tree whispers things to those who can hear it.* Was the tree trying to tell me something?

"Whatever you are trying to tell me," I whispered back, "it won't work. I'm still going to burn you down." A pit formed in my stomach. I knew a tree was a living thing, but was the Whispering Oak of Dodona more alive than a regular tree? Would I be killing its spirit too?

The tree was even more beautiful than the day I had first seen it, now full of buds and blooms. Which of these flowers represented Kris and Domenico? Their happiness had blossomed instantaneously—would Kris ever forgive me for destroying this symbol of their love?

My hand slid into my pocket and pulled out the folded photo of me and Bryan. I stared into his eyes, suddenly desperate for his presence. "Things would be so much easier if you were here, Bryan."

I heard footsteps and quickly shoved the photograph back into my pocket. Adrian had finally arrived. "What took you so—"

It wasn't Adrian. It was Damian. The last person in the world I wanted to see right now.

"I've found you alone at last."

"And I want it to stay that way. Now walk away!"

Before I could say another word, there was a blur of motion and I caught sight of a dagger as it was plunged straight into my stomach. I was thrust backward, staggering, and fell to the ground. Pain radiated from my belly, and my chest became tight. I pressed my hand against the wound and felt wetness. I put both hands against the ground and tried to push myself up, but before I could sit up properly, he grabbed the collar of my hoodie and slapped me repeatedly. When he was satisfied, he grabbed me by my hair and dragged me away.

"I'll make my family proud, you know. I've finally caught the last Stavros. All I have to do now is bring you to the Faction, then they'll crown me as their leader."

My face stung; I could feel his handprints all over my face. My stomach bled as I tried to struggle against his grip. Through blurry vision, my eyes met a pair of green ones. It was only a split second before the figure vanished. My eyes fluttered closed, the darkness enveloping me, and I had no power left to fight.

The pain burned like fire, then slowly faded to an icy numbness. My breath came in ragged shallow gasps. I heard footsteps, then voices. I felt people swarming around me, trying to save me.

My consciousness was floating through an empty space filled with infinite darkness and my heartbeat echoed in my ears. I wanted to be saved. Three familiar faces came into my vision. The three strange ladies from the Hyped—but they were dressed differently. Instead of the usual dull-brown uniform like the rest of the Court workers, they were now cloaked in white robes. Their skin was blistered and their eyes were bloodshot. Each of them had one hand on me, the other reaching out to the oak.

My vision went black again. I lost time; I felt nothing but numbness.

Then I saw Adrian. His dark-blond hair was messier than usual. His emerald eyes were in pain. I longed to be in his arms, to feel his soft kiss on my lips. I longed for my body to feel the fire that I had felt when he had kissed me, his exploring hands ravishing wherever he could touch.

Then his face was gone and darkness returned.

Now Vlad's worried face appeared before me, a deep frown settled between his brows. He, too, looked like he was suffering. And all I wanted was to comfort him—to make his pain go away.

I did not want to die. Even if it meant that I would spend the rest of my life continuously being hunted down for being the ancestor of Hades.

Everything went black once more until I heard a woman's voice. I couldn't grasp the meaning of what she was saying, but I strained to hear anyway.

"You came!"

"Of course. How could I miss the rare chance to see my little sister?"

Then the voices wafted away.

"There are different types of love," the first voice said.

Blackness and deathly quiet.

Then the first voice came again: "*She*'s going to kill me."

Finally, a voice I realized was my own spoke, "This was all your fault!"

A concerned face appeared in my vision. The last face I expected to see, but it soothed me just to behold her. Queen Rhea. I could feel her hand on mine as she whispered for me to please wake up.

I knew I was dreaming then. And just as I realized this, I regained consciousness.

Kris was the first person I saw the moment I was able to lift my heavy lids. She was beside my hospital bed, her hand in mine, looking down at me with sadness in her eyes. I saw her eyes widen, not believing what she was seeing: me looking back at her.

"You're awake!" She jumped to her feet, hands covering her mouth as happy tears streamed down her heart-shaped face. "I've prayed to every god imaginable to bring you back. Someone must've heard me." She hugged me and I winced in pain, but I was grateful to be awake, to be with her, to rejoin the land of the living.

"What happened?" I pushed myself up into a sitting position with Kris's help. "I mean, I know. I think—" I paused for a second. My head was throbbing, and I felt a little disoriented. The pain felt like someone had taken a baseball bat to my skull.

"Ave, are you okay? Should I get the nurses now?" Kris sounded frantic.

"I'm okay, I'm okay," I said, trying to calm her down. "I think it was Damian. Was it?"

"Yes. I still can't believe it. But you're safe. He's in prison, he can't hurt you again."

Though I wasn't sure about the safe part, I was glad he had at least been arrested. "He sure takes rejection badly," I joked.

"I know everything, Ave. I've been told that you are a Stavros and that he's a member of the Faction."

My eyes widened in shock.

"They ordered him to kill you after their attempt in jail failed. Hudson and Drake are investigating how the Faction knew your real identity. They believe Damian has an accomplice and could be used as a source to catch all the Faction members. If Vlad wasn't there, I don't know what would've happened."

"Wait, Vlad was there?"

"He was leaving the Court on his way back to the trial he's been working on all month when he saw Damian dragging you to his car. He called Commander Hudson."

"I must thank him." I made a mental note then turned my attention to her and noticed light glittering off of a gold band with one square diamond encircling Kris's ring finger. "Oh my Zeus! Don't tell me that's what I think that is!"

My best friend blushed. Holding one hand up, with tears glimmering in her eyes, she said, "Domenico proposed." She continued, "We're not going to get married right now, or next year, or even in the next two years. I don't know when. But we're engaged!"

"I'm so happy for you!" I shook my head in disbelief that I had missed all of this. "Engaged at eighteen, at your first Gathering!" She giggled at that and I gave her a gentle hug, mindful of my wound. "I want details! Tell me how he proposed."

"The second he thought of asking, I knew." Kris giggled. "And then he knew my answer. But I said it anyway: 'Domenico, I love you. It's a definite yes.' And voilà! Ring on my finger."

"You've got to be kidding me." Before I could ask any more questions, we heard a knock at the door and watched as Hudson stepped inside. I rested my head back on the pillow as he was followed by Hawke and Lincoln.

"I see that you haven't lost your way with words, Lady Stavros." Hudson using my new name in front of Kris brought goose bumps;

it felt more real now that they were openly acknowledging it. I wasn't sure I'd ever be comfortable being called lady after growing up as a Regular.

"Thank you for your concern, it's greatly appreciated." I nodded at Hawke and Lincoln, who stood behind him. "What are you two doing here? Don't tell me you've been worried too."

Hudson answered for them. "They have. I figured the only way to shut up their incessant questions about your well-being was to bring them here so they could see you with their own eyes."

I thought I was just a case to them. A job. But their expressions proved me wrong. There were tears in Lincoln's eyes, and Hawke hardened his jaw to keep his mouth from trembling.

"Since you two want to see me, why don't you come take a closer look?" They both moved to the side of my bed. Once they were close enough, I flung my arms around them and pulled them into a three-way hug. I knew that they didn't love me the way parents did a child, but I also knew that they did care for me in their own ways. And for now, that was enough.

Hudson clenched his jaw, eyeing me and crossing his arms. I knew something was troubling him. Sure enough, once the tender moment was over, he came forward. There was urgency in his voice when he spoke. "Once you're feeling well enough, the queen has requested you attend an audience with her."

"May I ask why?" I said, surprised and also a little concerned.

Lincoln gasped. "You just received a royal invitation! You don't question it."

"Isn't it better if I know what she wants? To prepare?" I asked.

"It's classified."

Lincoln whispered under her breath. "You're supposed to say, 'I accept.'"

"Fine. I accept. Thank you. Why does all this royal business have to be so complicated, anyway?"

Then I suddenly remembered seeing the queen by my side in my dream—or what I'd thought was a dream. She seemed to care for me in that moment. Then I recalled that look she'd given me at the Awakening Ceremony on the first day. She had probably known then that I was the last Stavros. I wondered if she had known my parents? I had so many questions for her.

Soon, Hudson, Lincoln, and Hawke left, their work taking them away and leaving me alone with Kris once more. When Kris finally had to leave as well, I was forced to stare at the ceiling, wishing my recovery would speed up. Kris had promised me that she would bring me my book tomorrow so that I wouldn't be so bored here at the Court Hospital now that I had regained consciousness.

It was close to midnight when I heard noises on the other side of the door. Was it the Faction? Had they found out that I was still alive and Damian had been arrested? Had they sent someone else to finish the job? I double-checked my surroundings, trying to find anything I could use as a weapon to defend myself. My eyes fell on the fruit basket someone had sent to me. No, I refused to throw fruit at them. I looked for an alternative and decided that the trash bin would have to do.

I gingerly crawled out of bed and grabbed the bin with both hands as I waited for the assassin to come in. When the door swung opened, I threw the trash bin, unfortunately causing Lady Jane Ambrosia, who was holding a lit-up birthday cake, to stumble backward. If Domenico hadn't been behind her, I doubt there would still be a cake.

"Sorry." I moved back toward the bed then sat on it.

"Well, that didn't go as planned." Jane shrugged it off, then beamed, she and the rest of the slightly stunned crew behind her starting to sing "Happy Birthday" to me.

When the song was finished, Jane said, "We're still waiting for more people. They're bringing up the gifts. They'll be here in a bit." Everyone continued to sing—but this time in Greek—to stall while we waited.

I peeked at the clock; it was two minutes until midnight. As if on cue, right when the Greek version of the song finished and the minute hand of the clock passed twelve, the door swung open. Vlad and Adrian walked in carrying gifts, which they placed on the nightstand before coming over to my bedside. Vlad went to my right and Adrian to my left. They each held one of my hands and wished me a happy birthday. And that was when it happened. It was like the sound of a pin dropping. No, it was more like a door being opened. Now that I'd heard it in my head, I knew why it was called the click.

I looked up at Adrian and Vlad. They both looked like they'd heard it too.

What is this?

Montgomery, is this happening?

Birthday cake and candles forgotten.

The two guys stared at me and I didn't know where to put my eyes because I hadn't expected this to happen. I *didn't* want this to happen. But the gods, once again, ignored my wishes. Maybe they'd known my plan to burn down Zeus's precious tree. Perhaps this was their way of punishing me for even thinking about doing something so drastic. My eyes found my best friend, who was looking between the three of us, confusion all over her face. "Could one of you please explain what the hell is going on?"

Then, before I could answer, both Vlad and Adrian said, "Avery and I just had a click."

Now everyone's eyes were on me.

Jane blew out the candles on my cake and set it down on the nightstand beside my gifts before ushering everyone out of the room, leaving me alone with Vlad and Adrian. Jane closed the door behind her, giving me a sheepish look as she did so.

Not knowing how to proceed, I fix my gaze straight ahead, not looking at either of the guys standing on either side of my bed. "Okay, look, having you two in my head is really weird."

What? Why don't I hear her thoughts in mind? Isn't this supposed to be a two-way bond?

"Who just thought that?" I asked.

Adrian looked at Vlad, then turned to me and raised his hand. "I did."

Are you able to read my thoughts, Vlad?

Vlad answered with a curt nod.

"Okay." I scratched my head. "Vlad can hear my thoughts?"

I tried to send another message to confirm. *Well, this is awkward.*

Vlad nodded his confirmation. "You think that this is awkward."

"Yes." I looked at Adrian, who was watching me expectantly. "Okay, you know the whole drill about me wanting to break free, so I'm gonna explain to Vlad."

The second the thought was in my head, Vlad said, "Okay. I got it. You both were planning to burn the tree."

Both of our jaws dropped on the hospital floor. "Geez, Zeus, so that's how it works?! This is a—"

"—total breach of privacy." Vlad finished my sentence.

"Okay, you." I pointed at Vlad. "No more reading my mind or being cocky about it."

Then to both of them—ignoring the fact that Vlad got it before I even opened my mouth—I finally said, "I didn't even want one soul mate to begin with, and now the gods have given me two. Let's just make a pack. I won't kiss you." I looked at Adrian, who quickly groaned. "And I won't kiss you either." I looked at Vlad, who shrugged as if it was not a big deal. Adrian's groan ceased once he heard my last sentence. "Good. Now I really need a good sleep. My whole body is sore."

"Um, Montgomery." Something was off. He was different, perhaps slightly nervous. "I'm sorry I was late."

It took me a minute to get what he was referring to. "Oh."

"Yeah. Althea told me that Caitlin had gotten worse all of a sudden and that I needed to get to the hospital ASAP." Adrian's face was in utter torment.

"It's okay, Adrian." It seemed to be pointless arguing about the past as it wouldn't change anything. Furthermore, I couldn't blame him for caring about his little sister. "Is she okay?"

"No. I mean, yes, Caitlin is all right. Althea lied, Montgomery. She was one of them."

I shook my head. "I don't understand."

"I found out Althea has been spying on us this whole time. She found out about our plan. She knew you would be at the tree during the Panhellenic closing ceremonies," Adrian explained.

I knew I had heard something that day at the suite when Adrian and I first came up with the idea to burn down the tree. She must have followed him then. I felt so stupid; I should have been more careful.

"She told me that things at the hospital had gotten worse. But Caitlin had been released. When I confronted Althea, she told me I was spending too much time with you and she knew that telling me something had happened to Caitlin was the only way to get me away from you." He shook his head. "Obviously that raised alarm bells. Why would she care about us hanging out? She never gave a shit who I hung out with." Adrian paused. "When I discovered what had happened to you, I put two and two together and it made more sense."

"She was the only one, other than you, who knew where I would be," I added.

"Exactly. So, I reported her to the Court Guards. Hawke and Lincoln had already suspected her when they saw her leaving your suite one day. She's being held at Court Guard Headquarters under heavy surveillance and in line for questioning. I'm so sorry I wasn't there, Avery."

"Holy Zeus." I had no other words. Damian, Althea, and the woman from jail had all managed to infiltrate the "heavily guarded" Court walls. I wondered how many more Faction members were still hiding in the Court, waiting for a chance to strike?

"It's okay, Montgomery. You're safe now."

Was I safe? Would this be the last time I had to go through this?

Carlo's voice mail suddenly replayed inside my head again:

Avery, you have to run. The Court isn't safe. You are in grave danger there. The Faction will find you and you won't stand a chance against them. There are things that you don't know—that I wouldn't know if I hadn't found your file in my father's safe. Come to Seattle and I'll show you. I'll explain everything. But now you have to ru—

It now made perfect sense. As long as I was here, I wasn't safe. At the same time, wouldn't I be in greater danger outside the Court walls? I couldn't tell who was a friend and who was an enemy.

"I know."

Maybe he had heard what had crossed my mind or he could feel it in his heart—whatever it was, Vlad suddenly held my hand and whispered so low that only I could hear, "I know it's hard. But if you don't trust anyone, not your friends, not your family, then what's the point?"

They both bid me good-bye and left. Right before Vlad closed the door, I called him. He stuck his head back in. "Thank you for saving my life."

Of course, Avy.

Ω

I remained in the Court Hospital for three more days with both Lincoln and Hawke lingering. It was awful. I had missed the Christmas celebrations, and the hospital had been eerily quiet with everyone celebrating in the garden where the famous Oak of Dodona had already been decorated. With my current predicament, I couldn't go anywhere. There were even two Court Guards standing outside my door at all times.

When the doctor finally cleared me, my joy at finally being released was ruined immediately when the whole team—including Commander Drake and Officer Warwick—came to pick me up and take me to the palace to meet with the queen. I had forgotten her request. Being pushed through the hospital halls in the wheelchair with Court Guards securing the area made me feel uncomfortable, so I kept my head ducked throughout the journey. No matter how much I asserted that I was perfectly capable of walking, they insisted on driving me to the palace. The drive itself didn't take a long time, but the security check certainly did. They were very thorough; they even checked Commander Drake and the other Court Guards. After two hours, we were allowed to proceed. Two Palace Guards walked beside us as they took us to the Throne Hall.

Queen Rhea Christoulakis had been waiting for me. Everyone in my entourage bowed the second we were in her presence, but before I could even attempt to bow in my wheelchair, she stopped me. She was as perfect as the first time I had laid eyes on her. Her blond hair was styled in a chignon with a few loose strands curling along the side of her jaw and landing softly on her shoulders. The blue dress that she was wearing complemented the blue Christoulakis eyes that regarded me carefully.

"Lady Stavros." The queen greeted me with a smile. I still wasn't used to my new name, and having her address me as lady was particularly overwhelming. For a second I almost thought she was speaking to someone else. But I was the only Stavros alive, so that wouldn't be possible.

"Your Majesty." I tried to keep my voice steady and pleasant.

She launched right into why she had brought me here so urgently. "As you now know, you're the last remaining Stavros, which is why these Special Court Guards have been guarding you throughout your life." Everything she stated was information I already knew, but I kept my mouth shut as I listened to her further. "The Stavroses died for a meaningless cause." The queen closed her eyes briefly, and when she opened them, they were filled with sadness as she continued, "I still blame myself for my lack of ability to protect everyone."

She looked remorseful, but I honestly couldn't blame her for what had happened to my bloodline. The killings had taken place over many generations, starting with the Great Massacre. Besides, the Hellenicus lived all over the world. I understood how hard it must be to keep track of each and every one of us over multiple generations.

"Keeping you alive is now my utmost priority. And since there is no safer place than the palace, I'm inviting you to live here."

Live in the palace?

I knew I couldn't cuss in front of the queen. Remembering what Lincoln had said about always accepting a royal invitation, I tried to sound grateful for the offer as I responded, "I'd be honored, Your Majesty." I couldn't help backpedaling. "However, if I lived at the palace, would I still have my freedom?"

The queen smiled as if she knew what I was getting at. "Yes. Of course. You can leave the palace whenever you like. But you can only go as far as the Court gate."

Forgetting formalities, I blurted out, "Wait, what? Why?"

"Because you are in great danger, my child. You were nearly killed, and it happened inside the protective walls of this Court." She shifted her icy gaze to Hudson, making him grimace. "I will not take any more chances. You'll be guarded by these two." She gave pointed looks to Officer Warwick and the guy standing next to him. "Officer Brad Warwick, whom you probably already know, and this is Officer Joseph Hudson."

Had she just said Hudson? I looked at Commander Pete Hudson and he winked at me. Holy Poseidon! Were they brothers?

"I will protect her with my own life, Your Majesty," Officer Warwick said with a voice filled with determination, and I could see that he meant every word.

"However, I'd like to appoint one more person to guard you." Queen Rhea signaled to the Palace Guards and they opened the door, revealing a girl with blond hair and similar facial features to the queen. "This is your additional guard, Scarlet Christoulakis." She paused for a heartbeat before adding, "My daughter."

My jaw dropped and I noticed Hudson's did too. Hudson was the first to recover. "Scar, what are you doing here?" From his tone it was clear that he knew her, and from the way he used a nickname instead of her title—Lady Scarlet Christoulakis—it was also clear that he had known her for quite a long time. Scarlet was not a princess because according to our law, the next queen would be chosen by the gods, not by lineage.

Lady Scarlet only looked a little older than me. I couldn't believe that Queen Rhea had a daughter so close in age to me. I guess the queen just looked much younger than she actually was. Pure Royal beauty treatments, I supposed.

Scarlet smiled. "Why, Petros? Do you really need to ask?" She gave me a once-over. "Time to put my training into practice, of course."

Petros? Why did that name sound so familiar? I looked at everyone, expecting someone to tell me that this was all some kind of joke. Instead, the queen concluded the meeting just as abruptly as she began it. "You all may leave."

Commander Pete Hudson bowed. He may have been in a hurry to get back to his life, but I was still figuring out my new life and had so many questions that were still unanswered.

"Your Majesty, please." There was desperation in my plea. "I was told only you could answer all the questions I have." Where should I even begin? I took a breath. "Where are my parents?" Queen Rhea seemed hesitant, but I wasn't about to give up. "Please. I need to know."

"Yes. You deserve to know. But please understand some things must remain a secret for now. They say ignorance is bliss, but in your case, Lady Stavros, ignorance could mean safety."

I nodded in response. I would take whatever information I could get.

Queen Rhea reached out and held my hand, which only made me even more nervous about what I was about to hear. "All I can tell you is that after the Great Massacre, the killing didn't stop—as you know. The Faction tracked down any remaining Stavroses throughout the centuries until there were only five families left. We were left with no choice but to establish an order of our own, made up of the most trusted Court Guards. These guards were sent to protect these families and to track down the Faction, ensuring they would never harm another Stavros."

The Myrmidons, I thought to myself. They had been here on official duty to the queen, like Vlad, Kris, and I had suspected. Back then, I had been sure that they had something to do with the Faction—not that they were the ones fighting against them. Since my first official meeting with Drake, though, I had known otherwise.

"But one of the remaining families believed that one day the Faction would become powerful enough again to complete what they had set out to do—to kill all remaining Stavroses. They sent their son, your father, to live among the Nescient, hoping he would have a better chance of survival if the Faction were to rise up again. They cut all ties with him to make sure he couldn't be traced.

"Not long after sending your father away, their vision came true and the final Stavros families were murdered with Apollo's arrow."

I thought back to everything we had learned in Hellenic school about the Great Massacre and the final killings of the Stavroses. "Our history textbooks never mentioned a surviving member of those families. We were told this was when the bloodline became extinct."

"Because I didn't want anyone to know that there was still a Stavros out there. But the Faction knew—and they made it their mission to find him."

"How did they know that my father was still out there?"

"Your father was adopted by a Nescient family that happened to live next to a Hellenicus family, your mother's family. Your father, knowing he had to hide the fact that he was a Stavros, never told your mother, and your mother, thinking he was a Nescient, never told him she was a Hellenicus. They grew up not knowing each other's true identity. Until"—a smile stretched across the queen's face—"it was time for your mother's first Gathering."

I looked around the room. Everyone was enthralled by the queen's story. I was sure they already knew all this, being Myrmidons, but they were listening so intently that it was as if they were hearing it for the first time as well.

"Your mother realized she was in love with your father and decided to forgo her first Gathering. She finally told him that she was a Hellenicus but was willing to leave it all behind to be with him. Your father urged her to forget him, to protect herself. But she refused, even when she found out his true identity. She knew that being with him would mean she would be putting herself in danger. Still, she chose to live in hiding with him. The childhood friends got married and had a daughter." She gestured to me.

"But how did the Faction find them?"

"If we knew that . . ." She hung her head. "We would have been able to stop them. By the time we found out that the Faction knew of your existence, we could only save you."

I felt a nudge on my arm and turned to see Officer Joseph Hudson offering a handkerchief. I realized that my cheeks were wet; I had been crying. I may have never met my parents, but my heart broke and ached for them and the rest of the Stavroses. I could never understand why someone would want to kill an entire bloodline. I wasn't comfortable crying in public, so I asked to be excused. Even though I could see worry still dancing in her icy-blue eyes, the queen hesitantly agreed to let me go.

I was wheeled back to the Hyped with Officer Brad Warwick in the front and Officer Joseph Hudson in the back. Scarlet walked right beside me; she surveyed the surroundings like a hawk trying to identify potential threats. It was just a short trip back to my old unit in the Hyped, but the three of them were making it look like it was a major operation.

"I've read your file," Scarlet stated. "I'm curious about your double click. How does it feel?"

How did they already have that information in my file? I gave her a one-word answer, as I wasn't in the mood to talk. "Weird."

"Hmm." Scarlet did not seem to be satisfied with my answer. "Surely this can't be the first time something like this has happened."

"What?"

"I mean, if it's happened to you, it's likely happened before, right?"

"Do you know where I can find that kind of information?"

"The archives, of course." A knowing smile formed on Scarlet's rosy lips. "Do you want me to take you there?"

Officer Warwick hesitated, but after some convincing, the three of us found ourselves at Court Guard Headquarters. Scarlet led the way to the archives, which was hidden below the Headquarters. The elevator ride down to the vaulted room took almost ten minutes, plunging us deep toward the center of the earth. By the time the doors opened, Commander Hudson was already there and clearly hadn't wasted any time getting stuck back in his work. He was reading a file with eyes that could burn a hole in the paper.

"We meet again so soon, old man," I greeted him. He was visibly taken aback to see me here.

According to Scarlet, this was where the Court kept all their records. Top secret and all. Only someone with a certain level of clearance, like Commander Hudson, knew the passcode. Well, and someone like Scarlet too.

Not only was Scarlet a Pure Royal and a descendant of Zeus but she also happened to be the daughter of our queen, Rhea Christoulakis. I still couldn't figure out how on earth someone like her ended up being a Court Guard. Or why her mother allowed it. A mystery for another day, I guessed.

"Why are you here?" asked Hudson accusingly.

I stood from the wheelchair, no longer feeling any unbearable pain, and walked closer. I didn't feel intimidated by him anymore. "It's a free Court, Commander."

Hudson dropped the file he had been holding in a box labeled X2211. He replaced the lid on top, closing the box before I could see anything inside. "You didn't answer my question, girl." He narrowed his eyes and walked toward me with a domineering look.

"It's none of your business."

Just as I said that, Scarlet came up behind us with a file and yelled, "Found it!"

Commander Hudson squeezed his eyes shut and massaged the spot between his brows with his thumb and index finger as if that would release some of his frustration. I almost felt bad for giving him trouble, but at the same time, there was no way I was going to back down when I was this close to an explanation for my double click.

"What did you find?" Hudson gripped Scarlet's wrist firmly and took the file from her hand. She tried to wriggle away but failed miserably. He glanced at the cover, a stern look on his face as he turned to Scarlet again. "You cannot read this."

"Oh yes, I can. I went to school and learned how to read, so of course I can read it." Scarlet rose to the balls of her feet, her free hand reaching for the paper while Commander Hudson stuck his arm up, holding it out of her reach.

"You don't have the clearance."

"To hell with clearance."

As they continued their struggle, I walked behind Commander Hudson and stood on top of a box laying on the floor close to his right foot. It gave me just enough additional height to snatch the file from his hand.

Commander Hudson and Scarlet stared at each other, baffled. Hudson let go of her wrist and, flipping her blond hair to one side, she blew at a lock that had fallen on her face.

"What are you doing bringing her here, Scar?" Commander Hudson asked. "How on earth did you even get in here, anyway?"

"I made a mental note of the passcode the last time I was here with you," Scarlet answered.

Hudson took a deep breath to calm himself down. I'd thought Pure Royals like her got special treatment, but it seemed like Scarlet was no exception when it came to needing a certain level of clearance for this kind of thing.

"Anyway." She walked over to me and I handed her the file. She opened it up and placed the contents on top of a wooden desk. "This should be what we came here for."

I peered over Scarlet's shoulder and read the contents.

January 1867
Lady Isabelle Stavros (18) reported the unusual click she had with two men: Mr. Jonathon Chance (21) and Lord Icarus Christoulakis (24). She was able to read both men's minds, however, only Lord Christoulakis was able to read hers, possibly because Lord Christoulakis is a Pure Royal, like Lady Stavros, while Mr. Chance is a Regular.

June 1867
Lady Stavros and the two men were called to meet the queen in her chamber.

Three Court Guards were on duty: Travis Hawke, Todd Warwick, and Typhon Lincoln. Additionally, the usual four Palace Guards were guarding the door of the queen's chamber.

A scream echoed from inside the chamber, and when the Palace Guards burst in to check on the queen, it was discovered that Lady Stavros had disappeared.

Witnesses to the occurrence were sworn to protect the secrecy of that night under the queen's order.

– the report continued to Classified files –

– the queen's authorization needed –

"That's it?!" Scarlet angrily rampaged through the rest of the file. Some photos dropped onto the floor.

I bent to pick up the photos and then froze. Commander Hudson bent on his knee and took the photograph from my hand. He looked down at it with narrowed eyes then looked up at me.

"What is it?" asked Scarlet.

Scarlet put one hand on Commander Hudson's shoulder and peeked at the photo. "Holy Zeus with a capital *Z*!" Her mouth dropped open as the realization hit her just as hard as it had hit us. "She looks exactly like you!"

I had no idea what to say.

Ω

I stepped into the lobby of the Royal Quarters with my new entourage, Officer Warwick dutifully pushing my now abandoned wheelchair. I was about to head to the Ambrosias' suite to meet Kris when I bumped into Vlad. And the first line that crossed his mind was, *Damn it.*

"How flattering." I crossed my arms in front of my chest. I started to move past him when I suddenly recalled something. That promise. The one he'd mentioned when we were standing in front of the tree. Now that I could read his mind, I could finally find out what that was about. My hand reached for his arm as he started to walk away, stopping him from going anywhere. "I have to talk to you."

"Then talk."

"Tell me about that promise." I tried to read his mind, but I got zilch. Maybe I wasn't very good at this, or maybe the fact that I could read two guys' thoughts caused my signal to get disrupted from time to time.

"The one that stopped you from kissing me that time by the tree."

I heard collective gasps from Officer Warwick and Officer Hudson, and a light giggle from Scarlet, but I didn't care. I wanted to know the truth, and now that I had a chance to grab it, I wouldn't let it go to waste.

"I can't." Vlad shook his head.

"I'm going to ask again. What promise?"

"It's—"

I didn't give him a chance to finish his sentence. "Don't you dare say that it's none of my business because if you're going to look at me as if you want to kiss me but then pull away at the last second, it is my goddamn business to know what's wrong."

"—complicated." He completed his sentence as if I had not said anything. He was staring at me, a look of utter torment distorting his features. I felt my heart ache—perhaps this bond caused me to have more feelings for Vlad than I had before.

"You promised that you wouldn't have anything to do with me." He didn't say yes, but he didn't say no, either, so I took it that I had hit close to the target. "Who did you make this promise to?" I moved closer to him, and somehow—maybe it was my gut feeling—I could read him better now that I was nearer. "Tell me."

"I can't. I'm a man of my word."

"Vlad, if it involves me, then you need to tell me. I deserve to know the truth." I lifted both of my hands and cupped his face, forcing him to look at me. "Who was it?"

He didn't say anything, but an image flashed in my mind. It was a face I knew all too well.

Adrian.

ACKNOWLEDGMENTS

First of all, I would like to thank God for letting me have that dream when I was thirteen years old and then again ten years later. Thank you for being with me every step of the way; that's what sustains me through the years.

Loads of love for my family for being so understanding when I suddenly paused while walking—or doing anything really—fished my phone out, and started typing rapidly. My dad, Joe, who let me *dream* and *follow* my dreams. I realize now that it's such a privilege. I thank my mum, who's the strongest person I know. Mom, you always push me to do my best and honestly, I owe it to you. I'm lucky to be able to call you Mom and Dad. For my sister Elizabeth, who dragged me out to get food—I'm alive because of you; and my youngest sister, Sandhra, for being an inspiration and force to be reckoned with. My dear aunt and godmother, Intan—you once told me when I was ten to never leave any task incomplete and to always do my best to achieve my goals. I have taken that with me since. I managed to finish *Entwined* because of you. My brother Steven for simply being him, you're amazing, bruh!—I'm pretty sure he'd laugh if he heard I said bruh in my nonexistent accent. Also, I want to thank my generous cousin Ariel Yoe for giving me his phone in the most dire situation during the writing of this story when my five-year-old phone died in the most inconvenient way possible—Man, you honestly saved *Entwined.*

I'd like to thank my first readers who had to go through *very* rough drafts back in 2017: Cinderella Pharaon, Clara Quezado, Damini Thakur, Daniella R., Daniella Irewole-ojo, Donna Fieldhouse, Fatima Rafiq, Fernanda Lemos, Gia Hunter, Hafsah Nadeem, Jovana Mrdalj, Krissy Ash, Maggie, Mariam, Marsela, Mlaika Nadeem, Muhammad Rizqi Fadlillah, Nwezeh Joyce Chiamaka, Priya Chauhan, Sanskriti, and Zeinab Faour. You gave *Entwined* a chance even when it had no reads and fame whatsoever. Your constant support, enthusiasm, and love are something I will cherish forever. Also, the fact that this book is now getting published means that I have indeed lost the bet. Pizza on me, fam!

To my English teachers: M. M. Wahyu Utami and Stefanie Nike N. Since that day you gave me the chance to join the storytelling contest, I found confidence in showing my story to others, so thank you! I hope you'll continue to inspire and nurture our young generations.

Amanda Ferreira, everything changed when you put my story on the featured list a long time ago. It's truly a wonderful gift to have you on this journey. I will forever remember your words: *Your story is amazing, believe in it and don't let anyone tell you otherwise.* They're my secret mantra whenever I deal with self-doubt.

A huge thank you to publishing director Deanna McFadden, talent manager I-Yana Tucker, and Crissy Calhoun for your patience, motivation, and understanding. The space you gave me to breathe, dig deeper into the mythology, and run wild with my imagination made this book possible.

I want to give a big warm hug, a cup of hot coffee, a slice of pepperoni pizza, tiramisu, and a tub of matcha ice cream—all things that I love—to my editor Paisley McNab. She is *literally* the best—if

I start talking about words to describe her, we'll be here all day. I love you and I truly believe we are soul sisters. Cheers to two hundred more emails and hugs for Giggsy.

Thank you to Neil Erickson for the lovely typesetting, Rebecca Mills for your diligent copyediting, and Rebecca Sands for all your hard work behind the scenes to keep *Entwined* on track. I really appreciate it!

To Sir Gavin Wilson and the Wattpad Ambassadors, thank you for having me. I've learned a lot by being an Ambassador. Not only does it help me so much in writing and understanding content, but being a part of this family is something I will cherish forever. Thank you Sir Michael Walsh for the *many* times we had tea; your wisdom and friendship mean the world to me. For sharing his experience, I thank Sir Dan Greathead Ecrivain. Rachel Crotzer for being really supportive and caring. Tawni Suchy for literally listening to everything I said and providing good humor—I cannot wait to see the little ones!

My sister from another mother, Vanessa C. Yim. You made me laugh even in tough times. And when I really needed someone, I knew exactly who to call.

Michelle Bugante and Jue Lyn Ng for being the best 언니. Thank you for that wonderful time at the BTS World Tour: Love Yourself concert. I will never forget you both running around to help me get the ticket. Let's continue fangirling over the boys on Twitter every chance we get! Sending purple hearts all the way to Shenzhen and Petaling Jaya!

Nur Lestari Br Situngkir for being so patient with me (and my random questions). Tyas Indah Pakarti, we will definitely have that *gulai*! And Kathleen Zefanya Janvy for taking the ferry several times to meet me and drag my hermit self out for culinary hunts and sightseeing. For Katelyn, a.k.a. treeleavez, for being so supportive. And

Arista Vernanda Fajarin, my little 동생! Let's order some pizza and eat it at GB, ladies!

Thank you Ellie Pindolia, a.k.a. TahliePurvis—to whom I dedicate this cameo of Axel Teller from *The Girl He Left Behind*—for being an inspiration and a wonderful human being inside out. I thank Katherine Arlene and Tiana Pop for letting me borrow their names—thank you, ladies! Fallon Elizabeth for letting me be part of the *Remember December* anthology and for talking to me despite the time difference.

I thank Catharina Melisa, who gave me real advice on all things writing and publishing, and who is a solid friend and fellow writer. Coffee's on me at So-Ba, Cat!

Jordan Lynde for being an absolute sweetheart! Now that I'm free, I am watching *Hotel del Luna*; don't give me spoilers! Chanelle and Nicole Pierman for reading the ARC—I have an ARC?! Now I'm starting to believe that I'm a real author (not sure what that means).

Hugs to my angels: Katelynn Dang, Angelica H., Taylor W., Caitlin P., Judy H., Ana Luisa MS., Lakshmi P., Zita N., Emmchel D., Amber Boyd, Syeeda Nafeah, Margarita M., Umniah S., Katherine M., Rachel B., Marlena A., Shahwar A., Vera Q., Brianna G., Marsida K., Dhriti S., Evelina L., Aran S., Turyaga C., Aakanksha D., Tawonga P., Audrey W., Sarayu K., Sylvia M., Iman A., Elena M., Faizah A., Mia F., Cheryl D., Shalu P., Manisha R., Tayo A., Joasy, Celine J., Faith G., Rahma M., Meghna, Daphne N., Theresa N., Ashley O., Adrianna B., Tamara N., Osh K., Mila H., Areebah S., Grace S., Khushi T., Abena K., K.S. Ocean, Priyanshi S., Tasneem J., Preyankaa S., Antarjot K., Nadine A., Gale M., Isabella S., Mariam M., Nassandra M., Kimberly M., Saadiya D., Glory N., Reha S., Renesmee S., Marie A., Tazeen F., Sana A., Sophia B., Kathryn S.V., Zoha Q., Keyura Vadlamani, Madison Nolan, Fidan A., Benthe B., Chloe Deffenbaugh,

Enyinna Jane, Rida Fawal, Deena Qistina, Faith J.R., Nividha Rajan, Hanfa Qasim, Amena Begum, Adeyinka Razak, Raquel Ferreira, Purva Kulkarni, Agboola Comfort, Harshita P., Suhani S., Anahita H., Nassandra M., and Rao Nayna Singh, who sent a lovely message saying I inspire and motivate her to write. Thank you—that's literally my goal. I cannot wait to read your stories!

I would like to thank everyone from Wattpad HQ, Macmillan Publishers, Penguin Random House UK, Raincoast Books, Laura Mengsinga, and everyone who helped to make this dream of mine come true. BTS, Frank Sinatra, Halsey, Linkin Park, and Taylor Swift for their wonderful, inspiring music.

Last but definitely not least, I would like to thank ARMY and Swifties all over the globe who have graced my timeline with tweets that made me cry and laugh in public.

There are many more people I want to thank, but time, space, and modesty compel me to stop here. For those I did not mention, you know who you are and that I love you. Thank you for letting me be a small part of your life.

[illegible]

[illegible]

[illegible]

[illegible]

ABOUT THE AUTHOR

A.J. Rosen is a twenty-three-year-old Wattpad Ambassador who splits her time between full-time school and writing YA romance. She's the founder of online movements like #ilovemyflaws (which supports victims of bullying) and #CareforCancer (which supports the loved ones of those battling cancer). She currently lives and studies in Singapore. *Entwined* is her first novel.

Want more? Why not try . . .

FIERCE WARRIORS.
FIERY MAGIC.
FATED LOVE.

Want more? Why not try . . .

Cupid isn't a myth – he's Lila Black's perfect match. As arrows fly and feelings become stronger, can Cupid and Lila resist each other's magnetic pull?